Praise for Rachel Dove from readers:

'Whenever I pick up a book by Rachel Dove, I know that there will be engaging characters along with a story that has warmth, humour and heartwarming vibes'

'An entertaining and wonderful story'

'Great read and a great ending'

'I loved it so much, I sat up half the night to finish it'

RACHEL LOUISE DOVE is a mum of two from Yorkshire. She has always loved writing and has had previous success as a self-published author. Rachel is the winner of the Mills & Boon & Prima Magazine Flirty Fiction competition and won The Writers Bureau Writer of the Year Award in 2016. She is a qualified adult education tutor specialising in child development and autism. In 2018 she founded the Rachel Dove Bursary, giving one working class writer each year a fully funded place on the Romantic Novelists' Association New Writer's Scheme.

Also by Rachel Dove

The Chic Boutique on Baker Street
The Flower Shop on Foxley Street
The Long Walk Back
The Wedding Shop on Wexley Street

The Fire House on Honeysuckle Street

BY RACHEL DOVE

ONE PLACE. MANY STORIES

HQ
An imprint of HarperCollins*Publishers* Ltd
1 London Bridge Street
London SE1 9GF

This paperback edition 2019

First published in Great Britain by
HQ, an imprint of HarperCollins*Publishers* Ltd 2019

ISBN: 9780008330910

*Dedicated to my gorgeous, clever and unique sons,
Book Worm and Little Man.
And to all the Mama and Papa Bears out there –
keep fighting and keep smiling.*

PROLOGUE

By the time the first alarm had sounded, Samuel Draper was already up, out of his bunk and running full pelt to his gear and the rig. His firefighter comrades were hot on his heels, all snapping into action the second the bell sounded. A mere few seconds after that and they were on the truck, peeling out of Euston Fire Station at speed.

'House fire, Guildford Street. Originated in the kitchen. Suspected hob fire. All residents are out of the property, but it's going up fast.' Robert rattled off the details as they navigated their way through the streets of London towards their shout. Sam nodded, pulling on his helmet, ready. 'Understood. Robert, you and I will do front door. Lenny, you head round the back. Assess any damage, check for hazards and stray looky-loos.'

'Okay, ETA six minutes. You glad to be back?'

Sam flashed his colleague and friend a smile. 'I'm going back, two weeks.'

Robert's face dropped in surprise. 'Back up there? What for, midwife school?'

Lenny, looking as big and burly as ever behind the wheel of the fire engine, laughed out loud as they sat in the back.

'Good one, Rob. Why are you going back? Got something going on up there?'

Sam didn't answer, just nodded in his usual quiet way. Lenny and Robert knew not to bother pressing him. Sam wasn't a gossip, or one to judge anyone else. Whatever he was doing up there, it had to be important to him. Sam never did anything in life without assessing every aspect first. It made him the skilled fire-fighter he was, and he had all the lads' unconditional trust the minute he walked through the door on his first shift, all those years ago. The only real thing that had altered was his hairline. When they did school visits, the others liked to joke that his mop of dark curls had been singed off – frazzled off in a fireball. The kids loved it. Sam, not so much.

They got to the shout in record time, putting out the small pan fire and comforting the understandably very frightened residents. These were the best calls, the best outcomes. Quick in and out, put the fire out and have no casualties or structural damage. A new pan or two, a lick of paint and the memory would be washed away, freshened up, made anew. The lads all knew from experience that it could have been far worse than a scorched splashback and smoke damage. Before long, they were heading back home to the station.

'Come on then, Sam,' Lenny teased, as he indicated left and waved at a small gaggle of schoolgirls who were frantically blowing kisses and waving at them from the corner of the busy street. 'Why do you keep going up to God's country?'

'God's armpit more like,' Robert scoffed, wiping a black sooty mark from the side of his face. 'Helping that woman deliver her baby must have been the most action you saw, right? You starting to feel your age?'

Lenny banged his meaty hand against the steering wheel.

'That's it! He's getting some action! That's it, isn't it?' He beeped at a cyclist who swung out wildly in front of their truck, chuckling to himself as the cyclist jumped about ten feet in the air and peddled frantically back into the bike lane where he belonged. 'Bike lanes save lives, man!' he shouted genially out of the window. The cyclist nodded apologetically, face as white as a sheet. 'Finally, Sam! A real-life woman who is not your mother to talk to!'

'Hey,' Sam warned, 'watch the mother talk.'

Robert laughed. 'Come on, Sam, as if we'd dare rib her. She scares me more than you do with one of her looks!' The lads in the truck all laughed together.

Sam, as eager as always to shut down the talk about his life, shook his head.

'I delivered a wedding planner's baby, and she is now planning her own wedding, to the man she loves. As a matter of fact, they asked me to go be part of it. I like the country, the station lads are nice, and I'm due a change. No woman involved.'

Robert sighed dramatically. 'Sam, Sam, Sam. You make my heart bleed, bro. You really do. How could you leave London?'

Sam just sat back and smiled at his friend. His mother Sondra had said much the same when he had told her, but she understood, as upset as she was.

Being a gangly lad in primary school, a white boy with a loud, bubbly African mother behind him and an array of temporary siblings, he was used to people trying to suss him out, wondering aloud and questioning his life choices. The thing was, Sondra Okeke Draper, his larger-than-life foster mother, always taught him to ignore the stares, hold your head up at all times, and do what felt right. Westfield, as bizarre as it was to his colleagues, was right. It felt right, and it wasn't his life going forward he needed to sort out. It was his backstory. He loved London, sure, but aside from a few colleagues and his mother, he was alone here, too. Moving to the North wouldn't be such a wrench, and one thing that Sam wasn't afraid of was making the bold moves. He might be the strong silent type, but Sam knew exactly what was going on, and what felt important. This did, and without quite knowing what the outcome would be, Sam knew he had to at least open the puzzle box of his past,

3

and peek inside. A wedding was a new beginning. Maria Mallory and James Chance, the couple with the baby he had delivered in front of the fire house, had their happy ever after. Sam had decided to at least look for his, and all signs pointed north.

THE DAY OF THE MALLORY–CHANCE WEDDING

Sam waved off the happy couple, and went to collect his bag, to head to the night do at Maria's friend's restaurant.

The chief of the fire house came out to shake his hand.

'Well done, Sam, nice bit of publicity there. With us being a little local fire station, we need all the good news stories we can get. Keeps the penny counters happy. We haven't always had a dedicated fire service in this village you know, and we need to make sure these damn cuts don't change that.'

Sam shook his hand back, shaking off his praise.

'It's okay, sir, it was an honour. Nice to see a couple doing so well. It's a good station.'

Chief Briggs nodded. 'Beautiful baby too.'

Sam smiled, and this time it reached his eyes.

'Sure is, Chief, Hope is gorgeous.'

'Have you considered my offer?' he asked Sam, all business now. 'You've done a few cover shifts here, including the one where you were delivering babies, so have you decided what's next? I know we're not very exciting, compared to what you're used to, but we're a good group of guys, and we'd love to have you onboard permanently. Good scope for progression too, believe it or not.'

Sam looked around him at Westfield Fire House. It wasn't

what he was used to, by any means. Working in London was a world apart from here, and the fires were a lot different too, along with the other terrifying call-outs he had endured lately. He realised that his personal quest had become much more. Lately, instead of coming to Westfield to figure out his past, it had made him consider his future.

The day that Maria and James had slammed onto the drive of the fire house, he had done his job. He didn't hesitate, he didn't think twice. He reacted, he planned and he galvanised the others into action. The baby was born safely, and it wasn't till Maria had held the child in her arms, James wrapped around them both protectively, that it had hit him. He wanted to find out the truth, he needed to. He had to find out what his past was, before he could even think about forming a future. Every time he had tried in the past, it had ended in failure, leaving him more alone, lost and confused than before.

He looked at Chief Briggs who was watching him, as though realising that he was thinking it through. It was this quiet, unassuming air that tipped the scales for Sam. He liked his new boss, felt at home.

'I'll take the job,' he said, shaking his hand before he could second guess himself and back out.

The chief looked delighted, pulling Sam into an awkward spontaneous hug.

'Ah lad, I am pleased!' He slapped him on the back and Sam patted him back gently. Given that Chief Alan Briggs was half his size, he felt fearful of breaking his new boss.

'Family coming with you?' he asked, looking a little embarrassed. 'Sorry, Sam, I never asked if you had a wife, or kids.'

Sam shook his head, the sunshine shining off his broad bald bonce.

'It's just me, sir. I'll be moving from London on my own.'

The chief nodded, seemingly satisfied.

'There are some cottages in the village, they do long-term lets as well as holiday ones. I'll get you a number. You can't be staying in the pub B & B or hotels when you come for good. That's if you don't want to buy, of course.'

'Great, thanks, sir. I'll be off then. Will check them out later, I have a wedding reception to attend.'

Chief Briggs gave him a thumbs up and Sam walked up to the staff quarters to collect his stuff. He was booked into a hotel in Harrogate that night, and due back on the train to London the day after. He sat down on one of the bunks, thankful that the room was empty, and dialled a number.

'Hey, Gina,' he said as the line of the fire station he worked at down south was answered by their receptionist.

'Hey, Sam! How's village life? Did the wedding go well? Rob had a bet with Lenny that you'd end up getting off with one of the bridesmaids.'

'Yeah,' he replied, looking out of the window at the green fields around him. He could see the Mayweather Estate beyond that, and further still the cottages and shops, laid like pearls in the countryside. 'It was nice. Tell Rob and Lenny that they're idiots, and to get their own love lives. Listen, tell the chief I'm taking the transfer. Chief Briggs will be in touch with him later today, I expect.'

Gina sighed. 'Aww, honey, we sure will miss you. Are you positive this is the right thing to do? You can talk to people you know, people here. I know you've had a few bad shouts lately. Moving stations won't change that you know.'

Sam's large jaw flexed, and he stood and leant on the windowsill. Just looking at the scenery soothed him. The thought of going back to London filled him with dread, and frustration. He knew he was making the right move, and he always followed his gut.

'I'm sure, Gina. I want something different from life. I'm fine mentally, but a break would be good.' He straightened his tie, which felt like it was strangling his thick-set neck in his collar. 'I need to make a fresh start.'

She made all the right noises, not that Sam was really listening. He thanked her and rang off, promising to stay in touch.

After leaving the fire house and saying goodbye to the lads who would soon hear that he had taken the job, he got into his hire car and pulled away. He liked the team already, but he wasn't one for a big fuss. He would let the chief tell them. He headed out of Westfield, making his way to Harrogate and his hotel. A few days in London to pack up his life, and he would be on his way back here. To Westfield, to live a new life. Put down some roots, and finally find out the truth of how his story started.

Somewhere in Westfield was the father he had never met. A mother he wanted to find. And once Sam set his mind on doing something, he didn't let anything stand in his way. Westfield had a secret, and Sam was going to find out the truth. Surely, someone in Westfield knew something. They had to. After all, it takes a village to raise a child. If you took the child from that village, someone would at least notice. Wouldn't they?

CHAPTER 1

Lucy pulled Xander along the platform edge as best she could, whilst juggling her suitcase on wheels and heavy holdall. Iain would be annoyed that she had taken his favourite gym bag, but at this point that would be the least of her worries.

'Mum, what about school? It's illegal to play truant. Mr Elphick told us last week when Billy went to Mallorca but his mum lied and said he had diarrhoea.'

She smiled down at her plain-speaking son, trying to keep the worry from her face, the anxiety from her voice. He would pick up on it and the last thing either of them needed was a meltdown at the train station. He had pulled his ear defenders off one tiny ear to listen to her, and she could already see that he was tense; his hand pulling on the fingers of the other, his eyes darting from side to side, searching for unknown and unseen dangers.

'You'll only miss one day, sweetheart, and then it's the summer holidays. Your teacher said that your class was only going to be watching videos all day anyway. I brought your iPad for the train.'

'*Lego Movie*?' he asked hopefully, and she nodded.

'Yep, and I downloaded *Lego Batman* too.'

Xander smiled, and she felt the relief wash over her. Luckily, Xander loved trains, so the journey wouldn't be too much of a trial. Thank God for J.K. Rowling. King's Cross would have been

9

impossible without Harry Potter, but now with the shop there, Xander had made it to the train doors unscathed, a new Hedwig stuffed owl in his hand. The travelling wouldn't be the problem. It was what was waiting for her at the other end that worried her. What the hell was she going to tell Xander? Would he cope with all the changes? She had packed all of his notes, his medical letters, his medication, and his repeat prescription slips, so they could get his sleep medication, but the upheavals to his routine would still be immense. She shuddered at the thought, but pushed on, till they were sitting on the train, near the doors and toilets. She stashed their luggage on the racks behind them, putting her oversized grey handbag on the seat next to her. She sat backwards, facing Xander who was sitting looking out of the window, humming to himself. She saw a few passengers giving him a sideways glance, and she tutted loudly at one man who didn't hide his judgement. She motioned for Xander to take off his ear defenders, and passed him the iPad, his soft cushioned earphones already plugged in. It had a full charge, and the charger in her bag was on hand, along with a spare, just in case. Worst case scenario he could watch Netflix on her smartphone. He was halfway through a documentary on global warming, so he could watch that, or draw or read. She had even bought a paperback for herself, a delightful romance book that she had picked up in the station bookshop. She had heard some of the other school mums talking about it at the gates, from a distance of course. In another world, she could have shared it with them, been friends perhaps.

Lucy never usually got much time to herself, but she was hoping that this, as well as many other things, would change now. Xander put his headphones on and settled down in his seat, his coat now discarded and used as a pillow. She had felt bad making him wear it on this July day, but it had been both a good disguise for the neighbours and a means of transporting the coat to their destination. He was wearing his weighted jacket too, and she decided to give him a minute before asking him to take it off.

Maybe when the train had set off would be better. Nowhere to run then in the event of a tantrum. She took off her own coat, laying it on the seat next to her. She had reserved all four seats, with the table, so she could relax in the knowledge that no one was going to crowd them and they could spread out a little. Xander was engrossed in his iPad, and she took out her new mobile, tapping out a text that they were now on the train. She got a text straight back, and smiled at the reply before slipping it back into her bag.

'Excuse me, is this yours?' A deep voice came from the side of her. It sounded like it had come down from the heavens, as high in direction as it was deep in tone. She could see a flash of white in the corner of her eye. Xander's new owl.

'Hedwig!' Xander shouted, reaching forward to grasp the toy, his fingers opening and closing like pincers. Lucy winced as a past memory came to mind, and as she watched her son cuddle his new snow-white companion, she wished for the train to leave, fast, and spirit them both away from here, and the memories she was trying so hard to forget.

'Why does he even need that stupid thing? He'll only lose it.'

Iain's whining was already in full flow, and they had only just gotten onto the bus to the airport, the one that took you from the long-stay car parks to the actual airport itself. They were juggling cases and bags, and Xander was sitting next to her on the seat, backpack strapped to his shoulders, playing with a tangle toy. One of many that she had bought and stashed in her case, not that she would tell Iain that. A bored-looking couple at the side of them looked across to see what Xander was holding, and she gave them a pointed look as if to say, 'Mind your own beeswax,' and turned to her husband. He looked like he was chewing a bee or two himself.

'He needs it, for his anxiety. Airports make him nervous,' she hissed. 'It's only a toy, I'll keep an eye on it.'

'Bloody waste of money if you ask me,' he chuntered on, his jaunty holiday panama hat making him look all the more curmudgeonly atop his sour face. 'Half the stuff you buy him doesn't get used.'

Not true, but Iain had never let the truth get in the way of a good whinge and moan.

'Really,' she said, monotone, watching Xander watch the planes as they took off overhead. His fingers ever moving, bending and reshaping his toy. It kept him calm. She almost wished she had one herself. A large one, that she could tie around her husband and the nearest car park meter. 'Bit like your fishing gear then, and the model airplane in the garage? Perhaps we should sell those, then we will have more money for stuff to help our son cope, eh? This toy cost less than a fancy coffee, Iain.'

He looked out of the window like a petulant child, taking a swig of his large extra hot no foam rip-off, and said nothing else till they got to the airport. The gulf between them was getting wider than ever, and she'd hated it at first. Now, she was just beginning to hate him. Where was the man she married, the one who danced around the room with her, holding a positive pee stick? That Iain was gone, replaced by this bitter, twisted, work-driven man. As they stepped down off the bus, cases in hand, she tried to stay positive and lock her own snark away. This holiday had been hard work to pay for, and she had planned everything down to the last detail, so she was going to go for it.

This holiday was more than just Xander's first holiday abroad with his family – it might just be his last unless things improved. Make or break, as the cliché went. She was determined to save her marriage, and their father–son relationship. Here, all together, they might just pull it off.

'Xander,' Iain shouted, drawing attention their way. 'Pick up your bloody toy, now!'

Lucy sighed and, putting her shiny optimistic face on, picked up the toy and took her son's trembling hand.

CHAPTER 2

The day Sam decided that he was going to be a fireman, no one in the household batted an eyelid. It was written in the stars, pretty much, and had been since he was a small dot in someone's arms. To young Sam, though, it seemed like a revelation. That he, little orphan Sam, could one day be a hero. Someone who people would turn to on their darkest days; someone strong, sturdy. Someone who would never let you down, would always come to your aid, no matter what. The kind of person he wanted around him. The kind of people who had saved him.

When his mother tucked him into bed that night, kissing the top of his little head and smelling the shampoo scent of his baby soft brown hair, he snuggled down under the covers, and finally felt like he had a plan. Not a thing to be sniffed at, having a plan, especially at five years old. He didn't realise it at the time of course, but he had in one day achieved what many people waited half their lives to feel. Purpose. Little five-year-old Samuel had purpose. He had a plan. That sheer bloody-mindedness fuelled his whole childhood, and never once did he detract from his mission. He had learned from an early age if you wanted something, you went for it. No excuses. His future was all down to him. Or, as his mum would say, '*We make our own destiny in the*

13

face of fate, Sam. Fate dealt you a bad deal, but it's not the end of your story, just the start.'

Now, as he packed up his belongings and prepared to make the journey once more to Westfield, and his new home, he had another mission in mind. One that, yet again, he had no hesitation in. No fear that he wouldn't complete it, find what he was looking for. What he wasn't so sure about was just what he would find, and whether he could live with his decision afterwards. Even for a man who walked into flames, with a spine of steel, the prospect was daunting, and a little scary.

Packing up his flat had been easy, and what he hadn't got in his holdall and suitcase, he had boxed up and stacked up in a corner of his mum's garage. Two whole boxes, mostly books. His furniture in the flat had been sparse at best, so he had sold what he had, or donated it to charity. Clothes, toiletries, a stack of paperbacks, and one photo album was all he took with him. Easy to carry, even easier to unload at the other side. He didn't need much. So here he stood, underneath the departure boards at King's Cross Station, waiting to board, alongside the Harry Potter fans and bored-looking commuters.

'I'm going to miss you, my darling boy,' Sondra said, her greying thick black curly hair tied up neatly in her trademark bandana. 'It will be so strange not to be close to you.'

Sam felt a twinge of regret as he saw her wipe a tear from her eyes with her handkerchief.

'It's not forever, and it's only a couple of hours on the train. I'll come and see you when I get a few days off, and you can come stay with me, when you have a break between kids.'

Sondra wouldn't take a break, but the pair of them didn't say that to each other. Such was their relationship that a lot went unsaid. They both knew it, and so to them, that was enough. She would come if she could. Sondra had never been between kids in all the years that Sam had lived with her. He had grown up in a hectic home, one full of smells, and noise, and memories, and Sondra was always at the centre of it. The calm captain at the helm. Many kids from all kinds of life had come through those doors. Some came in the dead of night, shaky little ghosts clutching bedraggled teddy bears, traumatised by what they had seen and heard. Others came angry, aggressive, half dragged out of cars by overworked social workers, eager to get rid of their fraught charges. Sondra never batted an eyelid, and she always commanded respect. Sam had been the only child she had never let go of, and he was forever grateful for her.

The train announcement sounded, and Sam took the woman into his beefy arms, kissing the top of her head as she wrapped her arms around his middle and held him tight.

'I love you, my boy. I'll see you soon.' When they finally pulled away, she pressed a thick envelope into his hand. Her trademark cream notepaper and vellum-finished stationery. He smiled, a picture of her sat at her desk popping into his head. Glasses halfway down her nose, a glass of wine on a coaster on the wooden surface of the desk, her head bent over her paper as she scribbled away. 'Read it on the train or when you get settled. Not now. Okay?'

He nodded, not trusting himself to keep it together if he tried to speak. She raised her hands above her five foot six frame, placing them on either side of his stubbly face. He stooped to let her, savouring the warmth from her palms, the scent of her coconut hand lotion enveloping him.

She dropped a motherly kiss onto his lips, stroking his face and letting the tears fall for a moment.

'Just you remember, my sweet little Sam, you always have a home with me. Stay safe.'

He hugged her tight once more, kissing her cheek.

'I will, Mum, I promise.'

She nodded, smiling through her watery tears. 'And find someone to love, okay? Grandbabies need a mother, you know. I'm not getting any younger here.'

He laughed then, a deep throaty boom, and she laughed right along with him, each of them tucking the moment into their pockets, to pull out and cherish when they needed it.

They looked back at each other till he turned the corner, and he gripped the envelope to him. It smelled of her. He pushed it into his coat pocket and hauled his baggage to the train. The conductor looked twice at him as he went to enter the train, and Sam could feel himself getting annoyed. Looking down at the man, he nodded slowly, not bothering to raise a smile. The man nodded back, clearing his throat nervously and stepping aside for him to get onto the train. Sam was used to people thinking he was a meathead, a rough and tough bruiser, but realistically, it did start to grate when he was trying to go about his day. Made his job tougher too, with the louts that seemed to think it was okay to have a pop at a man trying to save lives, do his job. Idiots, one and all. He wouldn't miss them in Westfield, and he very much doubted that it would be as tough in the little village he was going to call home for the next few months. He could only hope, anyway. In his current state, he didn't have the energy for much else.

Still irked by the bloke, Sam stomped through the carriages till he found his seat. Moving to the end of the carriage, he stashed his bags in the luggage compartments. He noticed a woman and a small boy, sitting across from his table seat. The boy had headphones on, his face enraptured in the screen, his hair ruffled and sticking up at odd angles, pushed askew by his big headphones. Sam smiled, thinking of the kids he had grown up alongside. Half of them had never seen movies, let alone been lucky enough to have a portable screen to watch them on. He squeezed himself into the seat he had reserved, so he ended up sitting the opposite way from the lad, the same side as the woman. He felt eyes on him, and looked across to see the boy watching him intently. He looked away, aware that a man of his size looking at a youngster might be intimidating. He flicked his gaze across at the woman, and she was looking right at him. He was just noticing how blue her eyes were when she opened her mouth to speak, flashing him a set of pearly whites, that were currently bared at him.

'Do you have a problem?' Her tone was clipped, pushed out like pellets from an air rifle.

He laughed, out loud. Right at her. He didn't mean to, and he choked off the motion in his throat as soon as he realised.

'Sorry,' he said gruffly. 'I didn't mean to laugh. I don't have a problem.'

She clenched her jaw, and Sam said nothing, observing her. He noticed how alike the pair looked, the young boy having her brown hair colouring, little streaks of lighter caramel tinted hair running through her shoulder-length locks. She had it wavy, and loose around her shoulders. She looked tired, he noted, and tense across her features. The boy was still looking at him, the tablet now on the table, forgotten.

'Are you okay?'

He surprised himself by asking. Normally he kept himself to himself, off the job, but something about her made him want to know more.

'I will be,' she said, folding her arms. 'I just want to enjoy the journey in peace.'

She glared at him again, and then turned to look at her son.

'Xander honey, don't stare.'

The boy, who had one headphone off his ear, looked at her in surprise.

'He's staring! Tell him!'

'Xander!' his mum scolded, in the form of a whisper. 'Remember what we said?'

'Mum! He did it! You always said to tell the truth!'

'Xander, please!'

Xander huffed, and rolled his eyes so far in the back of his head Sam thought they would never return.

'Fine,' he spat out, giving Sam a sidelong glance that could spark a fire from across the county. 'I don't like you,' he said, matter of factly, sticking his tongue out at Sam before picking up his tablet and shoving his headphones back onto his ears. The woman blushed furiously, and Sam chuckled again.

'I'm sorry, Xander,' he said. 'You're quite right, it is rude to stare.'

Xander didn't take his eyes from the screen, but Sam saw him sneak a peek over the top at his mother and give a little grin.

'I see you,' she said, but her tone was softer this time. She looked across at Sam. 'Thank you. He speaks his mind.'

Sam looked at the woman, who looked so frazzled and on edge and nodded once.

'Nothing wrong with that.'

She raised her eyebrows, pulling a face.

'Not always, for him. He hasn't mastered tact.'

Sam looked out of the window at the man from earlier, who was now getting ready to blow his whistle.

'He has time, I know plenty of adults who haven't learnt that skill either.'

She laughed then, just once, and smiled at him for the first time. Her blue eyes flashed and he couldn't help but notice how pretty she was.

'Well, thanks.'

'Sam, Draper.'

She looked him up and down, as though deciding something for herself, and then looked at her son, who was by now engrossed in his movie and not paying any attention to their conversation.

'Lucy.'

She didn't volunteer a surname, and turned back to her book. As she folded the page out to crack the spine a little, he noticed that she touched her bare ring finger, as though out of habit, before stopping herself. He was about to ask where she was headed when the whistle blew, and the Tannoy started to detail the journey from London to Leeds, and all the stops in between. He had stashed his holdall and suitcase in the compartments, and he checked on them as the train started to move. He took his jacket off, folded it and put it onto the seat next to him, before reaching into the carrier bag he had bought in the station. He took out a bottle of water and the latest thriller and settled in for the duration. He couldn't bring himself to read the letter yet, when the smell of his mother was still all around him, on his clothing. He would wait to get settled in, and be alone. Then he would read the letter. No one wanted to see a six foot four man cry like a baby. As emotional as she had been on the platform, his mother wasn't an overly emotional woman. Whatever was in that envelope was going to hurt him, and help him. How much of each, he didn't like to hazard a guess.

A few chapters of his book in, and the train was racing along the tracks, the near empty carriage quiet and soothing. Xander was still in his seat, wrapped in his and his mother's coats, tablet propped up on the table, his head nodding as he fought sleep. The noise of a mobile phone broke the silence, and Lucy scrabbled to answer it.

'Hello,' she said, half whispering. 'I can't really talk at the moment, call you later?'

The Tannoy sprang into life, announcing that refreshments would be coming down the train on a cart, and Lucy jumped, cupping the phone between her hands for dear life and scrunching down into her seat frantically. *Shit!*

The voice prattled on, and Lucy listened as best she could to the voice on the line. He was talking about work, again. He hadn't even noticed the Tannoy, hadn't even asked where she was. She let him finish, and waited for him to ask her about her day.

'So,' he continued, a line starting to ring in the background, 'I'll be really late, so go ahead and have tea without me, I'll grab something here. We might end up going out somewhere, with it being Friday.'

'Hmm-hmm.' She looked across at her son, whose eyelids had now closed, and marvelled at how adorable he was. His long brown eyelashes fanned out into his cheeks, and even in sleep, he looked a little confused and anxious. Her beautiful, clever, misunderstood boy. 'Okay, fine.'

If her husband picked up on her tone, he didn't mention it. His voice was the same; distracted, far away. He acted as though letting his family know his whereabouts was an annoyance, a mundane obligation to tick off his to-do list. Speak to long-suffering wife. Check. Ignore existence of son bar the basics. Check. She thought of how he used to be, and her stomach flipped as she thought of where they were now. Miles apart from each other, now more than ever.

'Okay. Oh, honey?'

She took a deep breath in. This was it. He was going to ask her. He was going to ask if Xander got to school okay, or what she was up to today. Anything. He could ask her anything, and she would tell him the truth.

'Yes?' she asked on a shaky breath. Her eyes flicked to the man opposite, but he hadn't lifted his eyes from the pages of his book.

'I forgot to ask, sorry. Been so busy today.'

Here it was. *Ask me, damn you. Prove me wrong. I swear, we'll get off this train. All you have to do is ask.*

'If you get time today, get my dry cleaning would you? I have golf tomorrow, and I need my suits back for Monday.' Another phone started up again, his office phone, and he tutted crossly.

'I gotta go, okay? See you later.'

She opened her mouth to speak, but before she could even form the words, she heard the click of the line. He had gone, back to work. She looked at her phone, willing him to ring back. To have picked up on her tone and guessed that something was off. But she knew in her heart that he wouldn't. He had stopped noticing things long ago. Her wallpaper came up on the screen, a picture of her and Xander together, smiling in the Lego shop.

She remembered the day. Another bad day at school, another day of her son coming out of the school doors and running into her arms, crying. Kids were rotten, and some parents were no better. She had wrapped him in her arms and strode out of the wrought iron gates, mentally sticking a finger up at the judgemental mum set that watched them leave. She had gotten him straight into town, to the Lego shop that he loved so much, and they had sat there, at the activity table, till her son dried his tears and started to be himself again. One of the shop assistants had offered to take a photo, after her attempts at a selfie had resulted in either missing the model or chopping their heads off. The photo came out well, and it had turned into a good day. A day of hot chocolate in the coffee shop, of Lego models and little smiles. Another day where his dad had not been able to get out of work, or even taken a minute to give him a call.

She looked again at her sleeping son and brushed a tear away. Today was going to be one of those days, where it would end better than it began. She turned her phone over, took out the SIM Card from the back and snapped it in half. Just looking down at the pieces of plastic and metal made her feel better. She brushed them into her pocket, and settled back down to read her book. At least in the pages of this story, there would be a happy ever after. She never noticed the man across watching her with interest, and a flexed jaw.

CHAPTER 3

Marlene stood on the train platform, shuffling from foot to foot, checking her watch and then checking it again when she realised she hadn't even registered the time. Dot and Grace were sitting on the metal bench nearby; Grace knitting away, Dot tapping on her phone.

'It's late. What if she never got on it?'

Grace didn't look up, swapping needles over in her arms and flicking the multicoloured wool in her bag to allow more of it to escape.

'She got on it. The trains are always bloody late, calm down. You'll have no shoe leather left. You'll look like a knackered old tyre by the time you're done.'

'I'm worried! I can't help it. Dot, what time do you make it?'

Dot looked at the platform clock and checked her own watch. 'Eleven twenty-seven, dear. My clock is still the same as yours.'

'And every other bloody clock in the land,' Grace griped. 'We share time you know, it won't pass any quicker looking at the blasted thing.'

'Oh shut up, Grace, go back to your knitting!' Marlene snapped. 'Why did you even come if you aren't going to be helpful?'

Grace's needles clacked away, and she let out a little sigh.

'I came to support you, and to stop you getting arrested by station security. You look like a bloody nutter, running a track into the platform. She'll be here when she's here, same as the rest of the train. It's an eighteen-minute delay, not the end of time for God's sake!'

Marlene glared at Grace, and her friend eyeballed her from the top of her glasses, shoving her middle finger up the bridge of her nose pointedly and returning it to her knitting. Marlene gasped, and Dot groaned.

'Up yours eh!? Well, the same to you, Grace. Dot, tell her!'

'*Dot, tell her!*' Grace mimicked, her needles picking up speed with her fury. 'You need to chill out. That poor girl is going to get off that train and jump straight back on it looking at you. Knock it off!'

'Oh shut your face!' Marlene boomed, startling a man walking out onto the platform.

'Shut both your faces!' Dot screeched, standing and pushing Marlene into the seat she had vacated. Grace and Marlene hissed at each other and had a mini elbowing fight, Grace being the victor by jabbing her knitting needle into Marlene's thigh.

'Oww! Bugger off!' Marlene shouted, trying to grapple the needle away from her. Her hand caught in the strand of wool, and started to unravel the stitching.

Grace growled furiously, slapping Marlene's hand, making her reel back with a startled yip.

'Watch my blessed knitting, you ham-fisted old tart!'

Dot ran to the pair, pushing her hands in between them.

'Ladies, for chuff's sake, pack it in!'

Bing bong. The Tannoy sprang to life, stopping the sparring ladies in their tracks.

'The delayed train from London King's Cross is now arriving on Platform 2. Can all passengers please stand well back.'

Dot sagged with relief.

'Thank Christ for that.'

Marlene and Grace both jumped up, ready to greet the newcomers.

The train trundled to a stop on the platform, and the doors swished open.

'Can you see her?' Grace asked, putting her arm around Marlene, their fight long forgotten.

'No, you?'

Grace peered into the carriages as they moved along the platform, but the windows were tinted, making it difficult. A train employee stepped out, paddle in hand, and then the commuters started to disembark.

'Dot, you see anything?'

Dot stood open-jawed next to them, looking at something a little way down the train. She nudged Grace, who followed her gaze. Marlene was still looking frantically, Grace pulling on her arm.

'What Grace, give up? What?'

Grace tutted and, reaching across, she grabbed Marlene by the jaw and showed her what they were looking at.

Down the platform, just getting off the train, was a man. Well, they assumed it was a man, not a mirage, but, sometimes, it was hard to tell the difference. Grace dropped her needles and they clattered to the floor with a metallic tinkle.

'What, I ask you, is that?' she asked, licking her lips slowly.

Dot shook her head slowly, her eyes out on stalks. 'I don't know, but I want one.'

Marlene, slack-jawed, babbled twice before muttering, 'It's Bruce Willis, I tell you. Or that other guy, the Statham guy, what's he called?'

Grace giggled. 'Who cares what he's called, where did he come from?'

The three women watched as the man put down a suitcase and oversized holdall, and swept back onto the train, dipping his head as he walked back through the doors. A minute later, dressed in a long coat and jeans, he stepped back down off the train, more luggage in hand. A woman and a small boy followed, the woman taking the bag from him.

'Figures,' Dot whined. 'A man like that, had to be taken.'

'Lucky cow,' Grace moaned, looking down at her forgotten knitting. 'Bollocks, I dropped my jumper.'

She bent to pick it up, and Marlene practically leap-frogged over her.

'It's Lucy! She's here!'

Marlene half ran, half trotted like a pony, over to the trio, and patted the woman excitedly on the shoulder.

'Lucy dear, is it you?'

Lucy turned around and smiled broadly, throwing one of her arms around her beloved aunt.

'Auntie Marlene, hello!' Marlene threw her arms around her, hugging her tight. Over her shoulder, she saw the Adonis they were ogling earlier, standing a little way back with the bags.

'Did you have a nice journey?' She pulled back, looking at her niece. She looked tired and drawn. She didn't let her face betray her worry for her niece. A pair of little eyes fixed on her, and she looked at the little boy, holding his mother's hand so tightly. He was looking around him as though he was fighting the urge to run off.

'Hello, my darling,' she said softly, bending down to look the youngster in the face. 'Shall we go to the car?'

Xander looked at her, his headphones making him look all the younger, and smiled slowly, nodding his head. Dot and Grace came up behind them, pointing to the bags.

'These all yours?' Grace asked. Or rather, she asked the crotch of the rather tall bald man guarding them.

He nodded politely, pointing at two of them.

'These are theirs, I just helped. You need a hand to your car?'

Lucy shook her head, and opened her mouth to say no, but the women had already gone, cooing around the bloke that she had just spent two hours trying to avoid.

25

'You are lovely!' Dot simpered, reaching up and touching the man's arm. 'Ooo, have you felt this, Grace?' She squeezed his bicep, and Sam blushed.

Lucy looked down at Xander, and he giggled at her.

'Come on then, let's go sort these ladies out before they rip his pants off.'

Xander gasped, a shocked expression on his face. 'That's not allowed in public, you told me!'

Lucy laughed, cursing herself for not watching her phrasing.

'It's just a saying, that's all, love. Sorry. They won't touch his pants. Let's go, shall we?' She squeezed his hand and he squeezed it back, their little nod to each other. Their comfort to each other when out and about in the world. *I'm here,* it said to the other.

They walked towards their cases, but Sam had seen them coming, and picked up their holdall.

'I can take your bags,' he stated, throwing the holdall over his shoulder with his own and taking the case handle in his hand with his own in the other.

'No, it's fine, I can manage.'

The women were all flocked around him, rapture on their faces. Lucy wanted to slap the lot of them. What was it about him that had made them lose their mind like this? Sam paid them no notice, he was standing there, laden down, looking at her in his own quiet way. She felt naked under his gaze, like he could read her thoughts, and she swallowed hard. Why didn't he say anything? What was in that lofty head of his?

'I didn't say you couldn't manage. I have them. I'll see you to your car.'

The ladies sprang into action then, and she found herself being pulled along, Xander stuck to her leg. They left Leeds station, heading through the crowds of suits and shoppers, Sam a way in front, carrying their combined luggage with ease. Grace and Dot went on in front, heading towards the car park, and, once there, they both got into two different cars.

26

Marlene turned to her and smiled kindly. 'We took two cars, because we all wanted to come. See you, and help you.' She looked at Xander, who was looking at Sam, who was putting their luggage into one of the car boots. 'Are you okay?' she said lightly, looking at Lucy intently. She smiled faintly, a little movement of the head barely identifiable.

'We will be.' Marlene squeezed her shoulder, and the two women looked at each other for a moment, happy to be near each other finally. Sam turned to look at them, a frown across his features, and Marlene noticed.

'Nice man, isn't he?' she said softly.

'Yes, I dare say he is.' Lucy noticed that he was putting his own case into the back of the other car. 'What is he doing?' Her voice came out shrill, panicked, and Xander looked up at her, picking up on the change instantly. She squeezed his hand to signal that she was okay.

She looked at her aunt just quickly enough to catch a sheepish look passing over her face.

'Auntie?' she tried again, but Marlene had already taken Xander's hand and started off towards the car. To his credit, Xander didn't make a fuss.

'I'll take Xander with me, you get in with Grace. Come on, Xander. Let's get home, and then we can make some lunch, eh?' Xander looked back at his mum questioningly, so she just smiled and waved him off.

'See you there, honey. Make sure you put your seatbelt on.'

The others got into the car, and drove off, leaving Sam standing by Grace's car. Grace was seemingly busy playing with the radio.

'I hope you don't mind – your friends didn't really give me the option of refusing. I was going to get a taxi, but apparently we're heading the same way.'

Lucy nodded, pointing to the front seat.

'I don't mind at all. Please.'

He shook his head, taking off his coat.

27

'I'll be fine in the back. You go ahead.'

He opened the door, and folded his tall frame into the back seat, his coat on his lap. She walked around to the other side of the car, opening the passenger side door. Grace's large bag was strapped into the seat.

'Sorry, love, I like to have my bag close, for my pills.' She winked at Lucy, and Lucy blushed. *Subtle.*

'Okay, no problem.' She forced her face into a relaxed expression, even though she was utterly embarrassed. The rear door opened, and she saw Sam's hand pull back onto his lap.

'Thank you.' She slipped into the seat next to him, putting her handbag onto her lap.

'Please, use the middle seat. Don't sit with your bag on you, all squashed up. There's plenty of room.'

She eyed him, but saw the same calm expression. He was hard to read. She slid the bag off her lap and put it in the space between them.

'So, what brings you to Westfield then?' Grace asked brightly, pulling out of the train station car park at speed, startling a passer-by as she weaved into the busy morning traffic. 'Meeting your wife?'

Lucy winced, looking out of the window. She saw a pigeon eating some discarded food at the side of the road and suddenly wished she could change places with it. This pretty much felt like being pecked to death anyway.

'Er, no wife.' Sam's deep tones filled the car. 'I'm here for work.'

'Ah, I see.' She turned the wheel abruptly, flicking from lane to lane, heading out of Leeds city centre. Lucy's bag lurched forward, and she put her hand out to grab it, instead touching Sam's doing the same. They both yanked their hands back as the touch of each other burned like fire. He pushed her bag back along the seat.

'I got it,' he murmured, and she smiled at him gratefully.

'So, have you got a girlfriend back home? Is she coming to join you? Or a him, maybe?'

'No, no girlfriend or boyfriend anywhere. It's just me.'

'No family?' Grace pushed.

Sam looked down at his hands, and Lucy cleared her throat.

'Grace, what were you knitting, back on the platform?'

Grace started babbling away, telling them both about the jumper drive that the village was currently embarking on, preparing for winter for the homeless.

'We're going to send them to the foodbanks, the homeless shelters. Amanda and a few of the other women are sewing blankets too, so we should have loads by the time the winter starts to bite.'

She eyed Sam in the rear-view mirror.

'About a forty chest, aren't you, Sam?'

Sam looked shocked, but soon recovered.

'Er yes, good eye. You must know your knitting.'

Grace chuckled, a mucky laugh that belied her years.

'Aye, I know a good beefcake size when I see one.'

'Dear Lord, kill me now,' Lucy muttered to herself.

'Take me with you if you do,' Sam muttered back. They shared a look and both stifled a laugh.

He is really cute, she thought to herself. *Not my type at all, but I can see the attraction.* He had long lashes, which reminded her of her son.

She looked away, out of the window, and didn't speak again until they reached the village of Westfield.

Sam saw the fire station come into view, and leaned forward.

'Here's my stop, Grace, thank you for the lift again.'

'It's no bother, are you sure you're okay here?'

Sam nodded.

'Yes, I'd like to say hello to the lads before I do anything else. Check everything's okay.'

29

Grace smiled approvingly.

'Well, Mr Draper, we are lucky to have you.'

He looked at her in surprise, and she winked.

'It's a small village, duck, nothing much passes us old bats here. Why do you think we took two cars?'

He looked across at Lucy, but she was sound asleep.

'Say goodbye to them for me?' he asked, feeling foolish, and a little cheated that he didn't get to tell her it himself. He wanted to see her again, feel her eyes on him.

'I will, love. I'm sure you'll see her soon enough.'

As Sam watched the women drive off, he was pretty sure that Grace meant every word, and seemed to know that what she said would come true. He had a feeling that some of these villagers might be a bit of a handful. Throwing his holdall over his shoulder and grabbing his suitcase handle, he headed inside to the fire station to start his new career.

CHAPTER 4

Grace drove up the small lane where the holiday cottages sat like pearls threaded on a necklace. It was beautiful here, even more beautiful than Lucy remembered from her childhood. She used to come up here for long summers as a child, no bigger than her son was now. Not much had changed at all, and she felt happier just being here. Grace pulled the car in side by side with the other, and Lucy spotted Xander, sitting in the back seat, headphones on. No doubt he was watching his movie all over again. He seemed settled, so she got out of the car and headed up the path to the cottage with the wide open front door.

The smell of fresh flowers assaulted her nostrils, and she looked around at the neat and gorgeous gardens. The cottages were in lines of twos, hugging each other in little couples along the small country lanes. There was no car next door in the little drive at the front of the house, and Lucy felt relieved that there would be no neighbours, for today at least. Marlene came out of the front door and, seeing her, grinned broadly.

'Lucy dear, it's lovely in here. Just the ticket for you both. I left Xander in the car, will he be okay?'

Lucy looked at her son, who hadn't moved a muscle.

'He'll be okay, he'll come out when he wants to.'

Marlene nodded, motioning for her to come inside. After

walking past the blooming flowers that ran around the edges of the green grass in neat beds, she passed by a lavender bush by the front door, and walked through the painted mint green door. The smell of bleach hit her as she walked in, and she wasn't surprised to see Marlene scrubbing the sink, Marigolds on, cloth in hand.

'It's not dirty, the whole place is spotless really, I just love a bleached sink.'

Lucy nodded, going to open the window and putting it on the latch.

'Xander's not so keen on the smell, it bothers him.' She looked through the window and saw that he was still sitting in the car, Dot now sitting in the passenger seat, book in hand. She waved her away, motioning to her that everything was fine. Lucy waved back.

'Sorry,' Marlene was saying. 'We did ask at the library, but they don't really have any books on the subject. If we do something wrong, let us know love, we want to help.'

Lucy felt the familiar burn of rage in the pit of her stomach.

'He's autistic, not stupid or difficult.'

She spat the words out, looking out of the window at the pretty garden to stop herself from saying anything else. The water started running behind her, and she heard the swish of the cloth as her auntie kept cleaning.

'We know that, dear, but we are trying. The last thing we want is to upset him. We didn't have it in my day, dear. Well, I'm sure that we did, but we just didn't know about it like we do now. Us old bids were just trying to be down with the kids.'

Lucy turned to look at her.

'I know, I'm sorry. It's been a rough day.'

Marlene nodded, pulling off her gloves and placing them on the stainless steel draining board.

'Did you tell him, before you left?'

Lucy swallowed, thinking of the phone call on the train.

'He went to work early. I spoke to him on the train but it didn't seem like the right time to tell him. I left a note, at home.'

She thought of her plush house back home, immaculate as always, the show house of his dreams. She had left everything neat and tidy, including the envelope she left on the kitchen island telling him that she was leaving him, to spend time with her family and think things through.

'Did he really deserve that, Luce?' Marlene asked. 'I know that things have been hard, but does he deserve to come home from work to that?'

'He barely comes home at all. I'll be amazed if he even sees the note.'

Marlene pursed her lips, but said nothing.

'I put your bags in the master bedroom, so Dot and I will leave you to it. We have yoga at the community centre this afternoon anyway. We put some food in the fridge, but you might want to do some shopping soon. If you need a sitter, let us know.'

Lucy nodded, not trusting herself to speak. She heard the door open behind her, and the waft of lavender filled the kitchen. She could hear the women speaking to Xander, and car doors open and close. She headed to the front door, and watched her little boy carry his belongings into the house. He wrinkled his nose at the smell.

'It's just cleaning smells that's all. Do you like the house?'

Xander looked around him at the cosy cream kitchen, the dining room table set for two, fresh pink peonies in a little vase on the table.

'It's different from home,' he said, his voice flat. 'It's not as shiny.' Thinking back to her state-of-the-art kitchen, she laughed a little to herself.

'It is; it's a country look, more wood than shiny surfaces.'

Xander walked around the space, staying clear of the kitchen sink, and touched the surface of the wooden table.

'I like it. It's smaller. Can we see my room now?'

Lucy smiled, pointing to the stairs.

'Lead the way, little man.'

Xander ran up the stairs, dumping his bag on the table before he went. There were no special hidden cupboards here to stash life away in. She looked at the backpack, and felt a wave of relief rush over her. Maybe, just maybe, this would all turn out for the best.

'Mum, come look!'

'I'm coming!' she said, kicking off her shoes and racing up the stairs.

It was late by the time Sam had eventually said goodbye to the lads at the fire station. As soon as he had walked through the door, the thought of the woman on the train fresh in his head, he had been dragged in and made to feel welcome. Chief Briggs was a burly man, his moustache the only tiny thing about him, a whisper of a thick bristle seemingly stencilled on his broad face.

Being lunchtime, the men were all sitting at the large scratched wood table, chatting and laughing away. Norman was at the stove, dishing out plates of hot chilli on baked potatoes. Sam's stomach gurgled.

'Come on in,' Danesh said, pointing to a clear space at the table. 'You eat meat, right?'

Alan patted him hard on the back.

'A man this size? Of course he does!'

'Er, actually no, I don't. Not much anyway. More chicken, eggs. I tend to stay away from red meat.'

He waited for the usual explosion of *what? why? how?* but none came.

Alan shrugged. 'Ah well, more for me, Dan!' He took a seat at the head of the table, and Danesh placed a steaming plate in front of him. Danesh returned to the cooker, taking the lid off a different pot.

'Here's yours.' He spooned some chilli onto a huge baked

potato. 'Meat free chilli, Norm's spesh. It's pretty good, but hold judgement till you've had it three times in one week.' Norman jabbed him in the side, and he laughed.

'Cheeky bugger, you love my cooking!'

Danesh groaned. 'Love, really? It's a strong word, Norm.'

Norman flicked his tea towel at Danesh as he headed to the table, putting a plate in front of Sam.

'Thanks,' he said gratefully, and Danesh sat down next to him.

'So,' Norman called, turning off the heat on the stove and coming to sit down. 'What made you come up here from London?'

Sam took a bite of his food and his whole body embraced the flavour. Proper food for once.

'Nice,' he said to Norman, pointing to his plate. 'I came for the job really, a change of pace.'

Danesh guffawed, slicing his potato up into smaller pieces.

'Well, you'll get that here, we don't get much action. You must have seen some things in your time.'

Sam thought of the call-outs he had had recently, back home, and nodded slowly.

'A few, yes. What have you got on today?'

'We have the rigs to clean out, and the general station main-tenance. We need to get things ready for the summer crowds, and the holiday lets will all need checking over. We do things differ-ently up here, Sam, as you might have gathered from your shifts.'

Sam nodded once, not feeling the need to answer any further. He knew what the job was, and it suited him just fine, for now at least.

'Agatha's on the warpath again too; she's coming down later. Something about the Langthwaite Farm and a bull.'

Norman groaned. 'Christ, can't she just call Ben at the veteri-nary surgery and get him on the case? The poor lad is obviously just trying to get his leg over; Old Man Langthwaite just needs to set him to work.'

Alan shook his head. 'Reg has been showing him to the females, but the bull is just not interested. It keeps jumping the fences to get onto Agatha's land. I think he fancies Archie's new cow.'

'Wow,' Danesh quipped. 'Quite the dairy disaster, eh?'

Alan gave him a look that could curdle milk. 'Anyway, we'll have to speak to Agatha, she'll not rest till she gets her way.' Sam finished his food, feeling very intrigued as to what kind of woman Agatha was that she could get a fire station full of burly blokes quaking into their safety boots.

Sam had hung around for the rest of the shift, filling in his paperwork, picking out a bunk and helping out where he could. Or where Alan would let him at least.

CHAPTER 5

Lucy woke up with a sharp pain in her back, like someone was trying to poke something through her spinal column. Wincing, she rolled over to her side, reaching behind her to move whatever piece of office crap Iain had left on the bed. Opening her eyes, she froze. She wasn't in her bed, or at home. The events from the day before came screaming back to her in a flurry, making her groan loudly and fall back on to her bed. The sharp object stabbed her again, making her jump up to a sitting position, bolt upright.

'Muuummm!' Xander moaned behind her. 'You crushed Bobba Fett!' He pushed her arm away, reaching under her to pull out his beloved toy. 'Grrr!'

He growled loudly, a sure sign that he was both upset and angry. He used to do it all the time as a toddler, unable at the time to verbalise his feelings. She felt a wave of nostalgia so strong that she half expected to see a toddler staring back at her when she looked back.

'Sorry, poppet,' she said softly, holding her hands out palms up. Xander eyed her warily, looking from her face to the toy with its now separate arm.

'Be careful, Mummy,' he said, giving her a final glare before placing the pieces into her waiting hands. She grinned at him, blowing an errant strand of light brown hair out of her eye line.

'I think you know by now, my darling son, that I—' she put the arm back on with ease, making Bobba wave at him '—am a master builder.'

Xander pressed his cute little lips together tight, but she could see he was dying to laugh.

'All fixed!' She grabbed him, pulling him closer to her. 'Cuddle for Mummy!' He squealed, grabbing Bobba tight to his chest, before turning and setting him down on the bedside table.

'Cuddle fort?' he asked, and she nodded.

'Cuddle fort it is!' She pulled him close, his little PJs smelling of the fabric softener she washed his clothes in. He snuggled tight into her, his nose inches from hers. She covered the quilt over them both, stacking the pillows to make a tent of sorts. He nestled closer to her, and she held him tight.

'Did you sleep well?' she asked, looking into the eyes that were so like her own – a bright blue that made his dark, thick lashes all the more striking against his pale skin. Marlene had them too.

'Yep, my room's nice. It's empty, I like it like that. I need my Lego from home though, I don't have enough. Will Dad bring it?'

Lucy winced, thinking of home. Iain would have noticed they were missing by now. He was due to have his golf weekend, but he wasn't leaving till that night. She wondered if he would still go. Would he have called Marlene? She knew her aunt wouldn't lie to him, it wasn't in her nature.

'Well, you remember I said we were coming here for the holidays, and we made that holiday scrapbook to bring? That means we won't be going home for a while yet. We have to leave what we didn't bring at home, till we need it.'

'I need it now,' he whined. 'I need more Lego! I can't do nothing, my brain won't let me.'

Her mouth curled up at one side, a slight grin showing. She ruffled his hair gently, and touched her nose to his. He let her, and stared right at her, just as she had taught him.

'We will have a lovely summer here, and have lots of things to do and see … your brain won't have to be doing nothing. I'll tell you what, you pick some Lego from Mummy's phone, and when it arrives, we can build it together.'

'Will Daddy bring it?'

'We'll get it delivered to our cottage, but we might even see something in town. We are going exploring today, remember, from the calendar?'

Before they had left, she had bought a calendar for the wall, and gone through with Xander the dates and plans that she knew they had, to prepare him. Many days were blanks, and she feared these days more than the ones with her loopy handwriting filling the squares. These were the days where she would feel lost, guilty with a dash of panic. Xander feared them too, the difference to his routine being so huge already. They both had a mistrust of the unknown, but here they were, together. She had a flash of memory. Xander, standing by the pool, screaming. Iain standing over him, shouting and demanding. Holiday-makers, openly gawping at the resort's prize exhibit. She pushed the thought away, willing it to dispel from her brain, riding the bolt of ice water she felt zipping down her spine. This would be a better holiday. It had to be.

'Breakfast first though, Mummy,' Xander checked.

'Yes, my darling. Breakfast. I think holiday pancakes are in order.'

Xander's nose scrunched up. 'Ordered from who?'

Marlene bustled into A New Lease of Life and flopped down on the chair that Grace had her leg on, shunting it to one side.

'Hey, my knee hurts you know!'

Marlene shot her a look. 'Don't moan, woman, it never stopped you doing samba last night, did it? Thrusting your hips at a man half your age, I ask you, where's the dignit—arrgghh!'

She rubbed her left bottom cheek as Grace stuck her tongue

39

out at her, her needle flicking back to her work after a successful stabbing. Marlene narrowed her eyes, looking around her quickly before opening her mouth.

'You do that again, woman, and I'll tell everyone about you and Ted Wilson, you see if I don't.'

Grace jumped forward, horror etched on her face.

'You promised!' She hissed. 'Since 1974 you have held that over me, you buzzard!'

'Buzzard?' Marlene frowned, before realisation set in. Followed by anger. 'You mean vulture, you bloody wizened old crow!'

Grace jabbed her wool-free knitting needle out in front of her menacingly.

'Crow! Crow? I'll stab you in the throat, you blackmailing witch!'

'Ladies, ladies, please!' Amanda, owner of the shop, and proud host of the Westfield Craft Club, pushed the two ladies gently back into their seats, prising Grace's needle from her white knuckles and placing it behind the counter. 'You can have this back when you stop trying to attempt ABH, okay?'

Grace opened her mouth to object, but thought better of it. Instead she mouthed 'you're dead' at Marlene, who ignored her.

'How are you, Marlene?' Amanda asked, putting a tray of tea together, and arranging some biscuits on a plate. 'Did you get the brandy snaps for Agatha?'

Marlene reached into her bag, producing a posh-looking pack.

'Yep, although why she can't just eat Malted Milk like the rest of us is anyone's guess.'

The door opened, the tinkle of the bell heralding someone's arrival.

'Guess what?' Dot said, striding in with her bags. 'It is rather glorious out there today, I had a lovely long walk here. I'm at 6,000 steps already!' She waggled her wrist at them all, her red fitness band's screen lit up.

'Agatha's posh biscuit demands, that's guess what. Six thousand is nothing, I've smashed my target.'

Dot looked at Grace suspiciously. 'How did you beat me? You came in the car, didn't you?' She looked outside the shop, at Baker Street, where Grace's car was parked near the pavement. Marlene, still incensed at the stabbing incident, joined in.

'Yes, Grace, how did you do that?'

Grace pushed her remaining needle into her wool ball, and dropped it into her bag.

'I just did, I'm a very busy woman.'

The two women's gazes centred in on her wrists. Amanda started laughing, setting down the tea tray on the table in front of them and heading back to her workstation. She was used to these ladies coming into her business and taking over. Today was an average day. Quiet even. Dot suddenly inhaled sharply, pointing excitedly.

'It's on your dominant knitting arm! You bloody well cheated! Stitches are not steps, Grace!'

Grace poured a china cup full of tea, the smell filling the shop with a homely aroma.

'Tell that to the app. I bet I'll win weekday warrior this week.'

Dot, who always won the weekday warrior challenge, was furious. 'By cheating and sitting on your fat arse, yeah!'

The ladies all spoke to each other at once, the decibels increasing as they tried to get their points across, shouting to be heard over each other. Their cacophony of noise drowned out the shop bell.

'You can't win every week, it's not fair on the rest of us!'

'It's a competition, Grace, you don't just get to win for nothing because it's your turn! I walk every inch of this village, so if I win, I win on merit!'

'Er, hello?' A quiet voice could be heard, but only Amanda looked at the shop doorway.

'You always did have to win, didn't you? You were always the same, even when we worked together.'

'Hello?'

'Oh here we go!'

"Yeah, let her have it!"

'Hi,' Amanda said finally, moving through the shop and reaching out her hand. Lucy stepped forward, Xander gripping her other arm, and shook Amanda's hand. 'Ignore the ladies here, they will settle down soon.' She turned to Xander, leaning forward, hands on her knees to get on the same level. 'And hello, young sir. May I interest you in some cake, and a glass of juice?'

His eyes opened wide at the mention of cake. Cake was one of Xander's horcruxes. Cake, Lego and superheroes. Not necessarily in that order. The boy was obsessed, and his obsessions were all-consuming at times. Lucy still knew all the names of the dinosaurs from the Cretaceous period, including half of the Latin ones, from having picked them up over the years, when his dino love was in full flow. She could go on *Mastermind* with that specialist subject, and feel completely at ease. Xander had learned all there was to know about the subject, and then moved on. Now it was all superheroes and Lego. Which was a real hardship to Lucy. Really, she did suffer. It was cruel really, this parenting lark. From learning about extinct scaly creatures to having to watch every superhero franchise movie, complete with half-naked sex gods? Parenting was indeed very tricky sometimes, but she did grin and bear it. Especially when poor Thor lost his long hair. That was terrible. She didn't get any cleaning done that day, that's for sure.

Amanda leaned in a little further, as though she was sharing a secret.

'Come with me to the counter, and I'll cut you the biggest piece.'

Xander nodded slowly, a happy smile crossing his features, and Lucy watched as he let go of her hand and trotted along behind the lady. He really was anybody's for a slice of cake. She pushed down the mild thought of terror that sprang to her throat when she thought about that simple truth, and shook herself out of it. The ladies were all still sniping at each other, Grace mumbling something about a needle weapon, so she walked forward and sat down in an empty wooden chair next to her aunt.

'Hello!' Marlene seemed to start a little when she noticed her, and the conversation stopped, turning to cheery hellos. The women transformed before her eyes from the cast of *Hocus Pocus* to something from *The Darling Buds of May*. In a split second they were all sitting contritely, arms clasped together on their laps, looking straight at her. *Great*, she thought, panicking slightly and looking longingly at the door. *Here comes the inquisition.*

'So, did you sleep well?'

'I did thanks. We both did actually.'

'Lovely,' Marlene said, holding up the pot in question. Lucy nodded and watched the steaming hot tea pour into the cute china cup and saucer. Looking around the shop, she could see why the ladies raved about it. It was like a home from home; little corners full of interesting trinkets and pieces of furniture, with the tables front and centre for people to come in, have a cuppa, do their hobbies in company. She couldn't imagine coming to one of these herself, back home. Perhaps she should have done, made more effort to get out of the house once in a while. She knew why she hadn't though. being in public meant dealing with people, and the human race loved to revel in the differences of others.

'Everything okay back home?' asked Grace, never one to shy away from an awkward question.

'Fine thanks,' Lucy replied, in as neutral a voice as possible. 'It's nice to get away, have a break.'

Grace nodded slowly, before looking out of the window. 'Agatha's not coming till later, so how come Taylor's here?'

Amanda groaned loudly, distracting Xander momentarily, who was sitting at a table beside her, chewing on a huge doorstep-sized piece of red velvet cake.

'He's here on official Mayweather business, for the wife. Christenings, and the seasonal run-up. Agatha's bugging all the shop owners. Once the Austen open air event is done, she's like a dog with a bone.' The door opened, and she hushed immediately. Sebastian Taylor, dapper as ever, even in his relaxed checked shirt and jeans, strode in, a clipboard under his arm and a lazy grin on his face. Lucy smiled back at him, and his grin widened in response. She couldn't help it, the man just seemed to shoot Valium into the shop space. She sneaked a peek at the other ladies, and saw similar expressions. The man was like a walking tranquilliser.

'Been shooting eh, Tex?' Dot quipped, and Lucy looked at her in confusion. Dot nodded to his feet. 'Cowboy boots. I swear, since you got wed, I think your dress sense has gotten worse, not better.'

'Hey!' Taylor stuck his lip out. 'Don't knock my cowboy boots, they're good for riding.'

Lucy heard her son gasp behind her, and turned automatically to see what was wrong. Xander was staring at the boots too, a look of awe on his cute little face.

'You're really a cowboy?'

Taylor chuckled. 'I wish, lad. I drive a car to get around, and I don't shoot bad guys. I do ride horses though, is that cowboy enough?'

Xander seemed to mull it over at some length, and Taylor just stood there, waiting as though he had all the time in the world. Lucy wanted to hug him.

'Not really, no, but I won't tell the real cowboys.'

That got another laugh from Taylor, and the ladies laughed along with him.

'Okay, thanks very much.' Taylor walked forward to the table, but instead of sitting down, he knelt to a crouch at the side of the boy. Holding out his hand, he offered a handshake. 'I'm Taylor, what's your name?'

Xander shook his hand immediately, so hard that Taylor's hand banged on the table a couple of times. If it hurt, Taylor didn't acknowledge it.

'I'm Xander Iain Walsh, pleased to meet you.' He pointed to his mother. 'That's my mum Lucy, we've come on holiday for the summer. Dad stayed home for work.'

'Ah well, we are glad you came, Xander. Tell me, have you ever been on a horse?'

Xander shook his head. 'I tried to go on a donkey once, at the seaside, but I didn't like it. It pooped on the sand.'

Taylor chuckled again. 'Well, if you ever do want to be a cowboy for a day, let me know, and I will show you our ponies.' He looked across at Lucy, and she found herself nodding, despite her misgivings. This summer was all about Xander, so if he wanted to ride a pony, he would ride a damn pony. 'Great, so, Amanda, can I borrow you for a minute?' He brandished the clipboard with an apologetic grin, and Amanda eye-rolled him into the back room.

The ladies all waited till the door closed behind them, then leant forward, closer to Lucy.

'If Agatha tries to rope you in, just shrug it off, tell her you are here on holiday, and far too busy to help. Taylor's married to her, and Amanda is like family. They are already damned, but we can save you.' Dot patted the hands on her lap. 'Honestly, she will accept it if you are firm.'

Grace snorted. 'Like you were, about the community centre bake sale? My fingers are still sore from mixing all those ruddy cupcakes!' She pointed out of the shop window, eyes focusing on Lucy. 'I tell ya, that woman was a menace. We all said no, that we were busy, but did she listen? Did she 'eckers! Then, come the day, she springs a bloody cupcake competition on us and stands there dissing our work! She was like Simon Cowell on acid.'

Marlene smoothed down her jumper. 'I didn't think she was that bad.'

Dot guffawed. 'Of course you didn't, you ruddy well won!'

Marlene pulled a happy face at Lucy. 'I know.' She stage-whispered the rest. 'I just like you lot remembering that important fact.'

Grace looked around the room. 'Whatever, Nigella, where is my blinking needle?'

Marlene shrank away from her, her hand covering her rump protectively.

'Well, I think we shall be off, anyway.' Lucy stood to leave, her duty being done. Her aunt had asked her to come, and be friendly, and she had. Xander was still at the table, holding his fork midair with the last piece of cake on.

'Noo, my cake!'

Lucy headed over to him, ruffling his hair as she always did.

'Finish it up, then we can have a look for some Lego.'

Dot frowned. 'I'm not sure you'll get any round here, honey. You might have to order it in.'

Lucy's heart sank. She thought as much.

'Shall we order it online then, Xander, and have a look around the shops anyway?'

She passed him her phone, but when she looked back he was frowning.

'It's saying that we can't go online, Mum.'

Shit. The SIM Card. He was frowning at the screen, jabbing away at the buttons.

'Mum, it's not working. Does that mean Dad can't call us?'

Lucy felt the air in the shop change, and the conversation trickle to a stop. Xander was now looking up at her, his eyes wide open and focusing on her. It was his anxious face, an expression she knew so well. She licked her lips, trying to get them moist, looking around her at the women, but they were studiously pretending not to be listening, fiddling with their crafts, rummaging in their bags.

'Xander,' she started, coming to sit in the chair next to him. 'Mummy and Daddy love you very much, and Daddy is working hard at home while we are on holiday. Mummy and Daddy had a little bit of a fight, and so I got cross and took something out of my phone to stop it working. I'm sorry. Shall we see if we can get a new number while we are shopping?'

Xander still had his worried face on, and she gave him the time he needed to process what she was saying. The ladies were all speaking in hushed voices now, and Lucy could feel her face flushing as her dirty laundry was aired out in front of them. God knows what they thought of her! She didn't even know why she had done it herself. She just remembered sitting on that train, wanting to protect her son from the world, if only for a few weeks. She wanted to protect him from the kids at his school, who picked on him, laughed at him. Called him names. She wanted to get away from the stares he got in shops when he couldn't cope with his senses. Most of all, she wanted to protect him from his father. And that was what hurt most of all.

'Mum, are you not listening to me? Can't you just put the thing back in? Dad could send us the Lego then, from my room.'

Lucy sighed, and pulled herself out of the chair.

'Let's go get a new SIM Card and see about ordering that Lego. Goodbye, ladies!' She gave a cheery wave that she did not feel and motioned for her son to follow her. He stood up and went to follow, but then, almost as an afterthought, he returned to his plate and proceeded to dip his face right into it, licking all the crumbs off with his cute little pink tongue.

'Xander,' she whispered, trying to get his attention. 'Love, what did we talk about?'

She turned to the women, who were all looking at the little boy, and automatically started to explain. What she didn't expect, however, was the look on their faces. There was no judgement there, just amusement. Marlene was even laughing a little as he made his way around the plate, getting every little bit of cream cheese frosting off it and into his mouth.

'Sorry, he has a thing about dirt, but he will always lick his plate clean when there is cake involved.'

Xander finished and put the plate down on the counter.

'I'm autistic – we don't like change, but we love cake!'

Lucy's eyes bulged. Marlene looked just as shocked. Xander's autism wasn't something they hid, but Xander himself never referred to it. Maybe time apart from home was going to be worth all the grief she would get when she went back. It wasn't anything to hide after all, so why had they?

'Well,' Grace said, getting up and heading for where Amanda had stashed her needle. She was shaking like she was having knitting withdrawal symptoms, which she probably was. 'I'm impressed, Xander.' She located the needle, and punched the air triumphantly. 'I'm a little jealous too. I would love to enjoy cake as much as you do!'

The ladies all laughed, and Lucy found herself laughing along too. Xander bounced out of the shop all smiles and sugar highs, and it made her heart soar. She was started to really like these ladies. Aunt Marlene was right, a change was as good as a rest.

CHAPTER 6

Sam's first morning in Westfield was uneventful. Waking up in the cottage he was renting, he listened to the quiet of his surroundings. It had been a long while since he had lived with his adoptive mother in her full and noisy house, but he still found himself missing the noise of little feet on the stairs, music battling for supremacy in different rooms, the heartwarming belly laughs of his mother as one of the children made her laugh. Even in his flat in London, he would be awoken by the sound of the streets outside his window, the sound of the fire engines starting up in the middle of the night. He rented near to the station, so that when things got bad he could be called in. There in six and a half minutes from the time the call came in to him walking into the fire station. He liked to be near.

He stretched out his arms in front of him, working out the kinks from sleeping on the unfamiliar and rather hard mattress in the master bedroom. It was a cosy cottage, homely and clean, with some nice touches throughout. Milk and bread and other essentials were in the fridge and cupboards when he had finally come in last night, and he was only connected to one other cottage, seemingly occupied judging from the lights that were in the window when he had arrived. No car though, so he couldn't get a read on who was staying there. Still, he couldn't see them

49

receiving many night call-outs, so he shouldn't be a nuisance. He was used to making himself smaller around people by now. Sometimes in life, he had to, despite what his mother taught him. He needed to fit in, or at least fly under the radar. At least for now. Toe the line.

Westfield Fire Station was a feeder station, as well as catering for the residents of Westfield. They often helped out on call-outs in Harrogate and other surrounding areas. Little villages mainly, dotted around the vast green fields and forests of the area. It sure made a difference from the concrete jungle he was used to, but it had great value all the same. This wasn't an easy job, by any means. He had not come here for an easy ride, job wise. True, he had his own agenda, but the job and the guys at the house were great. It had felt welcoming from the first moment he had worked in there, all those months ago. Filling a staff need and looking for answers.

Heading downstairs a short while later, wearing nothing but a pair of sweatpants, he made himself a coffee using the complimentary sachets and made a mental note to get some shopping in after his shift, or at least book an online delivery. Back home, he would place the same order week after week, to be delivered the same day. Convenient, but, tasting the coffee in his mug, he realised that change perhaps wasn't such a bad thing. He opened up the patio doors in the kitchen, standing just outside the door, his bare feet feeling the cool of the neatly decked seating area outside. A barbecue stood in the corner, covered up and tucked away from the elements, with a large seat on the other. Perfect for family holidays, he was sure. Lucky for him that this had been available. The thought of living in a hotel had filled him with dread, but a holiday cottage? He hadn't been keen when the chief suggested it, picturing plaid and crocheted doilies, but he actually rather liked living in a house. It felt homely, in an odd way. He was busy looking out at the countryside that stretched out beyond the garden borders when he heard a noise to his left.

Sitting on one of the chairs, wrapped in a teal fluffy robe that he recognised from his own welcome pack, was the girl from the train. He opened his mouth to say hello, but then she started talking.

'I know you're not happy I left, but we needed to get away. Don't you get that?'

She was sitting side on from him, twirling a piece of lavender in her free hand, and he found himself taking a step back, closer to his porch. He could slip back through the patio doors, but he found himself hesitating. She sounded upset, and he had a feeling that this was something to do with why she was here. The irony wasn't lost on him. He had come to find answers, and perhaps she had escaped whatever she had to find her own.

She stood suddenly, dragging her fingers through her unkempt morning hair and sticking the lavender behind her ear. The movement made Sam yearn to lean in and smell the fragrance that it left there, near her hair.

'No, you can't speak to him, he's asleep! I'm not waking him up for you to interrogate him like you normally do! We are here on holiday, he needs this. So do I, come to think of it. I asked you to come away with us, for us to sort things out, but you couldn't do it. What do you want us to do, hang around at home for you all summer whilst we wait for you to grace us with your presence?'

Her head snapped back, the phone suddenly thrust forward in her hand. She forked it vigorously before speaking into it again. The sprig fell from her ear and landed on the stone slabs under her feet.

'Iain, I don't give a shitting shite about your shirts! Is that really what you care about?' She flumped back down on the seat, shaking her head. She was angry. Even a stranger could tell that.

'I know I don't talk like that, but you pushed me, Iain.' She

51

sighed heavily, and her voice cracked a little when she spoke again. 'I'm just trying to help my son.'

Whatever the caller said didn't help. In fact, she started to cry softly.

'Iain, you know where we are. I shouldn't have changed my number, but you ...' A sob escaped, and her hand flew up to her mouth. 'You know what you did, Iain. I just can't spend all summer living like that. He can't cope and, to be honest, neither can I any more.'

Sam decided he had heard more than enough. Turning to go back into the house, he didn't see a ceramic blue plant pot there, a topiary tree potted in it, and ended up kicking it with his bare foot.

'Arggh!' He tried to trap his pain in his mouth, but it squeaked out. He immediately looked to his right, to see if she had heard. Funny that, how a human's first reaction after kicking a ceramic pot and being 'punched' in the scrotum by a ball-shaped tree is to look around to see if anyone was a witness to their failure. She had heard. She was up out of her seat, looking right at him. The phone was still to her ear, and after a moment of panic crossing her features, she narrowed her eyes and made a shushing sound with her finger.

'Iain, I have to go, okay? Xander is waking up.' She flinched, nibbling her bottom lip as though considering something. 'I'll ask him to call you, yes. I have to go.'

She ended the call and put her hands on her hips.

'Earwig much?'

Sam held up his hands in surrender.

'I'm sorry, I really wasn't. I just came out here to drink my coffee, and then ...' One look at her and he forgot what he was trying to say. Her robe had come undone a little, showing a white t-shirt and pink shorts underneath. It was distracting, and he wasn't a great liar in the first place. Lies and secrets were two things he abhorred. He dragged his eyes back up to her face, but

52

not before she noticed what he was looking at, covering herself with her robe. Her cheeks flushed, and Sam was conflicted by the action. He had invaded her privacy and then ogled at her, which was bad. The flush in her cheeks wasn't though, nor the biting of her bottom lip, which she seemed to use as a comfort motion when stressed. That was good. It lit up her whole face. He couldn't help but think about how he could make her cheeks flush that way again.

'And then?' she prompted, hands firmly back on her hips now, with the added movement of a foot tap. He noticed her feet were bare, pretty polish adorning the toes. Polish that was a little wonky.

She followed his eye line and crossed one foot over the other, hiding one set of toes with its counterpart.

'Xander did my nails last night. Or did you already know that?'

He pulled an action like she had wounded him, reeling back a little and putting his hand over his chest as though shot through with her words.

'Guilty as charged. I'm sorry, I am not normally nosy. I honestly just did come out here for coffee. You on holiday then?'

She already knew that he had heard her phone call. That this was more than just a holiday. She took the bait though, smiling a fraction of a second at his attempt to smooth things over.

'Yes. My Auntie Marlene lives here, she's always at me to come. She asked me to stay with her, but Xander likes his own space, and her house is a lot to take in.'

Sam nodded. 'Autism, right?' He said it easily, as he would any other word. He had seen his fair share of kids with different needs over the years, picked things up. On the job, too.

He felt her scrutinise him, as though she was weighing him up and finding him lacking.

'Yes, he has autism. It's not been diagnosed long, but I knew.'

Sam nodded, putting his coffee cup down on the table across the deck. Moving a little closer to her.

'Mothers always know. He got a good school system set up?'

53

Her face pinched, and the flush disappeared. He regretted asking, if it took that away from him.

'Kind of. Not really.' She shrugged. 'They put things in place, things work for a while. Till someone says something, or there's an event.' She looked down at her polish, her face lighting up as she saw the haphazard blobs of polish on her nails. She loved the bones of the boy, Sam didn't need to ask a question to know that. 'July was hard, you know. I just needed to get away.' He waited for her to elaborate, but she was looking at him now. 'How did you know?'

'I've been around a lot of kids, on the job. My mum is a foster parent too, so I picked a few things up.'

'I'm sure you did, but living with it is a little different.' He wanted to counter that he had lived with it, many times over, but what would the point be? He wasn't a parent, so he didn't know what it was like to be raising a child, that much was true. Any further explanation would only bring questions back to him, and he didn't want to talk about it. So they both stood there a while, looking at the other, wanting to ask, to probe, to enquire, but not wishing to divulge anything themselves.

'Well, I'd better be off to work. You and Xander have a good day, okay?'

At that minute Xander shouted for her from inside, and she automatically took a step closer to the cottage. Her face was pinched, her shoulders up above her ears with the tension of the stress.

'Hey, listen,' Sam said softly. 'It's your holiday. Enjoy it.'

She said nothing, just waved her fingers at him and headed inside.

'You have a good day at work.' Her foot was on the step, when she turned and looked at him, biting her lip. 'Be safe.'

Sam nodded. No one but his mother had ever cared about him like that. Here she was, worrying for his wellbeing. He stood there, looking at the space where she had just been standing, and felt the bloom of warmth in his chest. It felt nice, having someone take the time to think about him. He thought of his mother and, going indoors, he opened one of the kitchen drawers and pulled out the letter that she had given to him at the train station. He took a seat at the small kitchen table, stretched his long legs out in front of him and, smiling at the looped handwriting he knew so well, opened the cream envelope. There were two sheets of paper inside, folded in half, and when he opened the sheaf, a photograph fell out, face down. He could make out his mother's faded writing on the back of it. He picked it up and read the inscription. It read:

Baby Sam, with his rescuers. November 1987, Euston Road Fire Station.

None of the description was anything new to him, the details were imprinted in his brain. His mother had told him all about his rescue, the firemen who had cared for him, and the social worker who had called Sondra that icy late November night, telling her a baby had need of a home. Turning over the photo, he saw the original of the photo that hung on the living room wall of Sondra's home. It was three firemen standing together, a tiny bundle of red cloth wrapped in the middle man's arms, all three of them smiling at the camera. In the background, on a table in the fire station, is a box. The box he had arrived in, marked 'Burgess Teas of Harrogate'. He'd been found just outside, after the half-frozen wails of a baby had gotten the inhabitants running outside, looking for the noise. That year, a new TV show had started, with the hero being a Welsh fireman called Sam. The men, all grappling to warm the baby up, feed him and wait for social services, hated to keep talking to him without him having a name, so one of them, a dad of a telly mad toddler, nicknamed him Sam. When Sondra took him in later that night, after the hospital gave him the all clear, she didn't have the heart to change it.

'Son,' she always said when telling him the tale of the day he found his family, 'I took one look at those beautiful big eyes of yours, and I knew, your name was meant to be Samuel. It was meant to be, just as much as you were meant to be found that night, right when I was looking for a sign to keep on fostering, to keep on trying to make a difference.'

Looking at the photo now, looking at the box, he once again found himself wondering at the differences between his two matriarchs. He had been found in that box, dressed in a thin Babygro, a spare terry towelling nappy tucked in with him, newspaper wrapping him up. He didn't even have a blanket to remember her by. The box had been searched for clues, but nothing of any value was found. A piece of cardboard and a bundle of paper. Not much to herald his entrance in the world, the Babygro was it. Second-hand at that. Sondra had offered him the piece of cloth many times, but Sam found he couldn't bear to look at it. It's tragic origins prevented him from wanting to be anywhere near it, but he knew that Sondra would keep it forever. He pushed the photo into the middle of the table, and looked at the letter.

It read:

Dear Sam,

I always knew the time would come when you would leave my arms and go out into the world. I've seen it so many times, and applauded when it happened even as I swallowed down my sadness. For you though, my dear sweet boy, it's always been different. My arms wept when I first held you that cold night. I remember seeing you, in the social worker's arms, as she walked up my front path that night so many years ago. I was a little beaten up myself, a little tired of the constantly sad stories that came etched on the faces of the children that came through my doors. I was due to finish that very next day. I was all set on stopping, on being on my own for a little while, to try to heal.

Helping others is the key to happiness, Samuel, and you gave me that key when you came into my life. The minute I held you, I knew you were home, but I also knew that I should make the most of every day after, because one day, this event would happen. You asked me once, where you came from, and I told you Westfield, but I didn't tell you everything. They traced the serial number on the box you were left in back to a Westfield batch of deliveries, sure, but that wasn't what made me so sure. After the police left, and the social workers had left you to my charge, I looked again at the box, and tucked into the flap, was the letter I attach. I followed the wishes, darling Sam, and I hope you can forgive me for that. I knew that your fearlessness would one day lead you to this, and I hope you find what you have been looking for.

Love, Mumma

He teared up as he saw her signing off with such a familiar moniker. He had called her Mumma from an early age, and it had stuck till well into his teens, if only in the privacy of their home by then. He swallowed to try to get rid of the sense of dread he felt, the lump of foreboding feeling like a dry piece of bread in the back of his throat. He looked at the last letter, and began to read.

CHAPTER 7

Given that she had started the morning with an argument with Iain, a half-naked encounter with her temporary neighbour and a morning of explaining to Xander, Lucy found herself feeling strangely upbeat. She had tried to explain that deliveries, even with Amazon Prime and the joys of modern technology, might take a day or two to arrive in Westfield. He had made the rest of his Lego up, and was now wanting to do more. Simply taking photos of his builds for posterity, and dismantling them to make other things wasn't an option. He didn't want them to be taken apart, not till he was ready. He wanted the whole set together, and wasn't about to ruin his models when they were incomplete.

'But can't we call them, see when it will come?' he whined as they left the cottage and headed out. They had been summoned again by Marlene, and her friends, but this time, they were headed to the big house. The Mayweather Estate was in the heart of Westfield, and it was a beauty to behold. She had seen it many times as a girl, but today she was to be a guest. Agatha Mayweather as was, now Mrs Taylor, matriarch and unofficial Queen Mother of Westfield, no less. One of the Craft Club cronies.

Xander was wearing his best clothes, which of course were soft and elasticated, and hated intensely by the wearer.

'Mummm!' he complained as they walked through the village.

'Do I have to wear a tie? It's a sign of toxic masculinity you know! You are oppressing me!'

Lucy giggled accidentally, not being able to keep her reactions in check for this one. She never dumbed things down for Xander, in fact quite the opposite. His vocabulary had most seasoned adults reaching for the dictionary.

'Xander, where did you read that?' She looked down at him, but he glared back, pouting.

'Google,' he said. 'It's right though. You always say that women shouldn't have to wear spiky shoes for men, but you made me wear this!' He brushed his hand across his chest, flicking the tie up in disgust. He did look cute though, smart grey slacks, a white shirt and a pastel blue tie, all pristine, ironed and shoehorned onto him that morning. She had given him plenty of notice, and warnings, but the holiday had been somewhat of an upheaval for him, and it was starting to show. The tie was seemingly the last straw.

'I've told you before about Googling things, be careful.' He rolled his eyes at her, having heard it so many times before. 'We have been invited as guests today, so it's nice to dress up. Be polite. We only have to stay for a few hours, and then we can go.'

'Hours?' echoed Xander with a loud woe-is-me wail. 'Not hours! There isn't enough conversation in the world to last that long! Nooo, Mum! We have to be home for the deliverieeesssss!' His voice was close to breaking, and she felt the beginnings of her earlier anxiety starting once more. She was wearing her best summer dress, a soft pastel blue peppered with violet flowers, and her favourite soft leather pumps in a matching blue. She felt like she was auditioning to be a villager, and she didn't like the sensation of being assessed. She had lived like that for months back home, having to justify her life to people: her parenting skills, her child, her marriage, her pregnancy. She'd come here to get away, to reassess her life from a distance, and to give Xander a taste of a different life. A taste of her childhood. She hadn't expected to be running the gauntlet of the Westfield elite. Finally walking up the driveway, she stopped at the fountain and bent down into a squat to look her son in the face.

'Xander, it's nice to visit people, and everyone here is nice, and they just want to meet you, that's all.' His little pinched face made her pause. 'I'm nervous too, but if we hold hands, we can face it together, okay? What is it we say?'

'Everything is A-okay!' he said loudly. 'Let's go, Mum.' His face screwed up in determination, a look that always made her heart melt. It meant he was focusing, getting ready to meet the challenge head-on. He squeezed her hand in his, and they walked up the drive together. They were almost at the front door when it opened, and a smartly dressed woman stepped out, heading straight for them.

'Well,' she said primly, a broad easy smile on her face, 'you must be Marlene's niece. You look so much like her! Welcome to our home.' She gestured behind her with little consequence, as though she was standing in front of a little shack instead of the Mayweather Mansion. 'Come in!' She very elegantly leaned forward and placed her manicured hands on her knees.

'Good morning, Xander, thank you for bringing your mother to come and see us, I appreciate it. Do you like dogs?'

Xander, preening with the praise and deference she was showing him, nodded slowly.

'Well, I have two big dogs, and I've put them in the grounds outside for a run about. I can show you them if you like. They are rather big though, and they get very excited, so I'll leave them outside for a little while. We can eat in peace then too.'

Moving forward a little closer, and looking at Lucy as though to check she wasn't listening, she whispered something to Xander. His eyes went wide, and he nodded vigorously.

'Shall we go in?' She raised herself to her full height, smoothed down her skirt and, in the same movement, ushered them all into the house before they could even think to object.

'Lucy!' Marlene exclaimed, her voice echoing in the huge hallway they found themselves in. Off to one side, in a room off the hallway there was a large sitting area, with comfy seating arranged around a large fireplace. At the other side, at the back of another expansive room, a table was set out with place settings, fancy crockery and cutlery, candlesticks and centrepieces in the middle. It looked beautiful, and very clean and organised. Lucy loved the look, and was almost glad to be there.

Marlene stood and trotted over to them both, enveloping Xander into a huge hug despite his weak protests. Dot and Grace sat like a couple of bookends at either side of the fireplace.

'They're here!' she trilled merrily. 'We have a lovely lunch planned, Agatha has gone all out!'

Grace, knitting something rather large and navy blue, snorted loudly.

'Well, the caterers she hired have done a little bit to help, I'm sure.' Dot scowled at her, but she ignored her friend, focusing on the visitors instead. 'Xander darling, how are you?' she asked kindly. 'Want to see what I'm making?'

Xander, intrigued by anything creative, nodded slowly and headed over.

'So,' Marlene said softly, taking Lucy's bag off her shoulder and dashing off to put it on a coatstand in the hallway, 'how are things at the cottage? Are you settling in?'

Lucy looked at Xander, being made a fuss of by the three ladies, and felt herself relax.

'It's good thanks, apart from the fact that Xander is waiting for an emergency Lego delivery and my neighbour is a big nosy drink of water.'

'Neighbour? Delivery? We do get parcels here, you know. It's not like we live in the Stone Age. Grace is always ordering bits from eBay for her hobbies. And as for the cottage, Cassie runs the holiday cottages, if you have a problem, we can call her.'

'Oh yeah, I'm really going to dob in the local fireman. The village will love me for that!'

Marlene puffed out her cheeks. 'Sam? You have a problem with Sam? Oh come on, he can't be that bad. He was lovely at the station.'

'Sure, lovely. I know what you guys all think of him, but you don't have to live next to him. Honestly, I am just trying my very best to avoid him at this point.'

There was a knock at the door, and Marlene ushered her further into the room, seating her on the large couch. Xander was sitting on a footstool next to Grace, focusing on a little row of stitches he had on a pair of smaller knitting needles. Grace was engrossed in teaching him, and Xander was doing his trademark cute move of sticking his tongue out when he was concentrating. Agatha breezed past, and Dot stood up to start pouring the tea.

'One lump or two?' she asked Lucy, and she was about to answer when the door opened, and a behemoth walked in. Agatha looked like a tiny little colourful bird as she fluttered around its mass, and she heard the women all make appreciative noises at the sight.

'Good morning, ladies,' Sam crooned, his voice soft and deep. 'Hello, Xander, you here looking after everyone?'

Xander beamed at him, lifting up his needles to show off his handiwork. Grace went over to him, giving him a hug and making him stand up straight. She held her work-in-progress up against his chest and whooped triumphantly.

'Excellent, it fits.' She reached up on her tiptoes and chucked him on the chin. 'Nice jumper for you, on the way.' She winked at Lucy and headed back to her knitting masterclass. Sam looked a little taken aback, but muttered his thanks in their direction before turning his gaze to Lucy.

'Hello again. I hope you had a good morning?'

Lucy frowned at him, but murmured something vague about walking in the village and cucumber sandwiches. Agatha, standing a little between them and the door, was watching the pair of them with an odd expression on her face.

'Sounds good,' he replied easily, looking her up and down slowly with his eyes. 'You look beautiful, if you don't mind me saying so. Reminds me of lavender, your dress.'

Lucy opened her mouth to say, *Thanks, it's just something from the back of my wardrobe*, but it erupted from her mouth as a little squeak. If he noticed, he didn't comment. The lavender comment was still smacking her in the face. He noticed. Every. Little. Thing.

'So, why are you here?' *Better, Lucy. Use your words. Nosy neighbour alert, get it together.*

'I ... er ...'

For the first time, she took him in properly. He was dressed in his firefighting uniform – a black fitted t-shirt and matching trousers, topped with a belt and huge black boots. The man was so tall, so big that even in this hallway, she felt his presence. It was disconcerting, especially when Agatha, an average-sized person, was at the side of him. She looked like a Funko plastic toy compared to his huge GI Joe looks. Lucy felt the urge to laugh bubbling up inside her, but she squashed it down.

'He's here to help me. I have some trees on the property that I thought might be becoming a bit of a hazard, so I called the station, and Chief Briggs was very obliging.'

'Shouldn't you call a tree surgeon for that, not a fireman?'

Agatha cleared her throat politely, turning to Sam and placing a hand on his arm. He smiled down at her, with no sign of irritation.

'A tree surgeon would do the job, of course, but we're happy to look at any issue that might be at risk of causing property damage or injury. Are the trees out back?' Sam, all business now, was already heading through the house, looking for the back doors. Agatha, not used to being controlled, stuttered a little and then followed him, her plummy tones ringing out as she click-clacked through the hallway on her heels. Lucy found herself sitting forwards, head bent, listening to them depart. She heard a door open and then a cacophony of dogs, barking and yipping. It reminded her of going to the school gates to collect her child back home, and she walked away from the memory in the company of the others.

What Agatha Mayweather called her back garden was laughable. In reality, it was a huge expanse of greens and browns, a lovely area to socialise in the sunshine, and large enough that the whole of Westfield could join her. She had paused in the boot room at the back of the house to take off her pink court shoes, placing them on a pristine high shelf and pushing her feet into a pair of Hunter wellington boots, which, oddly, also matched her outfit. They headed out onto the patio area, walking further out towards where a large crop of trees stood, one leaning more than the rest. Sam followed her patiently, taking in the scenery and listening to her speaking about the history of the house, and the renovations that they had undertaken to protect against the ravages of time and to keep up with modern conveniences. Finally, they were standing at the foot of the trees, and Agatha was silent.

'So, Mr Draper …' she began.

'Please, call me Sam.'

'Samuel?'

'Samuel's fine, Mrs Taylor, or is it Mayweather?'

She brushed him off with her folded hands. 'Oh please, call me Agatha. My first husband was Mayweather, but I go by both Taylor and Mayweather in these parts. Agatha to those I like. I'm grateful that you could come to help today. How are you settling in?'

Sam focused on the trees, assessing the situation before replying.

'I'm settling in fine, thanks. The cottage is comfortable; the lads are great. These trees are fine where they are, but this one that's leaning, it looks as though there was some storm damage to it at some point, so you might want to call that tree surgeon to take care of it. At this distance from the house and outbuildings, and in the condition it's in now, I don't foresee a problem at this time. Nothing the fire house need to deal with thankfully.'

'That's wonderful,' she said dismissively. 'We can eat then. Tell me, are you a coffee or a tea man?'

A boatload of sandwiches, scones, little nibbles and a vat of English Breakfast tea later, the party were all feeling rather full, and a little lazy. Even Xander was settled and happily dozing on the sofa, his head in Lucy's lap. Agatha was sitting in a Queen Anne wingback chair, a plate on one of the arms with a half-eaten prawn vol-au-vent sitting on it. Dot was snoring softly in her chair, and Grace's knitting was sitting in her handbag, Grace laid back in her chair, head nodding. Food comas all around, till Sam broke the spell by standing up from his position on the sofa in the corner.

'Well, ladies.' He did a little bow to them all. 'I thank you for the hospitality, but I do have to be getting back to the station now. Duty calls.'

'Whose duty?' asked Xander, suddenly wide awake and looking up at him inquisitively. 'What's he calling for?' Grace tittered in her chair a little, but the others looked at Sam. He was unreadable as always, and Lucy held her breath as he walked over and stooped to crouch in front of her son. Flicking his gaze to her, she saw that he already had stubble on his muscular chin, giving him a rather fetching five-o'clock shadow. Lucy didn't really look at men, but she was looking now. Sam was just so different from anyone she had seen before, she couldn't help but study him.

'It's just a saying, Xander, sorry. It means that I have a job to do, and I need to go and do it now, to keep people safe. Do you understand?'

'Yes, I do now.' He bit his lip before reaching over to the emblem on Sam's shirt and running his finger along the stitching. 'Can anyone be a hero? Even me?'

Lucy felt her heart constrict. They had never hidden his condition from him, or at least she hadn't hidden it from him. He knew he was different, but in this world, what defined normal? Iain was another story, and she knew this insecurity stemmed from him, and all the others free to give their opinions on the spawn of others.

'Of course,' Sam replied easily. 'Especially you, you look after your mum, don't you? I saw you, on the train, looking after her and making sure she was okay. That's just what a hero does, looks after other people. So you do that, yeah? That's your mission this summer, to look after your mother and to have a great holiday.'

Xander leaned forward and very seriously said, 'And the Death Star. Don't forget we need to build the Death Star. It's my dream.'

Sam leaned in and just as seriously replied, 'I understand. If you need any help, you know where I am.' He clenched his fist and offered it to Xander, who fist-bumped him back and made a shushing motion with his finger against his lips. Sam winked at him, laughing softly as he raised himself back up to his full height.

'Ladies, I bid you adieu!' He did a fake over-the-top bow, and took his imaginary hat off his head to complete the effect. 'Goodbye, Lucy. It was lovely to see you again. Xander, may the force be with you.' The ladies all watched him leave through the huge main doors, and stayed silent for a while after the wooden doors had closed behind him.

'Well,' Grace said dreamily, 'there is a man who can fill a sweater.'

The ladies all laughed, and Lucy found herself laughing with them. She didn't have an argument to the contrary, and she had even thought herself about what would be hidden under that woollen layer. That would be a sight to see, and one she wouldn't object to. What Lucy didn't see, and perhaps would have had strong objections to, was the ladies looking at each other, and the beginnings of a plan forming in their grey matter.

CHAPTER 8

Walking through the village after their huge lunch at the Mayweather Mansion, Lucy felt lighter than she had in a long time. When she thought of her life back home, she could feel her muscles clench up, her anxiety levels rising. It had been so hard to manage, to try to get through every day unscathed; making sure that Xander had a good morning, making sure Iain had everything he needed for work, getting them out of the door on time, ready to start the day. Here, Xander was blooming already, and she couldn't help feeling it was more than being off school that was a relief to her only child.

Iain hadn't been in touch since their call, and Xander had refused to call him, so she hadn't pushed or mentioned it again. If he didn't want to call his father today, they could manage that. When the next day came, and he still didn't want to talk to him, then that would be a problem.

'Mum,' Xander asked as they walked through the pretty streets back to the cottage, 'can we go and see the fire station one day, and see Sam?'

There he was again, in her thoughts, and it seemed that she wasn't alone.

'I'm not sure we can do that buddy, the fire station is a pretty busy place, and I'm not sure that children are allowed there.'

'Can we ask, next time we see him?'

Lucy grimaced, but found herself agreeing.

'Okay, we can ask, but don't be upset if it's not possible, okay? They do an important job so they need to focus on their work.'

Xander was a little way in front, stepping over the cracks in the pavement carefully as he hopped and skipped along the lane. He had a habit of spinning around and touching the ground when he moved about sometimes, when he was excited or nervous in new situations. It generated a lot of stares and odd questions back home, but here, no one batted an eyelid. One nice lady had even clapped him on her way past and told him he looked like a fairy king. Lucy could have sunk to her knees and sobbed like a baby right then and there. She knew that it was probably just in her head, but what was it about this place that seemed so much more relaxed, more open and friendly? They hadn't travelled to the ends of the earth, and the old wives' tale about Londoners being closed off wasn't true. There were tolerant people and close-minded people in every walk of life, so what was different about Westfield? Looking around her, she didn't have any answers, but the jolt of fresh air and the feel of the sun on her face went some way to soothe her busy mind. Maybe she would even get a little colour to her skin. Her tan was fading from their holiday to Spain, even if the memories of that day were still as fresh and raw as ever. Which left her thinking about Iain again, and what had happened to them that had evolved from a simple disconnect in their marriage, to her fleeing their life with their son in tow. She knew that this holiday was more than that, but she didn't think that Iain realised the same thing. Would he miss her? Them? Would he wonder why they had decided to leave, with so little notice?

They walked towards the cottages, and the two linked together came into view, Sam's and theirs. They really were the most beautiful cottages, with the utmost care and attention given to them both by the owners. As a holiday let, it was pretty idyllic. Truth be told, she felt more at home in the cosy warmth of their

68

temporary home than she ever had in the rather larger new-build house they shared with Iain. Another thing to contemplate when she went to bed tonight.

'Mum!' Xander was running through the gate now, up the path. She hadn't quite rounded the corner, so couldn't see him, but from his squeals and excited whoops she guessed that the deliveryman had been and followed her instructions to leave their packages in the storage bench on the front porch area. She could hear him laughing, and her heart sang with the sound, until she turned the corner, and saw him wrapped in Iain's arms, the boxes at their feet. It seemed her husband had missed them after all, and the delivery driver couldn't follow a simple instruction. Probably a male delivery driver too. Men. As always, she was ruled by their whims and actions. She plastered on the best smile she could, and walked up to the house.

'What the hell are you playing at, Luce?' He rounded on her as soon as the back door was closed. Xander was outside, having been coaxed by her to go and search for butterflies. Xander loved animals and insects of every description, and was always keen to go exploring. It would distract him for long enough, hopefully. She walked past him and headed to the kettle, keeping one eye on her son through the glass doors. After filling it with water, she flicked it on and set about making coffee.

'Are you not going to even say hello? Really?' His voice was shaking with anger, and she turned to face him, spooning sugar into the mugs as she did so.

'How did you find us?' was all she could think to ask.

He looked at her with such an angry look of contempt that it made her heart race.

'That's it!? That's all you care about?' He jabbed a finger at the doors, where Lucy could see Xander lying on the grass, looking up at the blue sky. 'You took my son on holiday without even bothering to tell me!'

'Don't shout,' she retorted, in a stronger voice than she thought she could muster. She heard the kettle click off and turned to finish the drinks, holding one of the mugs out to him and motioning towards the kitchen table. He glared at her, his jaw flexing as he gritted his teeth, but he eventually reached out and took the cup from her. They ended up sitting across from each other, Lucy facing the patio doors.

'Lucy,' he began again, running his hand over his clean-shaven chin. Considering he was so upset, he still looked immaculate, dressed in a smart shirt and trousers. His casual day at the office look. Not a hair was out of place on his perfectly coiffed head. *Hardly frantic, were you?* 'What's going on? Is this about Mallorca? Is that it?'

She sat back in her seat, taking a long drink of her warm beverage, feeling the jolt of caffeine immediately, the warmth of the drink comforting her. As love affairs went, Lucy did have a thing for the coffee bean. Strong, dependable and quiet. Just what every woman wanted. She found her thoughts drifting back to her neighbour, but she quickly batted them out of her mind.

'Spain was bad, I know,' he admitted, looking down at his fingers, clasping his cup. 'I said I was sorry. It just got a bit much, you know?'

She nodded. She did know. She understood, but it didn't alter her feelings about him, the feelings he had put there that day. She hadn't been able to shake that, though she had tried. God knows she had tried. That day had sharpened her senses, woken her up. She wasn't happy, but that day, she finally admitted it, and there was no going back. Not now.

'I know, I understand that, Iain, but it's not just that one thing, is it?' She waited for him to nod, to agree, to start talking, but he just looked at her expectantly. 'I had to get away. I'm sorry for the way I did it, but I was trying to avoid a big scene. I needed to get away, and Marlene has been begging us to visit for years.'

Iain said nothing. That much was true, but, with his job, they could never quite swing the time off. Which was funny, because he always found time for golf weekends.

'You're never home any more. You work late, and when you are home you're in your office on the phone, or sleeping. Xander hasn't spent any proper time with you for ages. He needs a father.'

'Really,' he said, in a deep tone. 'He needs a father, so you took him away from me? That's your logic? I work hard for this family—'

'This isn't about money! We do fine, and I do have a job, thanks. I earn money too.'

'Working in a deli is not exactly lucrative, is it? Doesn't pay the mortgage, and everything else. That falls to me!'

Lucy banged her cup down, sploshing coffee over her fingers and the wooden surface of the table.

'You wanted that big house, not me! I had a house, remember? When we met I was a teacher, with my own house, my own car. Not exactly in need of a rich husband, was I? *You* wanted the flashy car and the big house, not me. I was happy in our old house. And don't forget, my house money went into the new one, so you didn't exactly pay for it on your own, did you? Don't you dare throw money in my face! I quit a job I loved to be home for our son, to look after him, to make sure he wasn't stuck in childcare he couldn't cope with. What did you do to help him, besides slap him?' She clamped her lips together, biting them in punishment for speaking out. 'I'm sorry, I didn't mean that.'

'You're never going to get over that, are you?' He sounded broken, his voice a weary monotone of regret and realisation. 'It was one mistake, and I will regret it forever.'

'You slapped our son, at the side of the pool, in front of everyone! Do you know how much that confused and upset him?'

The pair looked at each other, saying nothing. Lucy brushed away a tear, and looked out of the doors at her son, who was now twirling in circles, his cute little button face turned up to the sun. She thought back to that day and how it had become the catalyst for so much change.

71

The holiday hadn't gotten off to a great start. It was the first time that they had taken Xander abroad for a holiday, and it had taken a lot of planning, forethought and cajoling to get both her son and husband on the plane at all. She had paid for the holiday herself, saving up her wages from the deli, so that Iain couldn't say that they couldn't afford it, or moan about the expense. She was determined to show her son the world and, with Spain being a short flight away, and having such a chilled-out family atmosphere, it was the perfect place. For the first couple of days, it was perfect. Iain left his phone in the hotel room, he and Xander were spending time together and Xander even made a few friends around the hotel. On an evening, she and Iain enjoyed a glass of wine whilst watching their son dance at the hotel disco. He didn't like unexpected noises, but he sure loved music. He had since he was a toddler, and the louder the better as far as he was concerned. The entertainment staff were amazing with him and, slowly, Lucy found herself relaxing, and really enjoying her family for the first time in a long time.

Till the pool day. Xander had not slept well, and Lucy felt exhausted, drowsy from the exertion of trying to settle her son in a stuffy room, the remnants of the wine on her lips making her head feel fuzzy. Iain helped at first, but then he fell asleep, and she was on her own.

That morning, Xander was up and ready to go to the pool at the crack of dawn. His parents – tired, angry and harbouring resentment – duly got up and took him to breakfast. Before they came to Spain, Lucy had paid for swimming lessons for Xander, so that he would feel confident in the water, and it had worked, but Xander still felt unsure. She was pretty sure it was a mixture of a fear of the unknown, and his sensory issues, but her husband had another theory.

'You mollycoddle that boy too much,' he sniped at her over the breakfast table in whispered tones. His voice sounded neutral, but his words were like hushed barbs, striking her over and over with their force. 'He'll never do anything for himself if you keep doing every little thing for him!'

The dining room was bustling with holidaymakers, families milling around at the different cooking stations, collecting what they wanted from the huge breakfast spread on offer. Babies could be heard crying in the background, people chatting and laughing, the noise of families, couples and singles on holiday. People enjoying their lives, how they wanted to. Xander was sitting eating his breakfast, shovelling waffles into his mouth, happily humming along to his headphone music.

Lucy leaned forward, pushing her bowl of fruit salad with her elbows.

'I don't do everything for him, I help him, that's all. I want him to live a normal life. I just don't want him to struggle, and he is only eight! Most eight-year-olds need help with things.'

Iain tutted and huffed at the same time, spearing a piece of sausage and shoving it into his mouth.

'He—' between mouthfuls of sausage, which Lucy could see rolling around his mouth like a meat grinder '—is not eight though, is he? Not really, with everything you do for him. He's like a toddler.'

Here we go again, she thought to herself. She should be surprised, but if she was honest with herself, this had been going on for a long time. Xander's autism was first dismissed, then denied, and then totally ignored by her husband. It had been a year since his diagnosis, and Iain had no intention of adapting.

'I can't do this any more. This holiday is supposed to be a chance to get back to us, to being a family. Can't you try?'

He finished his mouthful and started to butter his toast.

'I didn't realise I had to try. It sounds like you have it all mapped out, Luce. Why do you need me at all?' He threw her his very best shit-eating grin, and she wanted to punch him. He never had any input into Xander because he chose not to. It was ridiculous to throw her parenting skills in her face, when he was the worst absent father you could have. One that lived with you, shared your life, but didn't give a fig about how you were or what made you happy. He had dropped his son like a hot potato as soon as he was a problem.

'Is this about the school?' She raised her voice now despite herself, and they both looked at Xander in a panic. He was still tucking into his breakfast, looking out of the window next to their table at the pool area beyond. It was one of the major draws of the place, the fantastic facilities for children. Water chutes, lazy river, wave machines, huge pool areas of different depths. Everything that they needed to keep Xander happy and interacting socially. She had formed a vision in her head over the last few months, one where they all splashed together in the pool, teaching their son to master swimming, being happy together, sharing the memory, being present and enjoying their time together. The image popped in her head as Iain jabbed his fork in her direction, trying to get her attention.

'You're not even listening to me. Of course it's about the bloody school!' He jabbed another sausage and thrust it into his mouth, chewing hard and glaring at her. Looking at him, his face scrunched up in fury, his posture ready for the argument that was brewing, the food swilling around in his mouth, she felt sick. How did she ever love this man like she did when they first met? Right now, she was ashamed to be his wife. She was never less attracted to him as she was in this moment. No wonder they didn't have sex any more. It wasn't all down to her nights being taken up by Xander's scary dreams and her exhaustion at the end of a long and tiring day.

'I told you about this a long time ago, he's not a happy kid there. We need to move him so we can help him to make friends. The kids at his school are awful, and the parents aren't much better.'

A snort came from her husband as he shovelled more food in, no doubt wanting to get his money's worth from the all-inclusive holiday that she'd paid for. The man could peel an orange in his pocket without spilling a drop of juice.

'So I should pay for some poncey school, for him to be molly-coddled even more?'

Lucy sighed heavily. Iain was a good businessman. A shark, excellent at what he did, which was selling office stationery by bulk to large businesses. He was good at his job, an excellent provider, but his working world and hers were, and always would be, galaxies apart.

'It's a specialist school, fewer pupils, more one to one support. He'd be with other children with needs like his, not kids who mock his little quirks. He's not a bad kid, Iain, but there, he lashes out and gets into trouble. He doesn't understand what he did wrong!'

It continued like this through the rest of the meal, them whispering and shouting occasionally, trying to sort out their differences whilst their son devoured half the buffet menu and listened to his favourite band of the moment, which was the Beatles at that time. He devoured whole back catalogues of bands, learned all there was to know about them, and then moved on to the next. Something that his mother was doubly grateful for lately, because it shielded him from witnessing his parents' marriage implode. Once they had finished, they grabbed their pool bags and headed outside. A few hours later, it happened.

Lucy had been reading, laid out on her sunlounger enjoying the feel of the sun on her skin. For once, she could relax, knowing that there was no work to do, no laundry to fold. Xander was slathered in cream and in the pool with his dad, and she was finally catching up on the stack of books she constantly had at the side of her bed. She bought them to read, but then never got the time, so they sat there, taunting her. Most nights she barely got through a chapter before her head started to nod. She had bought herself a Kindle, thinking she could read it one-handed by the soft screen light, cuddling her anxiety-ridden son, but after a few nights of dozing off and having it land hard on her face, she went back to the paperbacks, and watched her stack of unused treasures get larger. Now, she was enjoying her downtime, and was just getting to the juiciest part of the book when her husband's voice boomed out across the pool. She jumped off her lounger, heading to the noise. In the queue to the water slides, right at the front, stood her son and husband. Xander was shaking his head from side to side rapidly, whilst Iain, an angry look on his face, was trying to drag him onto the ride.

'Come on, don't be a bloody girl! You'll love it, I'll come down with you.'

Lucy shuddered. Since when was being a girl a bad thing? Man up, stop crying, be a man. It had to stop. At eight, Xander didn't care about what kind of man he was going to be, he was simply terrified of his dad throwing him down a water slide. Lucy fast-walked towards them, trying to get their attention by waving, not wanting to draw any more attention. People were already looking, which would make Iain angrier and Xander more anxious. When he felt cornered, he dug his heels in. He was like his father in that respect if nothing else.

Reaching them, apologising to everyone in the queue as she pushed past, she smiled at them both and looked at Iain.

'He doesn't want to go, it's fine. I'll take him to the pool, you go on the slide. We'll watch from the bottom, won't we?'

Xander, tear-soaked cheeks and full bottom lip pout, shook his head vehemently.

'No! I want to go to the room!'

'You're not going anywhere.' Iain tugged his arm again, pushing his wife aside none too gently as he headed to the mouth of the slide. 'We're holding people up. Two minutes and we're done, okay? Let's go!'

Xander reached for his mother with his free hand. 'Mummy!'

Lucy took it, giving it a reassuring squeeze but taking care not to pull him her way. The last thing he needed was a parent tug-of-war.

'Iain, please,' she tried, but he glared at her, before pulling his arm again.

'I am his father, I know what's best. Come on, Xander!'

'No!' Xander screamed, pulling back against his dad, jerking his arm back in quick bursts to try to get free. 'No, Daddiiiee, I don't want to!'

'You're doing it!'

'Stop, Iain, you're scaring him!'

'Shut up, Lucy, mind your own business!'

'Nooooo! Daddiiieeee!'

'He is my bloody business! Let him go!'

'Dadd-dy, let me go!' Xander, now realising that he wasn't going to get free, screamed in frustration and then charged forward, head-butting his dad in the torso.

'Oofff!'

'Xander, stop that. Iain, let him go!'

'For God's sake, why can't you just be fucking normal, for once!'

Xander went to charge again, and that was it. Iain brought his open palm up towards his chest, and then backhanded him. Suddenly free, Xander careened into his mother, who wrapped him in her arms, tucking him into her side, away from Iain, as she lunged forward and pushed him in the chest with her free hand. She used all her might, feeling every inch the mummy bear.

'Don't you dare do that again! You hear me? You will never hit him like that again!'

She could feel the strain on her throat as she growled the words at him, the anger, shock and frustration zapping around every inch of her body, firing up every cell of her being.

'Xander, let's go to the room.' He gave a relieved squeak, his face hidden into her side. She turned back to Iain, jabbing her finger in the air in front of her. 'You even try to come into our room, and I'll have you arrested.' He looked for a moment like he was going to challenge her. She saw that familiar glint of annoyance cross his features, but he sighed deeply and nodded. She headed to the loungers, scooping up her bag and hers and Xander's things on the way. The romance novel, lying open on the towel, was flung off and ended up landing in a puddle of water on the tiled floor. She left it there. She didn't want to know how the story ended. Happy ever after was a concept that she had no hope or use for now.

'You'll never let me forget that, will you? I am the devil in your story, and that's it.' Iain was slumped at his seat at the table now, and for the first time Lucy saw real pain in his demeanour. 'I will regret that forever, you know that. That's not me, I was just frustrated. I love our son, I do. I just …'

'He's not the son you wanted, is he?'

She didn't mean it in a harsh way. She'd had her struggles herself over the years. You develop a picture in your head of what your family will be. What your children will become. Will they have your chin? Your love of reading? Their dad's business brain? When you have a child growing inside you, you envisage a big, beautiful, happy life for them. You will tear down any obstacle, you will stop any bullies, you will give your child the tools of life and then watch them build their own bright and shiny futures. You imagine Christmases with matching PJs, hot chocolate, leaving goodies out for Santa. Watching their excited faces as they come downstairs, their tiny feet padding down the carpeted stairs, bursting with energy and happiness because Santa has been. You imagine Easter egg hunts, family holidays, graduations. Standing in the aisle, best hat on, crying as your child ties themselves to their chosen person before God, or Elvis, or whatever deity they choose to wed under.

When your child is born, and they have needs, that picture is taken away, and you can find yourselves feeling cheated. For them, for you. Life will never look like that, and it can be a bitter pill to swallow. She wouldn't be without Xander, but she understood how people can struggle.

'I love him,' Iain said, for lack of any other explanation. 'I just had a picture in my head, you know? Playing catch, riding bikes, going to the footie. Xander can't do any of that. It doesn't mean you get to take him from me.'

She felt wretched then. The first thing she wanted to say was that Xander could do those things. It would be tricky sometimes, sure, but he was a person, with a life of his own. He didn't try to do those things with his son, so how would he know? Xander didn't even have a bike. Something else she needed to remedy. She made a mental note. He was autistic, not incapable. Lucy realised how little her husband actually knew about their son, and her heart ached for them both. For what they were missing out on from each other.

'How did you find us, anyway? I know I told you we were coming to see my aunt, but how did you know where you were staying?'

'I looked at your Amazon account. I saw the delivery order address. Bit much to spend on Lego, isn't it? He has Lego at home.'

'Wow, stalk much?' she asked, surprised that he had gone to such depths to find her. *Why didn't he just ring Marlene?* She knew the answer to that. Pride. Stubbornness. The same reasons she had decided to get away from him for.

He didn't laugh, just clenched his jaw.

'I had to "stalk" you as you say—' he used aggressive air quotes to punctuate his point '—because you ran off to the countryside and left me a note. You order a lot of expensive toys that he doesn't need, and don't have a thought for me, or what I have going on in my life.'

It took a while for what he said to sink in; she had to dissect his barbs in her head. Money was always a sore point with them both, with Iain feeling like he did everything, but it wasn't the case. Lucy was independent before she met him, and he had obviously forgotten that now.

'First of all, he did need the Lego. He spent his birthday money on it, and he needs something to do when we are in the cottage. Do you really begrudge him that? You spend four times the money on your golfing weekends, and I don't moan at you, do I?'

'Right, fine,' he snipped, standing up and looking around him at the surroundings of the neat and cosy cottage. 'How much is this place costing?'

Lucy felt her anger bubble up under her skin. Same old, same old.

'I've got it covered, don't worry.'

He nodded, sneering a little as he looked about him. 'Right, well I have the car around the corner, so we can get packed up and go when you're ready. I'm sure we can return the parcels.'

Lucy looked at him in stunned silence. Looking out of the doors, she checked that Xander was still okay and playing, and then stood and headed to the front door. She could hear Iain following her, and she steeled herself for what was coming. Opening the front door, she stood out on the porch. The light was still there, but fading a little as the heat from the sun died down. She needed to get tea on, and Xander in and bathed ready for bed. If his routine was messed up, he wouldn't sleep well. Not that Iain would care about that.

He followed her out and picked up one of the big boxes from the porch.

'I'll start taking these to the car. I'll park out front.'

Lucy crossed her arms. 'Put the box down, Iain, we're not coming with you. I booked the whole summer here, and we're staying.'

Iain's face was a picture, and she couldn't help but laugh. It escaped before she could stop it, and she covered her mouth with her hand. Luckily, the little lanes around them were empty.

'Funny, is it?' he jeered. 'What makes you think you can do that?'

Lucy looked at him, his face scrunched up in anger, the box in his hands, his knuckles turning white as he gripped it tight. She loved him once, but that seemed like a hell of a long time ago now.

'Iain,' she said softly, moving forward and taking the box out of his hands. He pulled it back at first, but then relented and let his fingers slip from the sides of the box. She put it back down next to the others, taking a step further forward. 'I don't want to fight, but you are never home, and Xander deserves a holiday. I wanted to get away, see my family. I got the time off work, and I'm staying here. We need this break, Iain, and I think you know that.'

Iain pulled his keys from his pocket. 'I'll go get the car, we can talk about it when we get home. I'm home tomorrow so we can sort it out then.'

Then, it clicked. The date popped into her head, she could see it. Right there, a snapshot in her mind of the calendar on her kitchen wall. That's why he was here.

'You can leave now, Iain, and don't bother coming back. We're having our summer, and we are not puppets for your amusement. You can't just pick us up when you need us.'

Iain threw his arms up in the air in frustration.

'What the hell are you talking about? I came to take my family home!'

'Really?' She raised her voice to match his, one ear and eye focused on the doors behind her. 'So it's not the fact that the annual ball for work is tomorrow, no? Face it, Iain, you don't give a shit about us! You're here so I can come home, clean the house, iron your shirt and hang on your arm all night to make you look good and talk about your perfect family. The son that you are ashamed of and slapped for being scared. Well, I'm not coming. You can go and schmooze all your little golfing buddies all on your own.'

'Really!' Iain exploded, right then and there. 'Really? That's it?' He squeezed the hand with his keys tight into a fist, and shook it at her. 'You really are a bitch sometimes, you know that? I don't think you know just how much I do for you!' He started to walk backwards down the path, and kept shouting at her the whole time. How hard he worked for them all, how much she had an easy life, how awful she was to him, how screwed up things were. All because of her and Xander. Everything was down to them. His long work hours, his need to golf all weekend and drink all night with his 'contacts'. She could almost hear the violins playing for him. The tiniest violins known to man, for this pitiful figure of one. Lucy was really starting to feel mad. She needed him to just go. The thought of even having to sit in a car with the man was enough to get her mouth moving. Enough was enough!

'Iain,' she said, as quietly and evenly as she could, 'you need to leave. You're not Tiger Woods, you don't need to golf every weekend to provide for your family. I managed on my own before you, and I sure as hell will after. You left, not me. You left your family a long time ago, as soon as things got tough. You want us when it suits you, and that's not a family.'

'A family!' He snorted with laughter, glaring at her from halfway down the path. 'Sure, blame it all on me, that's great. I'll just rattle around all summer, paying for your strop!'

'I don't need your money!' This came out as a scream, a vent of anger spewing forth from her. 'I need you to leave, so just go!'

'You know what, Lucy? I'm tired of your crap now. Go get Xander, and your shit, and let's go.'

He went to take a step closer, his eye on the boxes of Lego, and no doubt to the refund he wanted of his own son's money. She pushed the boxes back with a sweep of her foot, and crossed her arms in defiance.

'No, Iain. Leave. I'll tell Xander you'll call him later.'

He went to take another step forward, his foot lifting to take a step, but then it didn't connect, and it just hung there, half off the ground. His face turned from rage to confusion as he lunged forward again, but he just swayed from side to side instead.

'I think,' Sam's deep voice said from behind him, 'that the lady asked you to leave. I think you should do that. Now.' Sam's shoulder moved, and Iain almost fell flat on his face as he released him. He had been holding his clothing, making him immobile. 'You okay, Lucy? Where's Xander?'

'He's fine, he's in the garden.'

She didn't know where he had appeared from. Was he next door all the time, had he heard them fight? She didn't have chance to feel embarrassed, she was just grateful he had shown up before she ended up lamping her feckless husband with a Lego Death Star in front of her child. Iain was now looking between the two of them as though he was watching a tennis match.

'Who the hell is this guy?' He took a step towards Sam, looking up at him and puffing his chest out. Sam looked at him as though he was a fly in his drink. A mild annoyance that needed to be dealt with.

'I'm her neighbour. Lucy, you go see to Xander. I will just say goodbye to your friend here, see him on his way.' He flicked his gaze back to Iain, one thick brow raised. Iain looked at her over his shoulder, his expression a mixture of impotent fury and fear. It was what Xander called a poop face, one of his ways of understanding his dad. He had a point, at this moment in time.

'This is not over, Luce, we have things to discuss.'

Luce shook her head slowly, looking right at him with a resigned expression on her face.

'I have nothing to say to you, Iain. Enjoy the party.' She didn't hear what the men said to each other. She went inside, heading straight for Xander, who was still happily playing in the sunshine.

Half an hour later, with Xander watching a film on his tablet in the lounge, Lucy was just pushing a home-made lasagne into the oven when there was a knock at the door. Lucy felt herself jump, flinching at the noise. The kitchen was quiet and peaceful, but now she felt the crackle of tension in the air. *Please, don't be Iain.*

She closed the oven door and, wiping her hands on a tea towel, she headed to the front door, trying to keep calm and quiet so Xander wouldn't pick up on it.

'Hello?' she said through the door, one hand on the handle.

'Hi,' a familiar voice said. 'I have your packages here, if you have a minute.'

Sam's voice was friendly and her body relaxed at the sound. She unlocked the door, and there he was. The packages looked like matchboxes in his arms. He gave her a big broad smile, showing his pearly whites and she found herself smiling back.

'Thanks, come in.'

He walked in, dipping his head as he came through the front door and gently kicking it closed behind him. He was massive, filling her small hallway but looking like he belonged there at the same time.

'Xander okay?' he asked, making no moves to come further into the house.

'He's fine, he was happy in the garden. Thanks for bringing these in. I totally forgot about them.'

On cue, Xander wandered in from the lounge, his face lighting up when he saw Sam.

'You brought my Lego! Have you come to build it with me?'

'Err …' Sam looked at her, not knowing what to say. 'That's up to your mum, kid. I just wanted to say hi, see how my favourite neighbours are.'

Xander laughed. 'We're your only neighbours, so you have to say that!' Sam laughed, an eruption of deep reverberation from his chest. It was quite sexy. 'Mum? Can Sam stay?'

Lucy looked at her afternoon saviour, and found herself agreeing readily. 'We're having lasagne for tea, a bit of salad and garlic bread. Have you eaten?'

Sam shook his head. 'No, not yet. It smells amazing.'

Xander nodded emphatically at him. 'The only thing I like more than Mum's lasagne is chocolate.'

Sam laughed again, putting the packages down to one side of the hallway and bending to take his boots off.

'Well, that sounds awesome, thank you. Now, shall we open one of these packages, maybe do a bit before tea?'

Xander lunged for the biggest one. 'Yes, Death Star here we come!' Between them, they dragged it into the lounge, Sam winking at her as they went. Lucy locked the door and headed back to the kitchen.

Lucy could hear them both chuckling in the lounge as she checked on the oven a short while later. She had managed to finish her jobs, do some washing and set the table for three. It was only a small table, but there was enough room for the three of them. As an afterthought, she lit a few candles, scattering them on the windowsill, away from Xander. He loved candles but he was a little clumsy at times, and she didn't want to take the risk. It had been an eventful day already, to say the least.

She went into the lounge to tell them to come for dinner, and walked into a military operation. The rug in the middle of the room had been taken over as command central, and operation 'Build a Death Star' was in full flow. The two of them were sitting cross-legged on the floor, both poring over tiny plastic pieces and reading the instructions together. It took her breath away, and she stood stock-still in the doorway, watching them.

Sam was the first one to notice her there. He was laughing with Xander, throwing his head back, and his eyes found hers. She gave him a little smile, and he smiled back.

'You doing okay?' he asked gently, his tone neutral, easy. This man always made her feel at ease, safe even. She was no damsel in distress, but, this afternoon, she could have kissed him for appearing when he did. She wondered what he had said to Iain to make him leave. Had he said anything at all? He could have stuffed him into his own car trunk for all she knew. She hadn't heard a peep after the front door had closed behind her. He half wished he had done just that. She could just imagine the outrage he'd feel.

'I'm good, thanks to you,' she replied honestly. He nodded, an expression she couldn't read crossing his features before disappearing back into his easy stance. 'I had it handled though.' She added it as an afterthought, wanting him to know that she could handle her own business. Every time she saw this man, she felt like she was spiralling. No wonder he was concerned.

'I know, I got that. Just remember I'm next door though, if you need anything.'

She didn't trust herself to reply without appearing stubborn or rude, so she just smiled at him.

'Dinner's ready, when you are. Would you like a glass of wine? I don't have any beer.'

The two master builders followed her in, Xander sitting in his favourite seat and grabbing a piece of garlic bread from the plate in the centre of the table. Sam waited in the doorway, watching Lucy get the lasagne out of the oven. It looked good, and the smell was delicious, even if Lucy said so herself.

'I'm not really a beer man, but I'll have a glass of wine please. This looks amazing. It's been a while since I've had a relaxed home-cooked meal. The lads at the firehouse cook, but mealtimes there are not quite the same, or the conversation.' Last shift, they had discussed the inner workings of the offside rule whilst shovelling in mash, pie and peas.

Lucy giggled, serving the lasagne onto three plates and reaching for the wine bottle. Sam took it from her in one smooth movement and took the wine opener from the drawer in the sideboard. She looked at him in surprise, and he nudged his head to the wall connecting their cottages.

'Same layout as mine,' he explained. He looked right at home, and Lucy couldn't help but compare this moment with all the moments she had shared in her own kitchen, with her husband.

Generally, this was him coming in demanding something while she was cooking, or baking with Xander, or just sneaking a glass of wine to take the edge off the long nights while Xander slept. In truth, she had gotten used to the long weekends while he was off drinking, and potting tiny balls into tiny holes. They had soon become the times that she looked forward to the most, and she knew that having these thoughts wasn't exactly a good sign of marital wellbeing.

'What is it?' Sam asked as he opened the wine. 'Did I overstep?'

She snapped back into the moment and shook her head at him, or rather, up at him. The man really was rather tall. She wasn't a small person herself, but she really felt his presence in the room. It was comforting, especially after the fractious day she'd had.

'What does "overstep" mean?' Xander piped up, a mouthful of garlic bread muffling his words.

'It means to do something that's not really your business, not your place as a person,' Sam replied easily, unscrewing the cork from the bottle opener and putting it into the bin. 'Glasses?' he asked politely to Xander. 'Do you know where the wine glasses are?'

Xander nodded, jumping up from his seat and opening one of the cupboards for him. Sam took two wine glasses out, and a tumbler.

'You want some wine, or are you having milk? Juice?'

Xander gasped and Sam laughed. 'I can't have wine, I'm eight!'

Sam pulled a shocked face, looking at Lucy, his mouth wide open.

'What? You're eight! Wow, I didn't know that! I thought you were going to come and work with me!'

Xander giggled excitedly. 'I can work with you, I can learn!' He tapped Sam on the arm, motioning for him to move closer. Sam bent down so Xander could reach his ear, which meant almost folding himself in half. 'I'm nearly nine too. We could still

87

be firemen.' He sneaked a peek at his mum, who pretended to busy herself putting the food on the table. 'Just don't tell my mum.'

Sam smiled, looking Xander right in the eyes for a second before looking away and saying, 'That's a deal, bud. Just let me know when.'

Xander squealed and threw his arms around Sam, who didn't even move despite being hunched over and resting on the balls of his feet. He hesitated for a beat or two, and then slowly, gently, he folded Xander into his arms, and hugged him back. Lucy watched the pair of them, and felt the upset of the day melt away a little. After this, she knew that she had done the right thing, getting away. Sam was a complication she hadn't seen coming, but having a friend might not be so bad after all, as long as Xander didn't get hurt. Looking at him now, laughing and joking with Sam as they headed back to the table, she felt hope for the first time in a long time.

Two and a half hours later, Xander was all tuckered out and ready for bed. She left Sam downstairs while she settled him down with a story, but he was that tired she didn't even get further than a few pages. They were working their way through a fantasy series that he loved, and had been for a few months now. Once Xander found a writer he liked, that was it, so she always tried to go for series of books to keep him occupied. The room he was sleeping in already looked like his. Books on the nightstand, his nightlight by the socket near the door, lighting his way to the bathroom, his toys in neat piles in the corner of the room. She got out from underneath him, gently moving his arm and tucking him under the covers. He smiled in his sleep, and her heart melted as she watched his little chest rise and fall, his long dark lashes fluttering against his cheeks as he slept. He really was beautiful, and she still found herself marvelling at the tiny human she made. She couldn't imagine her life without him, or remember life before him. All the old clichés were true, and she was feeling better and better about her decision every day.

Heading downstairs, she could hear movement in the kitchen, the sound of running water, and the low hum of Sam. He was singing to himself, and she recognised the tune. Walking into the kitchen, she saw that Sam had cleared the table, wiped it down and was now washing the dishes. *An Adonis in Marigolds. Be still my beating heart.*

'Aretha?' she asked, stepping into the room and reaching for the tea towel. 'You don't have to wash up you know, but I appreciate it.'

'Least I can do for that meal. You like Aretha?'

Lucy grabbed a dish, brushing back her long brown hair from her face.

'Love her. My mother loved Motown; it rubs off when you hear it played at home.'

Sam beamed, nodding his head. 'Doesn't it just. My mother plagued us all with her music, especially when she was in a cleaning mood.'

Lucy did the same when she was at home alone, crooning along to her favourites whilst she got the house spick and span. It was her cardio, and given that she never got time to go to the gym, it was always a good workout.

'You have a lot of brothers and sisters, growing up?' Sam washed the last dish, and emptied the washing-up bowl, cleaning around the sink area with a clean cloth. Whoever his mother was, she had raised her boy well. The man was like Mr Muscle, literally and metaphorically.

'My mother's a foster carer, so we always had people in the house. She adopted me when I was a baby, so I got used to having a loud, busy house.'

Lucy didn't know what to say for a second, so she just kept drying up. If he wanted to tell her more, he would.

'Can I ask you a question?' He moved to one side, leaning against the sink with one hand, facing her.

She finished off the last of the dishes, putting them into the cupboards and throwing the tea towel into the washing machine.

'Sure.'

'The thing today, with your husband, is it always like that?' His face closed off, a serious shadow cast over it. 'He seemed a little aggressive.'

Lucy thought of the slap, but shook her head. 'He's not like that normally. He's mad at me. I didn't help matters really.'

Sam nodded once, but the shadow was still there.

'You sure?'

She smiled at him. 'He's not a bad guy, and he's never hurt me.' She looked out of the door, at the staircase, as though expecting Xander to be sat there, listening. 'He made a mistake, and I'm not sure I can forgive him for it. I think that we've been growing apart a while, and ...' She sighed before picking up her half empty wine glass from the countertop and taking a mouthful. 'It's complicated I guess. We came here for the summer to enjoy being away, but the longer I'm away from home, the less I want to go back.'

She picked up the wine bottle and turned to him.

'Do you want to sit in the lounge for a moment?' She was enjoying talking to him, and found she wasn't in a hurry to sit alone for the rest of the evening, watching TV and drinking the rest of the bottle alone.

'You sure I'm not stopping you from doing anything?'

She shook her head, heading through to the lounge. 'Nope, nothing to do.'

They sat on the sofa, at opposite ends, settling back into the seats and sipping their wine. The coffee table was clear of Lego thankfully, and she set the wine bottle down after refilling both their glasses.

'So, are you a full-time mum normally?'

She loved how he phrased the question. Usually it was 'Do

you work?' which always made her feel like a bum, even though she was a trained professional. In another life perhaps, but still. Some people thought that a lobotomy was performed after labour, a bit like the Bounty photographer who came around the ward to photograph your precious bundles. Like K, men in blacking every new mother with his flashy memory eraser. 'Look right here and smile!'

'I work in a deli part-time. I used to be a primary school teacher, but when Xander started struggling, I left to be home for him.'

'He's a lovely kid, you're doing a great job.' He looked across at her, leaning forward a little. 'Hard though, isn't it?'

Lucy sighed. 'It's not been easy, and Iain and I have struggled. I thought we'd pull together, but …'

'It's hard for a man sometimes, to see his son struggle. I'm not saying it's right, but I've seen it before. Have you talked about it?'

'We've done nothing but talk, not that it does any good.' She took another sip of her wine, enjoying the sensation of the chilled beverage as it both warmed and relaxed her. 'I think he blames me sometimes. I don't know why. Like because I noticed it first, I caused it somehow. I feel like sometimes he wishes I hadn't said anything.' She stretched out her feet in front of her, slipping off her pale pink pumps and flexing her toes. 'Anyway, I'm sorry you had to see that today. I'm not going to be a troublesome neighbour, I promise.'

Sam laughed, a deep rumble that made Lucy smile.

'I'm not worried about that. Especially after that meal. Best neighbour ever.'

She giggled, slapping him on the arm before she checked herself. He laughed again, rubbing his arm and wincing.

'Ow Lucy, I take it back! Worst neighbour ever! Not even your lasagne can be worth the bruises.'

She drained her glass, and he picked up the bottle and refilled it automatically.

'Thanks. You're such a gent, did they teach you these manners at fireman school?'

'They teach you to save lives and protect each other in fire school. My mum's a very polite woman, she brought me up right. I'll tell her you said that, she'll be pleased as punch.'

'You're really close, aren't you,' she observed, standing to turn off the main lights and switch on the standing lamp in the corner. It bathed the lounge in a warm glow, and, with the drapes pulled, it looked cosy and warm. It felt like home. 'Do you know about your birth parents?'

Sam looked uncomfortable and before she knew what she had done, she'd moved closer to him on the couch and placed her hand over his.

'Sorry, I shouldn't have asked.' He looked at her hand on his, saying nothing, and she went to pull it away, but he clasped his other hand over it, sandwiching hers between them. Looking up at her, she noticed his gaze flick to her lips, and she found herself licking them in response. He looked into her eyes and then slowly, gently, moved his hands away, his thumb leaving an imaginary trail of heat along hers.

'Can I tell you something?' he asked, his voice thick with something she hadn't heard before. It made his rumbling voice richer, sexier. 'It's weird, but I feel like I can tell you this, like I can trust you.'

You can tell me anything … she thought dreamily. *You're a part-time stripper in your spare time and you have tickets. Tucked into your pants. Grab and go.*

'Yes,' she said, rather more breathily than she intended. 'Of course you can.'

He sighed and turned away a little, reaching into his jean pocket. *Oh my God, if he pulls show tickets out, I'm going to faint. Sensational Sam and his big pole. Move over, Magic Mike. Thank you, next.*

He pulled out a piece of paper and held it out to her. Once she realised it didn't have a naked torso printed on it, she came to her senses and took the folded note from him. It was expensive paper, she could see an emblem on the top. The Mayweather coat of arms, with Mayweather Estates printed underneath it. It had been folded and unfolded many times, the creases less rigid, more like well-worn paper. She looked at him in question, and he nodded.

'My mother gave it to me. My real mother I mean. She left it with me, the day I was … the day I met my foster mother. I was only a baby, so I have no memories. It's why I'm here.'

She read the pretty cursive writing, taking in the words. As a mother herself, she could only imagine what the writer was feeling when she wrote these words, how torn and broken she must have felt. Someone would have to prise Xander from her cold, dead hands before she let him go. Iain included. She felt the familiar frisson of fear bubble in her stomach and squashed it down. This wasn't about her, or her son. She read it again, taking in every word. Sam, as ever, was quiet and calm. For such a big guy, he was a real oasis of tranquillity. She felt it every time she was around him, and she knew that Xander felt it too.

'You're here to find your family?' she asked gently. 'Your father, too?'

'Do you think I'm mad?' he asked genuinely, and her heart went out to him.

'No, I don't at all. I think it's great. Is that why you took the job?'

He nodded, taking the letter back from her and tucking it carefully back into his pocket.

'That's the plan, but now I'm here, it just seems like a bit of a bad idea. I knew I came from Westfield, but I didn't have this letter till I'd already decided to move here. My mother kept it till I was ready, I guess. The woman is never wrong usually, but I'm still no closer really.'

'You're trying to find your family, that's never easy. Can't social services help?'

Sam shook his head. 'I didn't go through the system too much. My mother, Sondra I mean, my foster mother, I went to her on day one—'

'And she never let you go,' Lucy finished. 'She sounds like my kinda mum.'

Sam's eyes wrinkled with warmth as he smiled at her. 'Yep, you are similar in some ways.' They both looked at each other, happy to be in each other's company. Both comforted by the other, and the privilege of finding someone to talk to about their problems and fears.

'Everyone's so nice here, it's more complicated than I thought it was going to be. I don't want to stride in with my big size twelves and stir up fresh pain and trouble for everyone. Who even knows what they'll think when I tell them.'

He drained his glass, sinking back into the overstuffed comfy sofa.

'I've managed without knowing my whole life, but now, I don't know. Mum's not going to be around forever, despite what she says, and I guess I just want some answers. To be able to fill in a form without coming out in a cold sweat. I'm fit and healthy, I got genetically tested, so that's not it. I guess I just want to know where I came from. One day, I might be a father too. I would like to sort this out before I think about the next step. I need to sort out my past before I try to make a future.'

Lucy's mind tingled at his words. It's just why she was here too. Why she had packed up her only child and headed for the hills. She wanted space to breathe, to separate the pieces of her broken life, to find out what she could salvage. What she wanted to let go, and what she could repair.

'Are you working tomorrow?' she asked, a plan forming in her head.

Intrigued, Sam cocked his head to one side. The movement reminded her of her son, when he was trying to decipher something, or someone. They were similar in a lot of ways, though they had no reason to be. Perhaps it was just their quiet looks, the way they both sized things up.

'No, why?'

'I want to help you. I need a project for the summer. I'll help you find your family, if you want me to. I know people here, and Aunt Marlene has lived here all her life.' He flashed her an uncharacteristic look of panic. 'I won't say anything to anyone, I promise.' She leaned into him a little. 'Let me help, please?'

He searched her face for what seemed like a long time, his face neutral, a blank canvas. She couldn't decipher what was going through the gentle giant's big bald head. Another eternity passed till he spoke.

'Okay, thank you. Not to lead you astray, but …' He looked at her devilishly, waggling his eyebrows. Lucy's thoughts bounced immediately back to the tickets, and she could almost hear 'Pony' in her head. Bop … bop … bop bop bop … bop … bop bop …

'Yes?' she said, imagining what he would look like in his fireman's uniform. And out of it.

'… shall we open another bottle? I told Xander I would finish this tricky bit for him, but my fingers aren't as dainty as yours. I could use the womanpower.'

The pony galloped off, leaving a deflated wah wah wah wahh-hhhh sound in its wake.

'Sure,' she said as cheerily as she could. 'I'll go get it.'

CHAPTER 9

'Muuuummmmmm! It's eight o'clock, we should be having breakfast now! Muuuuummmmmmmm!'

Lucy shook from side to side as Xander, clad in character pyjamas, straddled his mother's hip, pulling on her nightshirt. She felt rough, and she could taste the remnants from the wine on her tongue as she tried in vain to lick her lips. Wow, she wasn't drunk last night, but she was definitely not used to late nights drinking wine and talking with a man. She and Iain hadn't done it in years. Done anything like that, truth be told, not since Xander was born. IT was a bit of an abstract concept, like skydiving. It was out there, it was exciting, people did it every day, but it just wasn't part of her life. In fact, the rocking she was currently experiencing was the closest her body had been to that kind of movement in far too long a while. Xander added salt to the wound by jumping to her side, kneeling on her boob and pinning it to the mattress in one smooth movement.

'Ouch, Xander, be careful, honey.' She pushed him gently aside, cradling her bruised mammary to her chest and pulling herself up. 'I'm up, I'm up.'

She dragged herself out of bed, half rolling, half falling, till she managed to arrive in an upright position. Her head pulsated a little, and she was filled with a sudden sense of horror. The horror that only occurred when alcohol was consumed with someone else, or out in public. This was the time where people reached for their phones, checking Insta stories for drunken singing, ill-timed declarations of love, or just plain idiocy. #spiralling. She thought back to the night before, but nothing sprang to mind. She remembered going to bed, she was wearing actual night clothes, and her clothes from the night before had been folded and laid on the chair. All signs of adulthood, not drunken debauchery. Good start, aside from the Sahara Desert impression her tongue was auditioning for and the tiny little drummer man that was pounding out a fine tune in her head. Heading downstairs, half dragged by Xander who was excitedly talking about the blueberry pancakes she had promised him the night before, they hadn't reached the lower level before there was an insistent knock at the front door.

Xander wasn't interested, he totally ignored the door and headed straight to the kitchen to get everything out. It was past eight o'clock, so unless Dwayne Johnson was at the door, nothing would put her son off eating his already late breakfast. Even IF Dwayne swooped into Westfield, the pancakes would still be a necessity. Being here, uprooted from his life, the school he didn't fit into, Xander had coped. A lot better than Lucy thought he would, and she was so grateful. Routine was routine though, and Xander's belly liked a tight schedule. The knock came again, and groaning at the pain it produced in her frontal lobe, she wiped the remnants of sleep out of her eyes and opened the door, her breath held captive by her sense of impending doom. Who was at the door? At this point in the morning, it would be easier just to go back to bed, ignore the day entirely. Her heart pounded at the thought of Iain being at the other side of the door. Could it be Sam, about last night? Did she make a dick of herself? Was he mad? She felt the sense of panic flowing through her wine-clogged veins and a frisson of something else. Excitement? A flutter of romance? God knows. It was probably just the faint urge to go vomit everywhere and lie with her head stuffed under a pillow.

Pulling open the pretty painted wooden door, she saw Marlene stood there, shopping bags in hand. Her mildly irritated look turned to horror when she took in the sight of her niece, crumpled nightwear hanging off her frame, hair puffed out at all angles. She bustled in the door, looking behind Lucy and hurriedly closing and locking the door behind her.

'Not here, is he?' she asked, one hand still on the key. 'Iain, I mean.'

Lucy slowly shook her head, surprised by the question.

'No, he's not here. How did you—'

'I was told a flash git in a poncey car was by the cottages. I cracked the code pretty quickly.' She checked the lock and then pushed through to the kitchen, putting the bags on the counter and kissing Xander on the top of his head. He was sitting at the table, playing with some figures. All the pancake-making apparatus had been laid out neatly on the worktop, a frying pan placed onto the cold hob.

'Good morning, my little darling. Pancakes, is it? Want me to make them while your mother gets a shower?'

Xander nodded, beaming at his great auntie. Anything to get pancakes quicker.

'Mum drank wine last night with Sam, I think she got drunk. My breakfast is at eight o'clock, but she was snoring in bed, and I'm starving!' He pointed at the kitchen clock on the wall to punctuate his point, and the whole thing came out in one breath. 'I have been dreaming of blueberry pancakes all night,' he added dramatically, throwing a deep sigh in for effect. Marlene laughed.

'Sounds like a fraught morning. Blueberry pancakes coming right up.'

Lucy started to tiptoe to the stairs, the thought of the hot shower a welcome incentive to launch an escape bid. She was just at the bottom of the stairs when she heard the trill of Marlene as she got to cooking.

'Enjoy your shower, Lucy darling, I'll have the coffee ready when you come down, we can have a nice little chat. Take your time, dear. Run a comb through your hair too, while you're at it.'

Her voice was easy, sing-song light, but Lucy knew her aunt well enough to know that she was in for a grilling when she got downstairs again. Sighing, she started to climb the stairs, hugging the banister for comfort.

'Throw in a bacon sandwich from the stuff in those bags, and you have a deal.'

Marlene chuckled to herself and Lucy went to dunk her head under the hot water. With a bit of luck, it would prepare her for the onslaught she would face over breakfast. At this point, she would rather be waterboarded than deal with the Auntie Interrogation.

'So she was drunk? Was Xander okay?'

Marlene shook her head, stirring her tea with a little silver spoon and resting it on her saucer. They were in their usual seats in New Lease of Life, their various craft projects spread out in front of them. As ever, Grace was knitting furiously, looking intently at Marlene for an answer.

'She wasn't drunk, Lucy's a great mum. Xander was fine. The poor girl runs her life around that boy, she overslept by fifteen minutes, that's all. That's not the point anyway! The point is, Iain won't just leave things like that now. If he made the effort to come and find her, he won't stop till he makes her feel guilty for not being on his arm or ironing his shirts, and she'll go back. I don't want them to go back, not yet, and especially not now.'

Dot, tucking into a salmon pinwheel, nodded.

'I agree, she came here for a reason, and she needs this time. We can have a great summer with them and she needs time to see the wood through the trees.'

Marlene leaned forward, picking up her tapestry and eyeing

her fellow coven members. 'Speaking of wood, you haven't heard the best bit. Just you wait.'

Amanda, owner of the shop, finished serving her customer and came over to the ladies.

'Agatha holding up your gossip session again? Where is she?'

Grace smiled at her. 'She's on a new health kick. She and Taylor walk the dogs twice a day now, and she's always up the community centre, taking the fitness classes. Her knee started twinging, so she thinks she's at death's door. You ought to see her, she dresses like Hyacinth Bucket, it's hilarious.'

'It's Taylor I feel sorry for, the poor bugger. Those dog walks were the only bits of peace he got, and now she's in his ear all the time. Even the dogs are missing the break.'

Amanda swatted at her playfully. 'Give over, it's good that she's getting exercise. I love the classes myself. Taylor's happy enough.'

Marlene grabbed a mini sausage roll and chomped on it. 'Well, I don't care if she's doing ruddy *Strictly Come Dancing*, she needs to start respecting the schedule!'

'Who does?' Agatha said, bounding through the door in tight lilac yoga pants, pink floral trainers and a t-shirt that said 'One Just Does It'. 'What schedule?'

'Who the hell dressed you this morning?' Grace asked, laughing so much she snorted. 'Where do you think you are? L.A., with the other gym bunnies?'

Agatha, her hair immaculately curled and set on her head like the Queen, looked down at herself in confusion. 'What do you mean? Taylor took me shopping. The assistant told us this was the in thing, and Taylor had the t-shirt made.'

Amanda guffawed and covered her mouth with her hand. 'Well,' she said, trying and failing not to laugh in between words, 'you look amazing! Marlene is just itching to tell us some news.'

Agatha sat down, primly folding her legs and setting her handbag by her feet. She looked down at her t-shirt, straightening an imaginary crease and sticking her bottom lip out, miffed.

'I'm all ears, sorry I was late.'

'All ears?' Grace quipped. 'All legs as well. Your camel toe is showing.'

Agatha shook her head, her response almost regal it was so refined. 'I don't think so, darling, I'm very anti-fur these days. Even the mink coat has been disposed of.'

Amanda burst into laughter again, heading to the back room.

'Right.' Marlene banged on the table. 'So now that's over—' she shuddered inwardly '—we have to talk. Remember when we helped Ben and Amanda get together?'

Amanda hadn't always lived in Westfield, and in fact hailed from London, where she shed her high-flying job in a law firm to set up her own craft and upcycling shop. At the time, Ben, village vet and now husband of Amanda, hadn't been that keen, and the ladies had decided a little meddling was in order. Headed by Agatha of course, with Taylor and the ladies along for the ride.

Dot clapped her hands together. 'Remember? Of course I do, it was such fun!' Her smile dimmed. 'I don't know though; Amanda and Ben just needed a well-meaning shove. Iain and Lucy have real issues, and Xander? We might do more harm tha—'

'No! Not them two! Sam! I mean Sam.'

'Fireman Sam?' Agatha checked. 'He is a lovely man, and so very tall.' She tapped her fingers against her temple. "He does remind me of someone, but I just can't fathom it out as yet."

'Hot,' Grace said, stroking the jumper sleeve she was knitting as though Sam was actually wearing it. 'The word you are looking for is hot. You don't need to fathom that. The man is a cool, tall drink of water. Who's the lucky lady?'

She jabbed at herself with her index finger, making Dot giggle.

'Lucy,' Marlene declared. 'Lucy and Sam. They spent the night together last night, drinking wine. Xander told me. I think we should get them together.'

Agatha poured herself a cup of tea, her lips pursed. 'To what end?'

'What do you mean to what end, to make them both happy!'

Dot joined in, crossing her hands together as she did when she was nervous.

'I don't know either. We don't know this guy; he could be a lothario, and what about Iain? Amanda and Ben were both single, and we knew Ben already. It's different, there's a child involved, and a marriage.

'Do we know where his family hail from?' Agatha asked, but her question was lost in the hubbub. 'I know he's from London, but has he always been there?' Another question to slip by unnoticed.

Marlene bit the inside of her lip. 'I know my girl, and if my sister were here to help her daughter, she would. The poor girl is so used to being with that man that she doesn't know which way the sun rises any more, and with Xander ... I think she might end up going home just for him, and I know they're not happy. Iain's not a bad man, but he's not a great one either. Sam is all on his own here, why not try to make some people connect?'

Grace was the first to get onboard.

'I like him. I'm in. We need a bit of fun around here.'

She eyed Agatha, who was the mother hen of the group, and was rewarded with a cheeky wink.

'We need a plan, and I would like to get to know both of them a bit more before we start, but why not?' Agatha wasn't one to back down from a challenge, after all.

Dot, still anxious, shook her head.

'I don't know, matchmaking people can be very dangerous. If it goes wrong ...'

Amanda, having come to listen to their conversation, laughed.

'Dangerous is right! Which poor sap are you inflicting your meddling ways on now?'

Grace, back to her knitting, tittered. 'You didn't do too bad when we meddled in your life, did you? Husband and a beautiful baby? Are you saying we can't do it again?'

Amanda rolled her eyes, knowing better. 'Not a chance. Once you lot get your teeth into the poor buggers, they'll be no stopping you. I'd better go buy a hat.' She looked around the shop, an idea forming in her head. 'In fact, I'll stock them in the shop. A home-grown wedding always means good business.' She slapped her hands together. 'I'll leave you ladies to it, eh? I have some work to do!'

She practically bounced to the back room, the spring in her step punctuating her departure.

Marlene took a notepad and pen out of her handbag, turned to a clear page and wrote 'Sam' as a title.

'Right, ladies, let's collate our information, and get cracking.'

Agatha, flicking an imaginary piece of lint off her sleek trousers, sat forward on her chair and narrowed her eyes.

'For this,' she said dramatically, 'we're going to need more tea.'

Agatha thanked her husband with a smile as he opened the car door for her, and she turned and waved at the ladies who were all draining the rest of their cups and headed home.

'Good day?' he asked, grabbing her hand in his and dropping a stubbly kiss on it. She kissed him on the cheek, then rubbed off the lipstick mark she had left.

'Yes, actually it was. It looks like we shall be matchmaking again, very soon.'

Taylor laughed, pulling away from New Lease of Life and heading home.

'Ah good, I take it the lovely Lucy is the target? Marlene has a tricky one on her hands there. Still, perhaps we wouldn't have got together if we hadn't been up to no good before. It's contagious, that Cupid business!' Before, when Amanda had crashed into Westfield, fresh from London and full of big ideas, the women had all seen how she and the village vet Ben interacted, and the sparks that flew from one to the other when they met. During the course of their collective matchmaking, more than one match had been made. Sebastian Taylor, in love with his employer and friend for many years, finally got his girl.

Agatha rolled her eyes, distracted. She gazed upon her husband and thought about how much better life was now, with him by her side in life, as well as in business. A partner *and* best friend. She wanted that for everyone.

'I can't help feeling that this is important though. I feel like it's more for Samuel than anything else. Do you know the name Draper?' She looked to her husband who was a stalwart of the village just as much as she was. 'I get the feeling I know the name from somewhere; in fact he looks a little familiar. I can't place it.' She leaned forward a little in the passenger seat, rubbing her fingers in slow circles on her forehead, her eyes closed.

Taylor shook his head. 'Not that name no, and I've not really met him yet. Maybe we should have him over sometime, or go see him at work?'

Agatha, normally the first one to walk into a room and command it within five seconds, shook her head. 'No, I don't think that's needed. Not yet, anyway. It'll come to me. Don't tell the girls, they'll think I'm losing my ruddy marbles.'

Taylor chuckled to himself, taking hold of his beloved wife's hand again as he changed gear. He had loved this woman since before he was old enough to be able to peek over the hood of a car, and he couldn't love her any more. If she had a sixth sense about something, he knew her well enough to know that it would come to her. She'd figure it out. He didn't know whether to feel scared, or amused. Such was life with his dynamic bride.

'So, we off to walk the dogs again?' she asked, a little brighter. 'I wanted to work up a bit of an appetite.' Taylor nodded, driving along. Agatha reached over and put her hand on the inside of his thigh. 'I rather thought we might introduce the odd afternoon siesta. What do you think?'

Taylor looked across at his wife, grinned like an idiot and put his foot down a tiny bit harder on the gas pedal.

'Woman, you bring new meaning to this retirement lark. I'm not sure how much more I can hack!' She laughed as they headed home to see the dogs.

Sam was at work cleaning down the equipment when he heard his boss talking at the front desk. Chief Briggs was a strong man; a friendly, fair guy who commanded his team with a firm hand and an air of certainty. Sam himself, never one to trust people at first meeting, liked him instantly, and the fact that he was such a great man to work under had made the decision to move to Westfield far easier career wise. The lads all loved him, and the fire house ran like a well-oiled machine.

That man, however, seemed to have phoned in sick today.

'Well, I appreciate that, but … butbutbut … er … well, yes but … I appreciate that bu—'

Sam could hear the tiny tinny tones of a woman's voice speaking to him, and when he heard the resigned sigh, he knew the woman had won.

'Right, fine, but I have to tell you, as fire chief—hello?'

Sam could hear the clicking of the line, as the chief tried to get the caller back. Next came the frustrated dialling out, but whoever he was trying to get hold of either wasn't available to speak suddenly or was screening their calls.

'Fiddlesticks!' Chief Briggs cursed, and Sam smirked despite himself. The man fought fire for a living, but never would a curse word burst forth from his lips. 'Sam?'

Sam put down what he was doing and headed over.

'Yes, boss?'

'Ah, there you are!' He coloured, probably guessing correctly that he was in earwigging distance of the call. 'Busy?'

Sam shook his head, professional as ever.

'No, sir, just finished in the back.'

The chief's face relaxed a little.

'Ah, good. I have a job for you. Actually, it's a few jobs really.'

He straightened his tie. 'I haven't had the full briefing yet, but it's coming, I'm sure. Today, I need you to go to the holiday cottages, the owners there are wanting their smoke alarms and carbon monoxide detectors checking, and one of them needs some installation.' He picked at a tiny thread on the material. 'It will no doubt become apparent when you get there. Take your time, we can hold the fort around here. The master keys have been dropped into the wedding boutique over on Wexley Street – a friend of the owner keeps a spare set for emergencies, repairs and the like.'

The incident warning system fired up, and Chief Briggs patted him on the shoulder.

'Duty calls, you get off to the cottages.'

The lads in the house sprang into action, throwing their gear on and clambering into the truck. Sam watched them leave with a sigh, and headed to the back to collect his gear. The chief hadn't even had a chance to give him any proper paperwork, so he had his work cut out for him today carrying out the assessments without knowing the layout or status of the tenants in the cottages.

It had been a few days since Iain had been standing on her doorstep, shouting the odds, but every time there was a knock at the door she still flinched. It was a beautiful day, and Xander had been up late, worrying himself to sleep over something he had read on the news. He was always so hyper aware of the dangers – the dark side of the world – even though she tried to shield him the best she could. Even after he fell asleep in her bed, she ended up staying awake long after she should. Watching his face, troubled even in sleep, his dark lashes fluttering as his mind fought against whatever unseen peril it faced. Watching him trying to navigate the world had changed her own view of the way she prioritised things. He loved books and Lego, and hated big crowds. He loved rock music, but would bolt from the noise of a motorcycle in the street.

He saw the world differently, but who was to say which was the right one? The spectrum was a rainbow of struggles and achievements, the usual yardsticks and milestones thrown out of the window. He was a bright, beautiful boy, and although he hadn't found his place in the world yet, Luce knew that he would find his people one day. The hard part was knowing that one of his parents was struggling so much with who his son was, and would be. As a mother, she only wanted one thing for her son. For him to be happy. The thought that perhaps that meant them both moving on kept her staring out of the window till the first rays of the sun peeped through the clouds, stretching and yawning into life. This morning, after grabbing a solid two hours of fitful sleep before the demands of breakfast, she felt like roadkill. Warmed-over roadkill, with a jolt or six of coffee thrown in. She had been staring at the sink for the last three minutes, summoning the skills to wash up that she seemed to have forgotten.. Xander was stuffing toast and jam into his face, seemingly a little tired himself.

The knock at the door came again, and she looked down at herself quickly before opening it. Knowing her luck, last night's pants were probably stuck to her dressing gown. She hadn't had the energy to even try to get dressed yet, and Xander was encased in a fluffy hooded onesie. He looked a bit like Obi Wan Kenobi. If Obi had a pancake fetish and night terrors.

'Morning, darling,' Marlene sang as she came through the door like a whirling dervish. 'Oh, breakfast? Yummy!' She kissed the top of Xander's head (well, hood) and gave him a little squeeze. Xander allowed her but grumbled under his breath.

'It's too early, Auntie. I can't have a conversation with you now, I need my space.' His gaze fell on the two rather large shopping bags she had dumped by the front door. 'What's in the bags?'

She winked at him. 'Well, you eat your breakfast, and when you're ready, you can have a look.' Turning to Luce, who was now dazedly looking at the kettle, she frowned.

'Love, do you think you should get changed? Dressed, maybe?' She reached around her niece gently and flicked on the kettle. 'I'll make the tea. Cup of tea, Xander?'

She got a grunt in response and took out an extra cup. 'You go up, have a shower and get dressed. I'll take care of things here.' She pulled a piece of electric blue material out of one of the bags and thrust it into her hands. 'Go on, and pop that on.'

Luce, still half asleep and semi drooling, looked at her son but he just looked at her blankly.

'Okay, quick shower, brush my teeth. I won't be a moment.'

Marlene was already passing her in the hall, heading for the closet.

'No problem, darling, we'll be fine. I might just have a bit of a tidy up. Xander, you're okay, aren't you?'

'Yeah,' he trilled. 'Go and have a bath, Mum, you look really ill.'

Wow. Sometimes his honesty slashed her to the bone.

'Okay, honey,' she said resignedly. 'Won't be long. Love you.'

The hoover sprang into life before she had even reached the top step. She could hear her auntie muttering to herself as she whipped around the rooms, shuffling furniture around. Heading straight to the bathroom, she looked in the mirror. The woman staring back at her bore more resemblance to her mother than ever before, and the eye bags didn't help the look. Thirty, and she looked every minute of it. For a holiday, she certainly wasn't feeling any more relaxed. Her phone buzzed on the bedside table, and she padded across to it, squinting at the early morning sun as she passed the window.

It was from Iain. She'd had to give him the new number, after him turning up. He was back at home, but wanted to come up the weekend after next to talk. And he wanted to sleep over. 'Sleep over'? What were they, five? She knew what he meant. He was trying, making the effort. He was asking to spend time with them. Which was great, wasn't it? Wasn't it what she wanted when she booked the package holiday to Spain? She didn't answer, replacing the phone back on the nightstand. She would deal with that mess later. Time for a shower. She just hoped that she wouldn't fall asleep standing up and drown under the running water. Just her luck.

Bang. Bang. Bang. Again. All through the shower, there had been these little taps, leading to the odd banging noise. Then nothing. She even turned off the shower at one point and stood there, shivering, her head stuck out from behind the shower screen. No noise then. It stopped, but the shower was already ruined. The reality of motherhood is, unless your child is at school, or with a relative, you never really relax. Even when they are out, you still have one part of your brain focused on them. The days of long showers and lazy baths being a daily treat are long gone. Most parents can have a three-minute shower, including deep conditioning their hair, shaving their legs and either chatting to their child, who is having a dump next to them, or yelling, 'Stop fighting, I'll be cross. Final warning!' through the bathroom door as they towel dry themselves so fast they end up with friction burns. The fact that she was allowed a shower, without distractions, had seemed too good to be true anyway, but she still mourned its loss. The hot water had made her feel so sleepy that now she was out, she was dreaming of bed. Hopefully Xander would sleep well. She would let him get in with her tonight, and they could drift off together. Iain always hated it, spouting on about routine and 'making a man' of their son by making him sleep on his own, but never actually got involved with the routine or pretty much anything else.

Right now, she could sleep on a clothesline, and she still had the whole day to live through, and a child to raise. After slapping some moisturiser on her face, she tucked her hair into a towel turban, wrapped a soft bath sheet around her torso and opened the door to head to her bedroom.

The first thing she saw was a crotch. Just before her body smashed into it.

'Arrggghhhh! Oh my God, arrggghhhhh!' The shock and surprise of being presented by a pair of black trousers holding a man package was too much, and it was pure fight or flight. Or, in Luce's case, both. She let go of her towel and, bringing both her hands back, she slammed them in the man with every little bit of energy and aggression she had in her. The man toppled over with a resounding crash, but she didn't stop to watch. She was already halfway down the stairs, boobies flying, screaming at the top of her lungs.

'Heeelllpppp! Xander! Marlene!'

'Lucy, stop!'

'Luce?'

'Mum?'

She got to the bottom of the stairs, and was just pulling on her coat, grabbed from the hook, when Marlene grabbed her and pulled her towards her.

'What on earth?' She helped pull the coat around her niece, covering her unmentionables and pulled Xander to them, bending down to look at him.

'It's okay, Xander, that was my fault. Everything's fine, you come back in the living room and I'll get you a snack, okay?' Marlene looked at Luce, a mixture of apology and horror on her normally stoic features. 'Get dressed, dear, you'll catch your death. Sam, are you okay?'

Luce turned in abject horror, to see Sam coming down the stairs, her blue dress in one hand, a slight limp present in his gait. Behind him, she could see a small stepladder and a toolbox just visible at the top of the stairs. She turned to Marlene, but the space she'd occupied in the hall was empty, replaced by the soft click of the lounge door. *Those bloody women. She knew, right then, that the women had been brewing more than Earl Grey at that Craft Club.*

'I'm really sorry, I didn't mean to startle you. Marlene, your aunt, she told me I could go up there. I didn't realise you were in the bathroom.' He reached the bottom of the stairs and stepped aside, holding out the bright blue material Marlene had brought.

'I grabbed this from your bed, I hope that's okay.' He was talking to her ear, the wall, the ceiling. Anything but her face, and she was touched by his chivalry. And mortally embarrassed to be standing there like a lady of the night. Faux fur coat, no knickers.

'Thanks,' she said, awkwardly sidestepping him chest to … well … belly button. As he moved away, she noticed him wince.

'I'm so sorry for pushing you, are you okay?'

He broke into a grin, his eyes sparkling with amusement. 'I've fallen off a ladder or two in my time, don't worry. I am sorry I scared you, the last thing I would want is for you not to feel safe.' His eyes flicked over her. Just for a second. Blink and you'd have missed it. A split second later, he was back focusing on the wall, but Luce had seen him. She self-consciously pulled the top part of her coat together with one hand, but, to her relief, everything was covered. Just about. 'I'd hate that.' He spoke again, his voice softer this time, quieter. Speaking the words just to her. 'Especially if it was because of me. That would be hard to live with.'

Luce opened her mouth to comfort him, to reassure him that the fact she had gone all Kung Fu Panda on his ass wasn't down to him, but just the sheer shock of seeing him … or parts of him … when she least expected it. She tried, but her mouth had gone a bit dry, and her inner monologue was repeating his words over and over. It seemed so … sweet. The guy was a softie. Wrapped in a panty-dropping wall of muscle.

'I know I live next door, but I don't want things to be weird. We seem to keep seeing each other at very awkward moments, don't we?'

Standing there, feeling a slight draught from the front door, she totally understood what he meant. Carefully, and with as

111

much dignity as she could muster, she started to move up the stairs, slinking sideways up the steps like a crab.

'I can't really argue that point, given that I turned into a naked assassin a moment ago.'

Sam's laugh filled the hallway, echoing in the confines of the space.

'A cute naked assassin, to be fair. The injuries were almost worth it.' She could see the cogs turning in his head, as she hid her own response to his 'cute' comment. 'I ... er ... mean with clothes on, of course. I didn't ... I never ...' He sighed, threading his fingers together in front of him like a schoolboy in front of the principal. 'Do you know, some days, I wish I'd just stayed in bed.'

The bed reference floated in the air, visible, tangible to them both. 'I'll let you get on. Hopefully we can just forget this. I came on work business, to fix your smoke alarms.' He looked sheepish again. 'Of course, when I fell off the ladder, I landed on your new one, so I'll have to come back later if that's okay? I can call first of course.' She was about to tell him she didn't know her new number when he pulled a card out of his pocket and handed it to her.

'My mobile number is on there, just let me know when it's convenient. I'll let you get on.' He flashed her a quick smile, and before she had even had a chance to process, he was gone, saying his goodbyes to Xander and Marlene. She looked at the card, turning it over to see his handwriting on the back. Neat, small looping letters with his name and number, the fire station logo and emblem on the front. She pushed down the tiny flutter she felt in the pit of her stomach and took herself upstairs to get dressed. Passing the ladder, she noticed the old alarm in the corner on the floor, next to the broom from the kitchen. What was that doing there?

Sam left the cottage and nipped next door to make a sandwich before his next cottage. He'd already checked his alarms when he moved in, so his was automatically ticked off the list. He needed a minute, truth be told. He had enlisted the help of his neighbour to find his family, but now he could feel the first lick of fiery desire stirring in his stomach. She was different to other people he had met, and he was intrigued. How strong does a woman have to be to up sticks with her son and spend the summer away? He knew that she was married, but meeting her husband, he just didn't get it. The two of them together made no sense, and Xander didn't seem to even miss him. He had come to find his kin, and was somehow on the fringes of her family now too. He needed to be careful, especially if he wanted to make a home here. Work was going well, he was settling in, and had even put feelers out for a house in the area. He needed to stay focused, keep his head in the game, and get on with it. He needed to get to know everyone, and annoying the villagers by hanging around with a married woman he couldn't quite stop thinking about wasn't a great start. Somewhere, someone in this village had some answers for him. He just needed to winkle them out of the shell.

He didn't expect to just find his mother here, waiting, if he was honest. The letter asked for them not to look for her, and he couldn't imagine his mother being amongst the faces he had already encountered. No one struck him as familiar, or looked remotely like him. In all the years he had thought about his birth parents, he always felt like he would just know when he met them. That one day, he would turn around and there they would be, standing in the crowd, but so different from anyone else. Someone just like him. Maybe that was just wishful thinking, but it was far better than the alternative.

Growing up with Sondra, he knew how some parents could be, and the effect their behaviour had on their own children. Even as a grown man, he needed to protect himself, and his heart. Where his neighbours fitted into all that was less clear, and all the more confusing.

After making a sandwich and grabbing a drink, he left the

cottage and headed off to work. He couldn't resist a quick peek at Lucy's cottage as he went past, but all was quiet.

Lucy headed into the lounge, where Xander and Marlene were snugged on the couch watching a programme about a vet. Xander was hugging one of the couch pillows to his chest, tucked into the arm of his great-aunt, who gasped when she walked in.

'Oh, Lucy, you look wonderful! Amanda was right, that colour is perfect for you.'

She did feel good, truth be told, but she wasn't completely letting her aunt off the hook. The dress was a perfect fit, and with the stress of the last few months falling away, and a remnant of a tan on her skin, she actually felt beautiful for the first time in a long while.

'Do you know why the broom is upstairs?' she asked innocently, shuffling the pair of them up and wrapping an arm around Xander. He ran his hand over the material of the dress a little, and resettled. 'I know it was in the kitchen, because I swept last night and put it away myself after. Did you move it?'

Marlene, ever the canny woman, didn't flinch or take her eyes off the television.

'I don't know, darling, I didn't notice. I'm glad you like the dress, you should go and have a look in the shop. Amanda has some lovely stuff in, she makes a lot of it herself.' She looked over Xander's head at her. 'There's some make-up in the chemist's too, if you need any.'

Lucy's face dropped. 'Do you think I need some?'

Marlene was already looking back at the TV. 'A woman sometimes needs a perk up, that's all. Even feminists like a bit of blusher now and again, don't they? Cheer themselves up while they do their protesting. What did Sam have to say?'

Lucy scowled at her. This was looking more suspicious by the minute.

'You mean before or after he was in this house fixing a smoke alarm that wasn't even broken. Xander left the bathroom door open yesterday while he had his shower and set it off with the steam. I know it was fine, but, according to Sam, it was kaput.'

Nothing. Xander got up and headed out of the room, leaving the pair of them alone. *Now's my chance.*

'It was kaput, because it was dented.'

Marlene made a non-committal noise, seemingly engaged in a rabbit getting dental surgery. *It was Dot who worked in the village surgery, for God's sake. She was stalling.*

'Dented, with what suspiciously looks like a pole.' A slight lift of the eyebrows, but nothing else. 'Like the handle of a broom, perhaps?'

'Reeeaallllyy,' she replied, dragging out every single letter. *Playing for time are we?* 'How strange!'

Xander padded back in on his tiptoes, clutching a large bowl of grapes to him and settling back down between them.

'Did the rabbit get better?' he asked anxiously.

'Yes, pet,' Marlene said, patting his hand. 'He's just going home, look.' The pair of them looked at the screen and Lucy rolled her eyes. *Well played, Auntie, well played.*

'I forgot to say, Agatha is hosting a party at hers in a couple of weeks. Just a bit of a charity fundraiser, a select few. She's planning to split the money between the fire house and the swimming pool. Both projects are quite new, so Agatha is keen to keep the money coming in and the local papers talking.' She leaned in a little excitedly. 'There's even been talk of a pop-up coffee cart! Can you imagine!' She leaned back against the sofa cushions, a dreamy look on her face. 'Last time we went to Leeds, I had a vanilla-flavoured coffee.' Her smile faded. 'I haven't quite felt the same about instant since. None of the village coffee quite adds up.'

Lucy laughed. It really was a different world.

CHAPTER 10

Agatha woke up and turned to her side to look out of the window. She loved the view from her bedroom window, looking out at the fields and trees beyond. The window was open, letting the sound of birdsong fill the room. She leant forward to get out of bed, but a hand snaked across and dragged her back under the duvet.

'Mrs Taylor, where on God's green do you think you're going?' A gravelly voice came from beneath the layers of frilly floral pillows and thick duvet and comforter, muffled and deep. 'Trying to escape from the floral sweatbox that is our marital bed, are we?'

She giggled at his choice of words. 'Sweatbox is hardly the best word to use, darling, it's rather vulgar.'

'Ah, you love it.' Taylor slid his other arm underneath her, wrapping her into his arms and pulling her close. 'It's your own fault, I mean who has all these blankets on in the middle of summer? And don't get me started on the patterns.'

Agatha huffed indignantly. 'This room hasn't long been decorated! It might not be on trend, as Amanda keeps reminding me, but it is contemporary.' She dropped a kiss on his lips.

'Fair enough, but the throw pillows need throwing right off the bed, and never putting on the bed again. It took me ten minutes to get in last night!'

He kissed her again, snuggling into her.

'What's the plan for today then, with the girls? I know something's happening when you lot get together. What's brewing in the cauldron?'

'Marlene's niece, Lucy? She's new to town and the girls thought it would be good to show her a good summer, make sure her and Xander settle in.'

Taylor, as ever the quiet, observant type, let her finish.

'She's staying in the holiday cottages, but Marlene thinks she might move here, given the right opportunities. The cottages can be let long term, so she can extend her stay at a cheaper rate till she finds somewhere else. She worked in a deli back home, but those skills are transferable anywhere really. Retail is very diverse.'

Her husband was aghast. The woman was a powerhouse, and he could almost hear the whirring of the cogs as her mind ran through the scenarios, lightning quick.

'You know the fundraising afternoon tea party we're hosting?' He started to nod along, but she didn't draw breath. 'Half the proceeds are going to the fire house, and I just wondered, what do Alan and the boys do exactly?'

Taylor sat up in bed, bringing her with him and karate-chopping a few pillows for good measure as he got comfy.

'Well, the people who work there are actually called firefighters, and they're men and women who put out the fires. With water and foam, not by actually fighting them. Do you understand now?'

The resulting look she gave told him she did, and wasn't amused.

'What I was asking, is what in the village would be under their remit?'

'You mean, how can you get the new fireman to do things for you?' Taylor laughed to himself. 'I know what you're playing at, missus, I always do, remember? Archie told me about calling them in about the damaged tree. You know, our gardener? The one

117

who cares for the grounds? Poor bloke nearly had a fit at the prospect of losing some good firewood. You going to spill the beans, Miss Marple?'

She elbowed him and got out of bed, then padded over to her dressing table and brushed her hair. 'Don't tease your wife, help her! Didn't anyone teach you that?'

He threw a cushion off the bed in response, and it thudded to the floor behind her.

'That's one, and I have more. Spill, woman.' He looked around him at the huge king-size bed, which was encased in pillows of various shapes and sizes, with more in a stack on the ottoman at the foot of the bed.

Agatha had to admit to herself, the whole thing was a bit OTT. Not that she would ever tell him that. She turned back to the mirror, picking up her morning face cream and planting her daily kiss on the photo frames. One photo was a shot of her late husband, standing on the steps of the Mayweather house, and the other a wedding photo of the day she became Mrs Taylor. Both happy days, in such different ways. School friends, she and Taylor had been the best of friends for many years, Taylor being an employee of the estate, just like his father before him. Things had developed from there. Now, they ran the estate together, as they did for many years as friends and work colleagues. They ran it now as husband and wife, and Taylor couldn't be happier. Even when she was up to her devious shenanigans with the other cronies she hung around with, in the guise of family and community spirit. The woman was like a dragon clutching her eggs. You messed with someone or something she loved in this village, and you would get burned. She could probably teach the fire house a few things, never mind learn more about their vocations.

'Threatening me with pillows?' She looked over her shoulder at him, one brow arched. 'A little weak, my dear.'

Flumph. Thud. Another pastel pink pillow in the shape of a rose bud fired across the room.

'Spill. What's the deal with the new fireman? Are you match-making again?'

Agatha started to apply her make-up, a little smirk crossing her features. 'Sam's a lovely man, but he's just a little … lost. Yes, lost I think. I know we don't really know him, but when Amanda moved here we didn't know her either, and that worked out, didn't it? We got Benjamin a woman who loves him dearly, and they're happy.'

She looked at him in the mirror. 'We fell in love doing all that matchmaking, so it might be fun to do it again, and it's different this time. It's trickier, so we're being careful. There's a child involved, and—'

'A child?' Taylor queried. 'Whose child?'

His facial features turned from confusion to mild shock. 'Not Lucy? You can't meddle in a marriage, Ags, it's not right.'

She flicked the mascara wand down her lashes.

'That's why we are treading carefully. I'm not daft. Or a home wrecker! We need to get to know Sam, and see what's what. No harm meant, I promise. Brownie's honour.'

Taylor shook his head, throwing the next pillow down into the pile, toppling the lot.

'You were never in the Brownies for long. Brown Owl kicked you out for bringing that frog in!'

Agatha rose from her dressing table and headed to her walk-in closet to dress.

'Yes I know, Sebastian Taylor, and whose ruddy frog was it! We are doing this, with or without your help.' She turned in the doorway, blowing him a kiss. 'I'd rather have it though, even if it happens to come with a frog.'

He laughed and she headed out. Taylor was in on the plan, so that was the last piece of the team. Now, they just needed to put the plan into action.

It was Friday, and Sam had been working non-stop at the fire house. He wanted to get his head back into the game, so he'd picked up Norman's shifts while he was on a cruise with his wife. Today was the first day off he had had for ten days, and he felt like he should be doing something with his day. From the library archives back home, he had researched the local papers from around the time that he was found, but other than the original reporting and some follow-up fluff pieces on how the abandoned baby was faring, there was nothing. Of course, they only had the box to go on, and nothing else. No one ever came forward to claim him, and there were no suspects at the time either. He'd looked through the obituaries around the time of his birth within one year too, just to see if there had been any women who could have fitted the bill, but came up short again. There was nothing about a father anywhere, but he was out there somewhere. Maybe he knew, maybe he didn't, but since being here, no one had gotten his spidey sense tingling, or commented on his familiarity to someone they knew. Of course, not many people would look at a six-foot-odd bald man with a surprisingly soft voice and a cockney accent and recognise traits or features of people they knew. They didn't grow them like him in this village, that was evident on his first day of working and living here. Not that they said anything, in fact, everyone had been really lovely.

He had woken up late, not setting an alarm for once and letting his body get the sleep it needed, so it was after eleven when he finally opened his eyes. He stretched, feeling his muscles pop and stretch as he slowly rose from his slumber. He was feeling rested, and a tad restless. The summer was rolling on, and he was no further forward. No clue as to where to look, or who to ask. Things had been awkward between him and Lucy since the whole naked ladder incident, and when she had contacted him to go back to fit the alarm, things were a little strained. She basically hid downstairs while he worked, and seemed to be in a bit of a rush to get him out of the door after. The husband had been in touch again; he heard her talking to him on the telephone the other night out on the patio. Another conversation that hadn't gone well. The man wasn't nice when he got angry. He would come again soon, he knew it. The question wasn't if but rather when. Last weekend, things had been quiet, probably because he had found something to occupy his mind, something that conveniently made him forget about his wife and child. The man irritated him to death. Anyone who didn't try to make a family work got his goat big time. Which was precisely why he didn't put down roots. The fear of this. He needed to stay the hell away from his neighbours, and concentrate on his own plan.

His phone beeped at the side of his bed. A text. From Lucy. He opened it up and half expected a telling off for his opinion on her marriage. Which was barmy, of course. Instead, it read:

Xander is going to Marlene's for the day. Do you want to do something, to find your family? Lucy x

Was this woman psychic? He read the message over and over, looking for some hidden meaning or clue. It beeped again.

No problem if you can't or don't want to.

No kiss this time. Maybe she was feeling obliged, and was trying to be nice but get out of it at the same time. He thought of what the day held, him rattling around in the cottage, working out or wondering idly where the answers could be. He tapped out a reply.

I'm fine for today, if you're sure it's still okay with you. I was planning to go for a run first, then have some lunch.

He hit send and cringed rereading it. Shit! Did that sound like an invite?

Nothing. He sat watching the screen, hoping for a reply but got nothing. Bollocks. For a fireman, who could get girls just by saying, 'Hello, I'm a fireman. Want to slide down me pole?' he had zero game. Never had, to be honest. The whole dating thing had kind of bypassed him. What would he say on a date? Job, fine ... but the rest? He had no answers to the questions that people generally asked on dates. Family, where he was from originally, whether male pattern baldness was hereditary in his family. The truth was, he had no clue. Aside from the genetic testing, which told him he was fine, there was no magic wand to wave to get the answers, or red sparkly shoes to take him home. So he avoided it, and was now seemingly hitting on a married mother who was fleeing her marriage and trying to sort her life out. He thrust back the covers, flinging them across the room, and reached for his running gear. He needed to pound this out on the pavement.

He was just pulling on his trainers when the text notification rang again. He almost left it there unread. He could go out on a run, go eat, and deal with it later. If he didn't read it, it wouldn't ruin his day. He wouldn't have to respond to it. He was halfway down the stairs when he groaned, stopping dead. With a growl, he headed back to the nightstand, cursing his polite and curious mind.

Lucy blinked at the reply. Well, that was easy. Her heart had been in her mouth since she sent the text, wondering if she had just made a mistake. She wanted to help him, but there was more to it than that. Iain had been asking to come up, but she wanted him to stay away. When Marlene had offered to take Xander for the day, she wanted to say no. Firstly, because she worried about Xander whenever he wasn't with her, and two, what the hell would she do with her time? She had no job to go to, she'd finished all the books she had brought, and the cottage was as shiny as a show home. The thought of rattling around on her own didn't appeal, and she wanted to help him. He deserved her help. He was the definition of a nice guy, and he had helped her already. Since they had arrived in the village, hell, even on the train, he had been there. He was a calming influence, and she felt better just knowing that he was next door.

Ten minutes later, she was heading out of the door, yoga pants and trainers on, a slouchy top over her vest top. She wasn't a runner, but she did keep fit. When Xander was at school, and she wasn't at the deli, she got bored at home. There was only so much cleaning and tidying a woman could do, and her Netflix obsession had been ramping up. Only a few months before their holiday, she had found herself pouring a glass of wine at 11 a.m., safe in the knowledge that Xander was happily gaming in his room, enjoying the weekend reprieve from the school he hated. She only had the one, but when she woke up at half past four in the afternoon, Netflix playing to itself and her lying on the sofa, she made a mental note that day drinking was not something that needed to be on her goal list any time soon. Hence the holiday planning, the yoga sessions at the local gym, and the beginning of the end.

Sam was leaning against her gate, his thigh resting against the wood. He was wearing sweats, long grey jogging bottoms and a black vest top and white trainers. He was looking outwards, his form side on to her, and she was grateful because it gave her a second to collect herself and stop her jaw from hitting the floor. She knew he was muscular, but seeing the muscles under his vest top, the way his shoulder muscles tensed when he turned to look at her …

'You look nice,' he said, smiling broadly at her. 'Xander get off okay?'

Two perfect sentences, right there.

'Thank you, he couldn't wait to go to be honest. I think my aunt and his friends just ply him with cake and cuddles.'

He opened the gate for her to walk through, and the pair stood there awkwardly.

'So—' Sam broke the silence first '—shall we run up past the fire house and back? I tend to stick to a bit of a route. It's only four miles.' *Four miles? Shit. That's a bit more than a few downward dogs.* Her face must have given her away because he laughed.

'We'll take it steady, don't worry. I was thinking we could have lunch at the local café? I don't really know anywhere else local.'

'That sounds good.

Sam nodded. 'Good, I know it's nothing fancy but ...'

'It's not a date, Sam. It's fine.'

He looked away, and she felt bad. Stating the obvious of course, but still. She didn't need to point it out and make it awkward.

'Good. Water?' He handed her a water bottle, one of two he was holding in his huge meaty hands. She took it gratefully, and they started to jog.

'So, enjoying your stay here? Marlene tells me you came here most summers as a child.'

Bloody Marlene, what else had she told him? Her favourite food? Credit score? Bra size. Oh bugger, he could probably take a wild stab at her bra size from when she brandished her bristols in his face. She cleared her throat, pushing the embarrassment away.

'Yeah, I did. Mum encouraged it. She moved away for work, but she never quite got over leaving really. She wanted me to enjoy my time off from school, and I did. I hung around with the neighbourhood kids, spent time with Marlene, it was good.'

'And now? How did it differ from being a kid, to bringing your own here?'

They had picked up the pace a little now, weaving through the streets of Westfield. Every time they passed someone, they waved, said hello. Not one person ignored them. The sun was out, and even though her lungs were starting to burn, Lucy felt great.

'Xander really likes it here. He's really enjoying spending time with everyone, and he loves the house. It's probably because it's so snug. He doesn't like the dark, or huge spaces. I think that our house upsets him sometimes, our house back home I mean.'

They were running flat out now, though looking at Sam, he might as well be strolling to the park leisurely. Lucy felt like she was going to pass out, and she could feel the boob sweat pooling around her sports bra. *Breathable material my arse.*

'What about you?' They were rounding the corner onto

Honeysuckle Street now, and she could see the fire house come into view. 'Are you enjoying being here?'

They stopped a little way back, leaning on the low wall, near to the road sign declaring the street name. They could see the fire house; the fire doors open, gleaming in the sun.

'I ran here.' It was out of her mouth. Gone, uttered to someone other than Marlene. 'I came here with my son to get away. I used to be a teacher, you know. I used to have more purpose, more happiness in my day. I just ...'

'Needed to find answers,' Sam supplied. They locked eyes. Nothing else needed to be said. He straightened up, and tilted his head towards the fire house.

'Fancy coming in, meeting the lads? We can have lunch after.'

Westfield fire station was relatively new in the village. Times were changing, albeit slowly, and the population was finally deemed big enough to warrant the expense of a proper fire station, with support staff and paid firemen. One with the Westfield name emblazoned upon it. A lot of the lads had already worked in the service, working as on-call firemen, living in Westfield and travelling to the other villages and towns dotted around the jurisdiction. Now, for the first time in years, they had their fire house, and they were damn proud of it.

Jogging up to the main doors, Lucy felt self-conscious suddenly. What would they think about Sam turning up with a woman in tow? What would she say if they asked?

Sam opened the door for her and, as she walked through, he touched the small of her back with his hand, gently ushering her through. It touched part of her bare skin, and she could feel the heat from his palm. She almost backed into it a little, to strengthen the force of the touch, but then it was gone, and they were inside. Sam led her through the garage area, past the two fire trucks, and headed inside and up some stairs. Now, the decor changed. It was still professionally kitted out, signs and plaques on the wall, but when they headed further into the living area, she found it quite homely. Through a set of double doors, she could see a dormitory-type room, beds laid out in rows, all made up neatly. Sam headed in the opposite direction, and she suddenly found herself in a large open-plan living and dining area.

'Afternoon, Gary,' Sam said cordially. 'What's cooking?'

Gary raised a ladle at him in response, before clocking his companion.

'My world-famous chilli, it's nearly ready. You looking for some lunch?'

He laughed and shook his head. 'No, man, it's okay. I just came to say hello.' He rested his arm on Lucy's shoulder, just for a beat, and smiled down at her. 'This is my jogging buddy, Lucy.'

'Hey, Lucy!' Gary said jovially. 'You want some lunch? I've made plenty, and you look like you could do with a bit of warming up.'

Lucy started to shake her head, but then the other lads all ambled through, laughing, joking and pushing each other. They all stopped momentarily seeing the pair of them stood there, but soon recovered. Lucy could feel her face flush. *This was a bad idea.*

The chief wandered in, patting Sam on the back as he entered the room.

'Smells great, Gary, but I hope we don't have to put the toilet rolls in the ruddy fridge again. That vindaloo you made last week had me all turned around.' His eyes fell on Lucy, and his moustache quivered, his thick eyebrows shooting up to his receding hairline.

'Oops! I am sorry, my dear, I didn't see you there! Come for a spot of lunch, eh?' He clasped her hand between his and, before she knew it, she was sitting at the large reclaimed oak table, sandwiched between him and another spot that he motioned for Sam to take. The lads were all busy setting the table, passing warm, fragrant garlic bread around and bowls of salad and grated cheese, carrying dishes of freshly cooked chilli, still piping hot from the huge cooking pot on the stove. Sam took his seat, grabbed a bowl from his mate and passed it to her with an apologetic look.

'Sorry about this, I didn't think this would happen.'

The chief slapped him on the back again, a little harder this time.

'You didn't think we would feed our visitors? You should know by now, Samuel, we're all family here.'

Sam rolled his eyes a little at Lucy, and got another slap for his trouble.

'I saw that,' Chief Briggs said, laughing. 'Tuck in, everyone!'

The lads all dug in, passing platters and plates around, chatting and laughing. Lucy took what was offered and before she knew it she had a whole plate full of mouthwatering food. She started to eat, listening to the conversation.

'So.' Russell, a carrot-topped, freckled man who looked like a lumberjack started to speak. 'I have to ask, Sam, what's the deal?' The table quietened down, and Lucy, a mouthful of chilli, almost choked. 'I think it's about time you told us.'

Sam looked at him, a steady, closed-off expression on his face. 'Told you what?'

Russ's expression was serious. 'I really think you need to tell us … why you dress like Mr Motivator on workout days.'

The whole table erupted into laughter, and Lucy managed to breathe again without inhaling kidney beans through her nostrils.

'Seriously,' he continued. 'What's with the muscle tops? You make me feel like a weed!'

Lucy giggled. Russell himself was hardly tiny. The man had tree trunks for legs, and his fingers were like two of hers taped together and then some.

Sam pouted and blew a kiss at Russ. 'Don't hate me because you love me,' he teased, giving him a flirty wave across the table. Russ blew a raspberry back. 'Whatever, man, I'll stick to my old Van Halen t-shirts and battered shorts.'

'Those need to be sent to the shit clothes hall of fame, Russ,' Gary chimed in before taking a mouthful of chilli and closing his eyes. 'Mmmmm, that's good!'

Russ glared at him, but Gary just flipped him the bird. Sam flinched.

'Guys, lady present. Please remember your manners.' He had an easy expression on his face, but his tone was stern enough to make the lads mumble their apologies. He was looking at her with concern, and she couldn't look back at him. She could feel the bloom of heat spreading in her chest, and she didn't trust herself to look into his piercing eyes. Especially not around this lot.

'So,' she said, trying to break the mood, 'which one of you has to do the washing up?'

Lunch went smoothly from there. No mention of them at all. No one asked why she was there, or why they were together. *Had he mentioned her to them? Did they know about her?* She wanted to pull at the thread, but then things would unravel, and she was already stitching enough back together as it was. They chatted about some jobs they had been on, how much they loved the fire house, the locals, Gary's cooking skills. Before they knew it, lunch was done and the lads were all tidying up when the alarm sounded. The chief ran back in, clutching a paper printout.

'House fire, Sandwell Street. Let's go!'

The lads were already running, heading for their gear, heads in the game. Gary threw a tea towel at Sam. 'Wash up eh? I already started!'

The truck peeled out, sirens blaring, and then they were alone. Lucy started to clear the rest of the plates from the large table.

'Oh, you don't have to do that. You get off if you like, I'll stay and clean up. Sorry we missed lunch at the café.'

Lucy scraped the food on their plates into the bin, before pushing the plates under the hot soapy suds that were all ready to go in the large stainless steel sink.

'Gary started us off, we can do it while we're here. Besides, we had lunch, so I'm happy.' She turned away from the sink, and almost slammed into him. The plate he was holding squashed up between them, the remnants of the food smearing under his top.

'Shit! I'm so sorry! I didn't see you there.' She whirled around, grabbed a clean dishcloth from the stack on the side and ran it under the hot water tap.

'It's okay, don't worry! It's only a to—'

She squeezed out the cloth and started to dab at the black material, flicking off the bigger bits into her hand and chucking them into the nearby bin. She rubbed the cloth along his chest, the other hand gripping his upper arm.

'Lucy?' he said softly. She kept going, turning to wash out the cloth and squeeze it again. 'Lucy,' he murmured. She felt his hand touch her shoulder, and turn her around. He'd moved closer, and she could feel his proximity. 'I'm fine.'

She looked up at him, and the cloth in her hand fell down to her side. 'Sorry,' she mumbled, feeling the moment between them and not wanting to do anything to break it.

'Stop apologising.' His voice was soft like caramel, and she watched his jaw flex as he swallowed. 'You always look after other people, don't you?'

'It's a mum thing.'

'It's not just that, though you are a great mum. I should know, I had one. Xander's a fantastic kid. It's more than that. You look after everyone, and all you do is say sorry for it.'

'I get a bit helicopter mum, Iain always says t—'

'Iain is an arsehole,' Sam spat, his gentle expression clouding over. 'He doesn't deserve either of you. Hell, if I had a wife like you I'd—'

Her lips were on his, her hands around his neck, pulling him closer. He hesitated for about a half a second, and then he was on her, lifting her up off the ground, turning them both and

129

sitting her on the newly cleaned countertop. His hands moved from underneath her bottom to her sides, and up into her hair, his fingers encasing her, cradling her head. He slipped his tongue into her mouth, and she met it with hers, pulling him closer, opening her yoga pant-clad legs to pin his between them. She pulled away to draw breath.

'What are we doing?' he asked, his eyes unfocused and hazy as they locked onto hers. 'Lucy, what are we doing?'

He took a step back before she had chance to answer him, or lunge for him again, which is what every tiny cell in her body was screaming at her to do. She had never been kissed like that before. Never, and she wanted more. Her hands were still wrapped around him, and he gently held her hands in his, placing a kiss on one of her palms before placing them both on her own lap.

'That was my fault,' they said together. 'I've wanted to do that.' Together, again. Their feelings were in unison, even if their brains weren't.

Sam looked ruffled, his breath coming out in hard gasps. He looked so sexy, just staring at her like that. She wanted to go to him, but what then?

'I really wanted to do that, but it's not the right thing, Lucy, I apologise. You are a married woman. I just slagged off your husband and then kissed you.'

'You kissed me back,' she clarified, standing up and straightening her clothing and hair. Her legs felt like jelly, and she tactfully leant against the countertop for support. 'I kissed you, it's my fault.'

Sam was already shaking his head. 'If you hadn't done it—' he looked right at her '—I know I would have. I want to right now, but it's not right. I'll walk you home.'

He headed to the door, his shoulders slumped, his walk droopy.

'What about the dishes?' She headed to the sink. She didn't want to go home. She didn't want to spend the rest of the day thinking about kissing her neighbour. Or thinking about her husband, who she knew now she had to talk to. 'I don't want to be rude.'

She started to wash up, her hands flicking on the hot tap and reaching for the dish brush. She felt him before she heard him. He leaned into her, his head touching the back of her hair, brushing his forehead against her and settling into her, his cheek to hers.

'You could never be rude, Lucy.' He sighed heavily. 'I don't know what's going on here, but I don't think we should be hanging out so much.'

She pushed her cheek into his, turning her head slightly to nuzzle into his neck.

'I don't want that. I know it's complicated, but I feel—'

'I feel it too,' he said, his whispered words coming out in a rush. 'I feel it, Lucy, believe me, but it's not right.' He took a step back, and picked up the tea towel. 'Let's just get cleaned up and I'll take you home.'

They washed the dishes in silence, and after the last plate and fork was put away, they dared to look at each other again.

'Ready?' he asked, moving towards her. 'Let's go home.'

They left the fire house, and headed back towards the cottages. The sun was fading a little now, the hottest part of the day burnt off. It was beautiful, the flowers and trees in full bloom, the birds singing, butterflies and bees fluttering and buzzing around, doing their thing. Lucy would normally have loved a day like this. She'd be out with Xander, looking at every tree and leaf, rolling down the grassy hills screaming and laughing. Instead, she was walking home with a man who she had been kissing passionately half an hour ago. Hell, she probably still would be, if she'd had the chance. She thought of her husband, their marriage, and waited for the guilt to overwhelm her.

Okay, not overwhelm. Feel it though, she should be feeling guilty right about now. She tried to conjure up the conversation she would have with him, but she couldn't picture his response. Would he even care? Did she?

'What about your parents? I said I would help, I still want to do that.'

Sam didn't say anything, and she could feel how tense he was, standing far enough apart from her that they couldn't touch accidentally. *Was he mad at her?*

'I don't normally do that, you know.' She was babbling a little now. The cottages were coming into view, and the whole long walk home had been more awkward by the minute. 'I've never done that before.'

'Me neither,' he muttered glumly. 'I shouldn't have let it happen. I know better. I'm really sorry.'

He stopped on the pavement and she whirled around to face him. This wasn't how she wanted the day to go. She was sick to death of playing nice, of trying to make the best of things, of trying to please everyone and be the goody two shoes she had always been. She had done everything right, and none of it looked like the front of the bloody brochure. What was the point?

'I'm not sorry.' She folded her hands in front of her, trying to stop the shaking of her hands. She stuffed them under her armpits, tossing her hair back in frustration. 'I'm not sorry at all, and I don't want you to be either.'

She wasn't sorry! She had loved kissing him. It had felt like a slap in the face, a great big slap in the face to wake her up. She had just stopped living lately, and she knew it. Sam looked at her, and opened his mouth to speak. She held her breath.

'Iain,' he uttered. *Shit.* Trust her to get the hot sexy fireman with morals of steel. Maybe if he was a bit of a cad, they wouldn't be talking at all now. They would still be kissing against the sink. Which was better, she couldn't possibly answer reliably at this moment in time.

'Iain, I know. I'm married, and that's complicated, bu—'

'Iain's here.' Sam looked downward, brows pulled in towards his nose. 'His car is outside the cottages.'

Lucy turned around and could just make out his outline getting out of his car. Damn it, he must have left work early and come straight to them. He was still in his suit, by the looks of things. She turned to speak to Sam, but he was gone.

Sam ran till his lungs almost burst, his stomach protesting at his body being pushed again so soon after being fattened up by Gary's cooking. He ran up past the fire house, waving at the lads as he went. The shout must have worked out well, judging by their expressions. You can tell a bad job from a mile off, just by looking at the men who stand in the fires next to you, watching your back. He wished he could talk to them about how he was feeling, but he didn't know them well enough. He wasn't that guy anyway. Buttoned up, his mum used to say. *You're all buttoned up, my boy. Just remember, not everything stays that way. Sometimes, you have to let things pass.*

What was Lucy though, on that scenario? Something to button up against, or let in? There wasn't just her either, there was Xander to consider, and Iain. A boy needs a father. He would never live with himself if he was the instrument of someone losing theirs, especially when his heart ached to find his own. He'd lived without a father, and an absent one was better than nothing. He couldn't be a part of that, he needed to stay away. He kept running, till the burn in his lungs and the beating of his hurt heart drowned out the voice telling him to go to the cottages and tell Lucy what he thought.

'What are you doing here?' Lucy asked as she headed to the cottage, pulling her keys from the strap around her waist.

Iain was looking tired, and more than a little crumpled. He looked like a wad of paper in a wastepaper basket, scrunched up and discarded. He had been, in a way. She felt a pang of guilt, and squashed it down. Just standing here, she couldn't help but look back the way she came, half expecting to see Sam. Probably for the best that he had left. She had to sort things out, once and for all. Iain pushed himself off his car, where he had been leaning, and tugged on one of his ears distractedly.

'I came to see my wife and child, I want you to come home. It's been three weeks, it's time.'

'Run out of clean shirts, have we?' She threw the words at him, tiny grenades of pain and anger. To his credit, a guilty look came across his face before he screened it off, back behind his mask of wounded perfect provider. ''Cos I know that shirt you're wearing is your least favourite. If that's been paroled from the back of the wardrobe, I know things are bad.'

Iain blinked rapidly, taking a step forward. She opened the gate and walked through it, shutting it behind her and keeping it as a barrier between them. His knees bumped against it, and he glared at her.

'Going to be like that, is it? I've driven from Sheffield to be here, we had some client thing, and instead of driving home, I came to you.'

'For a laundry service, probably.' She folded her arms, keeping the ball of her left trainer propped up against the wood of the gate. 'It's closed sadly, so you can leave. You can make it home before dark.'

'Lucy, stop this!' He leaned forward to open the gate latch, and she took a step back. 'You can't just do this! You can't just leave me! I've got people asking me what the hell's going on. I know you don't have much family, but I do, and they're all wondering what the fuck is going on!'

He was breathing in short, fast breaths now, his face a blanched palette of reds and whites, shock, worry and rage fighting for supremacy across his features. 'I need to know, are you coming back?'

She stood there, on the path, staring at her husband and not having a damn clue what to say to him. He didn't understand at all.

'Lucy!' he boomed, and went to grab her hand. He closed his

134

fingers around her wrist and started to pull her towards him. 'Enough now, it's enough!'

She was halfway out of the gate, arm pulled out in front of her, tugged along by a now ranting Iain, when they both heard a voice.

'Let go of her. NOW.' It was spoken in a calm, authoritative voice. Iain flinched but kept heading to the car, Lucy still in his grip.

'This is private business,' he shouted over his shoulder. 'All fine, just leave us alone.'

Lucy stamped on his feet in her trainers, grinding the soles into whatever parts of his shiny black loafers she could.

'Let go!' she bellowed, kicking him in the leg as hard as she could and scratching at his hands with her fingernails to release his grip. He let go, making a hissing sound and examining his hands for wounds.

'For God's sake!' Iain screamed. 'Get in the fucking car, and let's go home!' He turned around and looked straight into the wall that was Sam, who was standing at his own gate, arms crossed, expressionless. 'Will you piss off, it's nothing to do with you!'

'Sam …' Lucy started, bitterly embarrassed and feeling the effects of being yanked in her shoulder. She rubbed at it, wincing, and Sam's eyes flicked to her, narrowing with concern.

'Are you okay?' he said, a different voice this time. One with emotion in, his soft voice. Sam's voice. He stood aside and opened his own gate. 'Go to my house, I'll be there in a minute.'

She didn't need to be told twice. She was just glad that Xander was still with Marlene and the girls, and didn't have to be a witness to this. If he had been standing there with her, would he have been dragged to the car too, shouted at? She thought back to the moment. The slap, his face when he realised that he had been hurt, and who had done the deed and she got angry again. Heading to the gate, she waited till she was halfway down the path and turned back to face her husband.

'I am never coming back, Iain. If you come here again, I'll go to the police and file a restraining order, for me and Xander. Please, just go, and leave us alone.'

'I'll never leave you alone!' he countered. 'You can't just run away, you need to come home. I have work to do, Xander has school …'

Lucy laughed then, a hollow, bitter laugh that burned when she released it. She felt it warm the blood in her veins, make her hands and legs shake. It felt like white hot lava, oozing around her body.

'You really don't have a clue, do you? He hates school! He hates every minute of it!'

She kicked at the paving stone in frustration. 'You don't know your own son, Iain! Do you even care what he's been going through? You never come to appointments, you make him do clubs he doesn't want to, just to fit in with your stupid bastard work mates, he's miserable!' She started to cry now, every feeling of frustration and isolation bubbling up. 'You don't know your own son, and you left ME alone!' A huge sob racked through her, and she wiped at her face, not even realising that her face was red from the tears she was shedding. 'You left us a long time ago, Iain. The only difference between then and now is that we are not waiting for you to come home and grace us with your presence any more.' She turned away, and headed into Sam's cottage. Shutting the door, she saw Sam still standing there, one eye on her, one on Iain. He was just standing there, a first-hand witness of just how much of a mess her life was. What a day.

Sam waited a moment or two before heading to his house. Iain was standing against his car, head in his hands.

'You were out together, weren't you?'

Sam stilled. 'We went for a run, yes.'

Clang! Iain pounded on the roof of his car with clenched fists. 'Don't treat me like an idiot! Did she come here with you?'

Now, if Sam wanted to be a dick, he could be here. He had the knowledge, the opportunity, and the articulation to tell this simpering bully of a man just what happened from that first day to this. He could tell him that not hours before, he was kissing his wife, and that mere days ago, he had seen her naked. That they had all travelled down on the train together from London. He could obliterate this man just by speaking the condensed truth. He didn't of course, but it took every fibre of his being not to, just for once, be the one to cause trouble.

'I rent the cottage next door. We went for a run. I work around here.'

All true, and it still produced a sneer from his rival. Was he Sam's rival? Could you have a rival for your own wife?

'Pretty chummy, running with someone else's wife.'

Sam laughed. Once, short. 'Last time I checked, women could run with friends, and vote, and drive. It's almost like she has her own mind, despite being shackled to a jackass who puts his hands on women.'

He moved to walk into the house, not trusting himself to talk to the bloke a moment longer.

'I'll come back you know. It's not over yet. I love her.'

Sam dipped his head to enter the cottage.

'Funny, that's not how I show love to people. Safe trip home.'

He closed the door and headed into the kitchen.

'Good job I left the door unlocked eh?' he quipped, for lack of anything else to say. 'Forgot my keys this morning.' *Because I was so eager to go for a run with you.* She was standing there in the window, obscured from view from the outside by the blinds up at the window. Sam stood next to her, and they both watched as Iain kicked out at the driver's door panel of his car, making a dent in the bodywork. He groaned and grunted, kicking it again and sagging against the car momentarily before wrenching open the door and throwing himself into the driver seat. He peeled off without a backward glance, and the street was quiet once more.

'I'll go now, Xander will be home soon.' She went to move to the front door, but Sam blocked her exit, taking a step backward towards the door jamb.

'I'll not stop you going. I wouldn't do that, but I think that you need to sit down for a bit, maybe have a drink. I can call Marlene, see if she can keep Xander a little longer. You have your phone, right?'

She nodded numbly, taking it out of her pocket space and handing it to him, her thumb lighting up the screen. On the display screen was a photo of her, standing with a class of school-children, Xander standing at her side. He looked at the picture, at the face of Lucy, so happy and beaming. Xander next to her however wasn't smiling, and he was tucked tightly into his mother as though he thought the lens was a black hole, waiting to suck him in. He motioned towards the lounge.

'You go and sit down, you know where the bathroom is if you need it. I'll make us a cup of tea.'

He didn't want tea. He wanted a Scotch, and a frickin' medal for not punching the douchebag that called himself Lucy's husband. He dialled Marlene's number and her cheery hello made him smile.

'Hi, darling, everything okay? Xander's fine. Did you have a good day?'

He could hear the jovial excitement and affection in her voice, and felt grateful that Lucy had people here. It was why she came, and she had made the right call.

'Hi, Marlene, it's Sam. Everything's fine. I just wanted to ask what time Xander would be coming home?'

Marlene hesitated for a second or three before she answered.

'Had a visitor, have you? Have they gone now?'

Sam's brows shot up. *This lot didn't miss a trick.* She could hear laughter in the background, one of the voices being Xander. He sounded happy.

'Yes, they've gone. We just … er … need a minute.'

Marlene cursed, and covered the phone. He could hear her speaking, firing words out rapid-fire, others speaking back.

'Tell Lucy that Xander can sleep here tonight, we're watching a movie about little bricks, so he's happy. Dot's staying over, so we'll be fine.'

Another murmured voice in the background, followed by Xander shouting, 'Go, Emmett!'

'I'll ask.' Another muffled exchange. 'Okay, Dot, keep your hair on!'

Sam could hear Xander asking Dot why her hair needed to be kept on, and where else it would be, and felt a flutter in his chest. The boy was so innocent, so curious about a world he didn't fully understand or relate to.

'Sam,' Marlene said, her voice saccharine sweet, 'will you be there?'

He turned to look at the lounge door, but couldn't see Lucy. There was a soft glow from the lamp in the corner of the room, lighting up the comfy chair.

'Well, she's at my house at the moment, but yes, I'll be here all night. I'm not on shift till tomorrow.'

Marlene muttered something to Dot. 'Okay, Sam, thank you so much. You have my number now, if you need it. Save it in your phone, just in case. We'll be round in the morning, around ten. That okay?'

Sam agreed, then put down the phone and made them both a cup of tea. Normally his mother would be in his head, telling him to bring out the teapot and cups and saucers, but this was his pad, his ways. *Sorry, Mum, man's not got a pot.*

He took the cups through to the lounge, putting them down on the coffee table. Lucy was asleep, sat propped up against the pillows. She looked so tired, even in sleep. He sat down in the comfy chair, bringing his tea with him, and picked up the open book laid across the arm. *I'm here, Lucy, if you need me.*

CHAPTER 11

Iain flew along the stupid, windy country roads, heading out of the podunk town his wife and child had chosen to hole up in, rather than their brand new London home. Taking a corner on two wheels, he saw a man stood outside a florist's shop, shaking his fist at him, ushering a woman inside the shop. He ignored his rantings, blasting a raised finger their way before leaving them in his dust. Bloody villagers, they had no idea about the real world.

Lucy was mollycoddled. Always had been. Her mother died when she was barely out of her twenties, and everyone had treated her differently since then. Well, not him. He was sick of pandering to her. What was he doing, flying up and down the country to try to sort them out? He was working his arse off to pay for everything, and she was renting some love shack next to some meathead who looked like he was chiselled from stone. God knows what was going on there, but he knew he didn't like it. She could find the time to palm her kid off on other people to go running with another man, but she couldn't find the time to support him and his career? The other wives were always there at the company events and nights out, their kids well groomed and quiet, the wives looking perfect and happily chatting to each other. Why did he have to have the ungrateful one?

Teaching wasn't exactly earning her big bucks when they met; sure she had money, but look at her now. She'd even given up her job to look after Xander, to be there 24/7. It was probably what caused half his drama. He was a mummy's boy, through and through.

He hit the outskirts of the village and roared down the road, heading to the motorway and home. He was wired, tired from a busy week at work, travelling and running around like a blue-arsed fly after her. Clicking a button on his dashboard, his car kit started to ring out.

'Gerald, hey!'

'What's up, my dude! You out tonight, or the ball and chain got you by the marital balls?'

'Heh,' Iain said scornfully. 'Not a chance, mate, I am out – I'm still driving back. Can you make it for ten?' He looked in the rear-view mirror, mentally kissing goodbye to Westfield. 'I'm in the mood to get utterly shitfaced. You in?'

The hoots from Gerald gave him his answer. 'First pint's on you.'

'Mate, the day I've had, the first bottle's my pleasure.'

Marlene was in her element. She was exhausted sure, her knees creaked a little as she bent to kiss Xander's head, but she didn't care. They'd had a lovely day, hanging out in the village, speaking to all her friends, introducing them to Xander. The boy was pure joy, all wrapped up in a little anxious brunette bundle. He looked the double of Lucy, thank God, and she kept catching herself remembering the little things that a younger Lucy had done over the summers. To have Xander here, happy and laughing, settling himself into her world, made her heart fit to burst.

When he had first been diagnosed, Lucy had been devastated and proven right in one foul swoop. She had known from an early age that something was different from other children around him in the play groups, baby massage, nursery. He'd almost been expelled from nursery for fighting, biting other children and hiding under tables and chairs. He'd run Lucy ragged, but then again, what little boy didn't? The realisation that he was autistic had been a relief in some ways, an answer. The thing was that the problem couldn't be solved. You couldn't magic cream away his struggles, so they learned to find ways to connect with him, to learn what made him happy, and what didn't. Autism was a puzzle with no answer, a riddle that no one had solved, and every autistic person had their own patterns and designs. The problem was, Iain had no intention of learning the patterns. He wanted to cut his son from cloth that just didn't fit, and he tore them all apart.

Looking at him now as she tucked him into her bed, Lego figures lined up on the bedside table, he was different than the boy she met off the train that day. He was calmer, less anxious, and she had never heard him laugh like he had today, not in all the years of talking to him on the phone, of hearing about his life. Now he was here, in the flesh, and she wasn't about to let anyone hurt her cubs. Mama Bear Marlene was well and truly prepared to get her claws out.

'Right, you have everything you need?' She plumped up the pillows for the fiftieth time, Xander already dwarfed by the frilly bedding. He nodded, snuggling down.

'Your bed smells lovely.' He stroked the quilt cover. 'It's really soft, I like it.'

She'd washed her bedding in the same fabric conditioner that Lucy used, she'd been doing it since they arrived. Towels, clothing, everything. She'd stopped using bleach in the kitchen as much, and switched to food that she knew Xander liked. She wanted him to feel at home, and what was a few brand changes between family? She would sell every stick of furniture she owned and go live in the forest if it meant being with them.

'It does smell nice,' she said. 'Your mother told me about it. Do you want the big light on, or off?' The bedside lamp was already on, and the landing light could be seen from the doorway. She could hear the TV on low, Dot's soap on.

'Off,' he said, looking around at the light before hunkering back down in his duvet fort. 'I'm not a baby, Auntie.'

She chuckled, standing and ignoring the protest of her knees to kiss his little face. He kissed her back, and after a moment's hesitation (and a wrestle against the covers) he reached out and hugged her tight. A little too tight, but Marlene loved every second.

'Goodnight, my strong young man,' she half whispered, moving to the doorway and heading downstairs.

'He okay?' Dot checked, one eye on the TV, where a resident love rat thrust his hands in his pockets, pushing his groin area into the eye line of a woman he was after. 'Why do men do that, it's like being a bloody peacock. I tell you, one day they'll just wop them out and waggle them at us, manners are going to pot these days. Where's the bloody romance?'

Marlene sank down into her armchair, her whole body feeling like a hot ember being thrust into water. She could feel the sizzle of her muscles as they relaxed and cooled down.

'I've no idea, Dot, I really haven't. Xander's fine, it's a good job Lucy had given me some spare sleep medication for him. He's nearly asleep, bless him.'

Dot turned down the sound a little, then stood and walked over to the little mobile bar, a two-tier trolley on wheels that Marlene kept bottles of alcohol on with fancy glasses. She filled two glasses with sherry from a cut crystal decanter, before passing one to her friend and taking a sip herself.

'Ahh, that'll put hairs on your chest, lass.' She looked back at the cart, and as an afterthought, grabbed the decanter and brought it over to put on the coffee table. Both ladies slid back the handles on the reclining armchairs, so their slippered feet were out in front of them. 'What did Sam say?'

Marlene shook her head, draining her glass and holding it out for another. When she spoke again, her voice sounded gruff, and she coughed once. 'Not much. He sounded fine, but he never really gives anything away, does he? The man is so calm, I swear, he'd even chill Agatha out.'

'But she was at his?' Dot refilled her glass, and the two ladies clinked them together, taking another swig.

'Yes, he said he'll be there all night. I trust him, she'll be fine.'

Dot nodded once, agreeing. 'So, the plan's off then?'

Marlene dead-eyed the TV, where the penis posturing male was onto another unsuspecting female.

'No, we stick to the plan.' The man on the television flashed his overly large and brilliant white smile, making him look shark-like in the camera lens. 'In fact, I say we ramp things up.'

'Operation Fireman's Pole?' Dot checked, a wry smile across her features.

'Yep, Operation Fireman's Pole is a go.' They grinned at each other, feeling the adrenaline of their meddling kick in. 'Text Grace, tell her to get knitting.'

Dot snorted, reaching for her mobile. 'Get knitting? That woman never bloody stops.'

Sam turned in his sleep, and felt his neck crick. He'd fallen asleep in the chair, book discarded in his lap. He sat up with a jolt. The room was empty.

'Lucy?' he called. No answer. The cushion had been plumped back into place, the cup of tea gone. He walked into the kitchen, stretching out his stiff neck. The cups were both washed and left on the draining board. *She's gone home.*

Pushing down the wave of disappointment that surged through him, he headed up the stairs to the bathroom. As he opened the door, she was there, holding the handle on the other side.

'Oh!'

'Oops, sorry!'

They both grinned at each other. Her hair was stuck up at one side, where she had been lying on the chair. She looked adorable. And a little flushed.

'Sorry, I woke up and thought you'd gone. I was just going to use the bathroom and go to bed.'

'I just tidied up a little. I should go next door.'

Shit. He'd been so happy to see her.

'Stay.' He pushed the words out of his mouth before Mr Logic could grab them back. 'You can sleep in with me, or in the spare room. No funny business, obviously. Well not obviously, but you know.' He rubbed the back of his neck with his hand, wondering why verbal diarrhoea always showed its ugly face when he needed to be articulate the most, around her. 'I mean, I have a spare room. There's no one next door, I'd sleep better if you stayed over here. Or you can share with me, I'll put a pillow between us.'

He was babbling, reaching for threads of something, anything that would keep her close.

She looked up at him, nibbling at her lower lip as she watched him in the shadows of the landing.

'If you have a spare toothbrush, I don't mind getting in with you. The pillow thing sounds okay.' A dark look crossed her face. 'I don't want to go to be honest. I'll be out of here early in the morning before anyone notices.'

This is wrong, Sam. A married woman in your bed, leaving in the early hours. What was she going to do, pole-vault over the back fence? His mother was going to go ballistic. He'd tell her too, like a little lemming having a stroll on a high cliff. The inevitable happened. That woman could smell blood in the damn water. He would open the blasted vein himself as soon as he heard her voice. Spill all his secrets. She had that effect, the woman was born with eyes in the back of her head.

'I can do that, I have plenty.' He thought of how that might sound, and held his hands out in surrender. 'I mean, I keep spares for work, that's all. Not for visitors. I don't have visitors, besides you. Overnight ones I mean, not that this will be happening ag—'

'Sam.' She put a hand on his chest, cutting off the stream of words. He could hear his heart beating a rhythm against the palm of her hand. *Babum. Babum babum babum.* 'Thank you.'

He gave her a purple toothbrush from his washbag and passed her a pair of his tightest sweats and a fitted t-shirt.

'I'll just use the bathroom, I won't be a minute.' She nodded, and he quickly washed and brushed his teeth, used the toilet and looked quickly around him to see if his cleaning would pass muster to a woman. It was easy to turn to slobbish ways living alone, but he was pretty neat most of the time.

Coming back out, he saw that she was sitting on his bed, clothing and brush in hand. They brushed past each other in the doorway, both ending up on the landing.

'We need to stop meeting like this, in hallways, near stairs.' She looked down at the things in her arms. 'Purple is my favourite colour.' She raised the toothbrush, showing him the colour of the handle.

'I know, I remember you telling me.' Her face dropped, and he cursed himself for sounding like a stalker. 'I remember you talking about the lavender in the garden, how your mother loved it, the colours and the smell.' He couldn't stop talking now he'd started. He could see her now, running her hands along the lavender bushes as they jogged. She'd slowed down to touch them, a wistful look on her face. It was something that he'd never forget.

'I did tell you that, didn't I.' She looked surprised at that, as though it wasn't something she spoke of readily. 'I'll just get dressed.'

She sidled past him into the bathroom, and he headed to his room, throwing off his clothes and putting on his loose cotton PJ bottoms. He normally just slept like this, ever ready for trouble in the middle of the night, but bare-chested didn't seem quite right. He reached into his drawer and slung on the first t-shirt he could find that had full short sleeves. Getting into bed, he waited for her to come out of the bathroom. He could feel his heart racing, and she wasn't even in the room. The thought of her sleeping in his bed all night? It was driving him crazy. He batted the pillows behind him, trying to get comfy. He wished he'd brought his book upstairs, so at least he could pretend to be reading. He was pretty certain that he wouldn't be able to comprehend a syllable at this moment in time. He settled for looking out of the window, at the night sky that could be seen in the crack in the curtains. There were so many stars here, lit up better by the lack of lighting outside.

He heard the bathroom door open and close, and she was there, in the doorway, highlighted by the shadows. He turned to look at her, and his heart clenched. She was dressed in his clothes, the drawstring pulled tight to form a kind of waistband from the oversized joggers. She padded into the room, and without taking his eyes off her, he pulled back the covers at her side of the bed. She got into bed, and he covered her over gently, being careful not to touch her. He didn't want to scare her, and he didn't fully trust himself not to jump into her arms. He lay down on his back, smoothing the covers over and clasping his hands together in front of him.

She moved the pillow a little, placing her hand underneath and turning towards him. He turned his head to look at her. Her dark hair was loose and curly, fanned out across the pillow. He could smell a faint scent of perfume, and soap. She smelled like heaven. *Down, boy. Gentleman, remember?*

'Are you comfortable?' he murmured, the low rumble of his voice cracking as he tried to keep his tone steady.

'Yes,' she half whispered. 'I'm not sure I can sleep though. I'm so sorry you saw all that earlier.'

Sam shushed her. 'You have nothing to be sorry for.' Something had bothered him since meeting the guy the first time, but he liked him even less now. 'Has he hit you before?'

Lucy shook her head, snuggling down under the covers. 'No, that's the first time he's done anything like that really. He's frustrated, I think. I didn't make the best exit.'

She nibbled at her lip again, and Sam found himself turning over in bed to face her better, being sure to keep his distance.

'No excuse, Lucy, not for that.'

'I know.' She looked straight at him. Her eyes looked shiny in the dark, and he could see that she was tearing up. 'He hit Xander. Just once, but it was enough. He didn't mean to, but still. Things hadn't been right for a while. I had to get away, and I have no real family, other than Marlene. I wanted to come here and think, get away, give us both a break. I knew he wouldn't get it, so we left.'

'And will you go back?' It flew out of his mouth and he realised that ever since he met her, he had wanted to know that answer. He wanted them here, with him, with her family. The thought of her going back to that man burned him more than any fire ever could. He moved his hand closer, letting it rest in the space between them. She reached up and covered her hand in his.

'I don't want to, no. The truth is, I don't really know what to do. I have a job to go back to, and the house … it's a mess.'

'You'll figure it out,' he whispered in his soft caramel-dipped voice. 'I'll help you.'

He turned his wrist, and claimed her hand in his, stroking his thumb along her soft skin.

'I'll help you too, to find your family.'

He smiled at her. 'I have something to show you about that, in the morning.'

She nodded, stifling a little yawn. 'Okay. That's fine.'

'Goodnight, Lucy,' he said, squeezing her hand. 'You want me to put some pillows between us?' He started to pull his hand away, but she held it tighter.

'No, I trust you. This is good.'

He moved a little closer, pulling the covers up a bit further around them both. 'Yeah, it is.'

They fell asleep not long after, hand in hand. They both slept like logs.

Sam heard a metallic bang coming from downstairs, and dived out of bed, banging his shin on the radiator under the window.

'Arrghh!' he roared, cutting himself off and listening intently. Half a second later, he remembered. Last night. His house guest. The bed next to him was empty, the clothes she had been wearing neatly folded on the pillow. He quickly donned his uniform, brushed his teeth, checked himself out in the mirror and headed downstairs. He could smell bacon and eggs, and his stomach rumbled. He stood in the doorway to the kitchen, watching her. She looked beautiful, all lit up with the morning sun streaming through the windows. Her hair was in a loose plait down her back, her clothes from yesterday on, with a little addition.

'Morning.'

She turned to him sheepishly. 'Oh sorry, I dropped a pan. Did I wake you?' Her smirk told him that she knew she had, and had heard his yelp of pain.

'Just a bit,' he laughed. 'Nice socks.'

She blushed, looking down at the black woolly socks. They were practically folded in half to fit over her tiny feet. He might never wash those again. *Smooth, dude. Creepy smooth.*

'Yeah, sorry. My feet were freezing when I got out of bed. Did you sleep well?'

He grinned, flicking the kettle on and getting two mugs out. 'Like a drunk baby. Coffee?'

She nodded, stirring a saucepan full of baked beans and keeping an eye on the frying pan.

'I made breakfast for us. I figured you might need a good meal before work. I hope you don't mind.'

He put a hand on her shoulder. 'Stop apologising. Make yourself at home here. Thanks for breakfast, it smells great.' He could have gone further, told her that the fact a woman was wearing his socks and making him breakfast was an alien and unprecedented event, but he stayed quiet as usual. He didn't want to make things awkward. He felt like giving it a name, discussing it, would break the spell. He didn't want that, he wanted more, so he was going to go with it. Risk his heart silently, without a fuss. The Sam way.

They both worked together, stirring and pouring, serving and plating up, and before long they were sitting at the small dining room table, rack full of toast, enjoying their breakfast together. Lucy took a glug of coffee and sighed appreciatively.

'Wow, that's nice. You working late tonight?'

He raised a brow. 'Yeah, till ten. Why?' He thought of the night before. 'You worried about Iain?'

She shook her head. 'No, I'm going to sort Iain. I just thought that we needed to crack on with finding your answers.'

He stood and headed over to the kitchen drawer. He took out an envelope and placed it on the table in front of her. 'That's everything I have. I'm thinking we start there.'

She went to open it, but he pulled it away.

'Ah-ah, breakfast first. I'll leave it with you, while I'm at work.'

She flashed him a cheeky grin. 'Tease.'

'Always,' he retorted, thinking of them lying together the night before. 'I'm a patient guy.'

She looked at him and smiled, her eyes twinkling at him. *Wow.*

'Yes,' she said softly. 'I know.'

Breakfast finished, they were both just heading out of the door when they heard the rumble of Marlene's car behind them.

'Shit! She's early!' Lucy was in a mad panic. Sam took her by the shoulders gently and ushered her out of the house by the front door.

150

'Do you trust me?' he asked. She bobbed her head up and down rapidly. 'Yes, of course!'

'Hang on then.' He reached down and, before she knew it, she was in his arms. He laughed a little as she squeaked in surprise, and then lifted his long leg and, a second later, they were standing outside her front door. He placed her down gently, never taking his eyes from hers. She clung to him even when she felt her feet touch the ground. She was so taken aback, and unsteady. And, if she admitted it to herself, a little turned on. What was it about women who loved a man who could scoop them up and carry them? What was the difference between feeling safe and intimidated? Why did she feel so different when she was around him? She had never felt like this before, not even in the early days of her and Iain courting.

'Sorry, it was all I could think of.'

'Now I know how the girl felt in *King Kong*.' He pretended to be hurt by the comment, beating his chest with an apelike expression on his face, scratching his head with a huge hand. A hand she had held all night, and woken up clasping that very morning across the sheets. They both started laughing together as the car pulled up. Dot was in the passenger seat, staring at them intently.

'You ready for this?' she asked. Sam waggled his eyebrows. 'Woman, I was born ready.'

'Good morning!' Marlene trilled, jumping out of the car, Xander already halfway through the gate.

'Mum, Sam! I slept at Great Auntie Marlene's, and she let me have cake that you don't let me eat!'

Lucy narrowed her eyes at Marlene, but her expression was happy. 'Oh really, E numbers galore eh? Bet that was fun at bedtime!'

Dot, following behind, waved her away. 'Nah, a tot or two of sherry, we were all out for the count.' She looked up at Sam, a broad smile plastered across her chops. 'Bit of exercise this morning, eh?'

151

The pair flushed. *Had she seen them bolt the fence?*

'Good morning, ladies.' Sam leaned down to Xander's eyeline, holding out a closed fist. Xander bumped it with his own. 'Morning, Xander, and good job looking after your auntie and her friend. You have fun?'

'Yeah.' He leaned forward and touched the embroidered fire station logo on Sam's shirt. 'When can we come to the fire house? You said we could.'

Sam looked across at Lucy. 'How about tomorrow? I'll have to check with the chief, but I'm sure it will be fine. I mentioned it to him the other day. That okay?'

'Yes!' Xander screeched, spinning his arms and legs around in a victory dance on the front lawn. 'I can't wait! One sleep!' He stopped abruptly. 'Can I drive the truck?'

'No you can't!' Lucy objected, a look of horror on her face at the thought.

'Sorry, buddy,' Sam chuckled, straightening up. 'I might be able to arrange you turning on the siren though, we'll see. Don't freak your mother out like that, okay?'

Xander's little head shook frantically. 'I won't, I promise.'

'Good job, look after your mother.' He straightened up to his full height, leaning to ruffle his hair as the boy passed him. Xander laughed, running through to the back garden.

'Bye, I will. I'm going to check for butterflies!'

Marlene and Dot were both clasping their hands, hearty eyes in full flow and aimed at Sam.

'You're so good with him,' Marlene simpered.

'You really are,' Dot agreed. 'Have you ever thought of having kids yourself?'

The easy smile died on his lips, and Lucy wished she was a bit closer to the women. Just so she could slap them around the chops.

'Err ... ladies!' she chided.

'I have thought about it, a lot actually, especially lately. One day.'

Both ladies looked triumphant, eyeing each other with a twinkle in their peepers.

'A child needs siblings though, so don't forget that! My mother always said big men were good solid stock, and babies are born bald anyway really, aren't they!'

Lucy could feel herself getting cross. Sam, to his credit, just stood there, watching them all with his usual relaxed expression.

'Yes, of course! Heaven forbid there should be a follicly challenged only child somewhere, that would be terrible, eh?' She looked pointedly at the ladies, and they blatantly ignored her, still grinning like loons at Sam and his apparently fertile physique.

'On that bombshell,' Sam winked at Lucy, 'I'm off to work, have a good day.'

He had almost reached the gate when he turned.

'I have my phone on me, if you need anything. I'll be home by eleven.'

He blushed as he left. It all sounded very domestic, very normal, couply. She must have realised it too. She cleared her throat, and discreetly took her key out and opened the front door.

'Tea, ladies?'

A familiar voice shouted from up the road. Grace was there, a large shopping bag in her hand along with her usual knitting bag.

'Two for me, duck. Am parched!'

The four women were all sat in the living room, tea tray laid out on the coffee table. They could see Xander outside from the back window. He was laid out under the tree, chatting away to himself. Talking to nature, probably.

'So, how did your night go? Sam said that Iain had been, did you resolve anything?'

'Did Sam punch him?' Grace asked, pushing herself forward in her chair to get involved in the conversation more. 'I bet he could bop him into the ground with one—' She banged her closed fist sideways on, onto the coffee table, making the contents dance. 'You should get on that you know, before the singletons in this village cotton on to the fact that a hot single fella is living and working here.'

Lucy stirred her tea, sitting back in her chair and shaking her head in disbelief. 'Get on that? He's not an exercise bike.'

'Oooo,' Dot chimed in. 'If he was, I might reconsider going to the gym.'

'I know.' Grace threw a Bourbon biscuit at Dot, who caught it and bit it in half with a hard chomp, pulling a funny face at her friend. 'Me too. What did you end up doing?'

Lucy's brows shot up as she thought of the night she had spent under the covers with the local public servant. 'Er, nothing really, just had a good night's sleep. Iain left, but I do need to call him, try and sort things out. I think I might need a solicitor.'

Marlene reached into her handbag, pulling out a card almost instantly. Given the fact that most women's handbags have an average of twenty things in them, and are like mini Tardises/Mary Poppins' carpet bags, it was obvious that this innocuous-looking business card had been waiting in the wings, for just a moment as this.

'He works from Harrogate.' Lucy took the card and looked at the name. It sounded familiar. 'He helped me when your mother … you know. He helped with the estate planning. He knows about your situation with your inheritance. Talk to him, protect your money, darling. Get some advice, if nothing else.'

Lucy placed the card next to the tea tray. 'I will, it's come to the stage where things do need sorting.'

The women all hmm-mmmed in unison, before taking a drink of their tea.

'So, fire station tomorrow with Sam eh? That'll be fun.'

There they go again. Lucy might be a little distracted this morning, with everything going on, but she still had her senses. And right now, she could smell a rat. A little grey-haired one.

'Yes, well Xander will love it, I'm sure.'

'And you!' Marlene exclaimed. 'It'll be lovely, spending time together there. What are you going to wear? Do you have something nice?'

Lucy looked down at herself. Fair enough, she was still in yesterday's jogging gear, and not quite looking her best, but she had managed to wash her face and brush her teeth this morning.

'Er, I hadn't thought about it to be honest. I'm sure I have something.'

Grace held up a finger aloft, reaching by her side and pulling things out of her shopping bag.

'Amanda's been making these, new stock for the shop. I said you'd try it out, see what you think. She's been stitching up a storm lately. I bet her and Ben will be making another little announcement soon.' She pretended to rub a pregnant belly in front of her, and the other two gasped.

'Oh, I do hope so,' Dot said, clapping her hands together. 'Be lovely to have another baby around here.'

Baby mad, this lot! Trying to impregnate people all over the shop!

'Here, love.' She handed Lucy two bundles and pointed upstairs. 'Nip up and try it on, eh?'

They were both wrapped in tissue paper, one looking like a muddy brown, the other a bright sunshine yellow. 'Why is there two?'

'One's for Sam. The dark one. Take it to him, would you?' She didn't wait for an answer before changing the subject. *Looks like I am playing delivery girl tomorrow as well.* 'I wanted to bring you a red one, but your auntie,' she jabbed her thumb at Marlene, an Elvis-like curl in her top lip, 'thought it might clash with the decor there. You know, too red. You'd look like a piece of equipment!' Lucy stood there open-mouthed. This was an utter stitch up. She felt like a bloody mannequin. She'd better not nap around these broads; they'd have her in the window with a metal rod up her jacksy sooner than you could say 'swipe left'.

'She'd look like a bloody pillar box too,' Lucy could hear someone say as she headed upstairs.

'Look after Xander,' she called to them, knowing that there would probably be no better babysitters than the women setting up camp in her living room. Placing the parcels on her bed, she opened the yellow one. Out spilled a gorgeous dress. It really was stunning. The label said '*design by Chic Boutique, Westfield*' and the dress had a flared, full skirt and a bodice design. It was classy, perfect for a daytime event, and the yellow was a tasteful sun-kissed shade. The skirt fanned out with a swish as she lifted it up, and she saw that the material was printed to look like a sunflower, the petals fanning out from the centre of the waistline.

'Wow,' she breathed. 'Gorgeous.'

She hung it on a hanger, suddenly feeling far too dirty and dishevelled to try it on in her current state of dress. She took off her bum bag, thrown back round her waist that morning at Sam's, and opened the zip. The letter that Sam had given her to read was in there, along with her phone. She put the phone on charge, and turned the bath on in the house bathroom, sitting on the side of the bath and closing the door. On opening the letter, she saw a newspaper clipping, and two letters in different handwriting. She began to read, and the more she read, the more she wanted Sam to be there. It was heartbreaking, and all she wanted to do was give him a hug. His adopted mother had done a brilliant job of raising him, and from reading her letter, loved him as much, if not more, than any mother could love her child. She knew without a shadow of a doubt that she loved Xander to distraction. She loved his nature, his smile, the way he took on the world and tried to find a place in it, carving a new Xander-shaped one along the way. She would die for him, kill for him, and endure anything just so he could avoid a moment's pain. Sondra and her would get on, if they ever met. Reading these, she knew just what she had to do this summer. Why she was here. How to proceed. She wasn't lost any more, but Sam still was. For once, he needed to be helped, to be rescued, and she wanted to be the one to do it. Folding the letters away, she slipped out of the bathroom, hiding the envelope and its contents in the pocket of her suitcase, and headed for the bath. She would play along with the little coven downstairs. The Witches of Westfield were preparing their brooms for battle, and she was right there with them, hopefully zapping some secrets loose along the way.

CHAPTER 12

Sunday morning, and Lucy was up before Xander even stirred. Which was unusual, since he hardly slept past six usually and was up and jiggling about like the Duracell bunny by ten past.

The previous evening, she had pushed the envelope back through Sam's door after Xander was in bed, and stuck a note into it.

See you tomorrow. I may hug you, so be warned. Ten okay? Let me know.

Lucy and Xander

P.S. I might have a plan.

She did have a plan, but whether he would go along with it was a different matter. He had morals, which wasn't a bad thing, but the lines were already blurring between them and she didn't know if he would be open to what she had to suggest.

Just after eleven, as she was dozing in bed with a book from a stack that Marlene had brought for her, her phone buzzed and vibrated on the nightstand.

Opening it, she saw a text from Sam.

Just got home. Ten is fine, and hugs are always acceptable. Meet you at the fire house.

Sam x

P.S. Am intrigued about the plan.

He seemed upbeat, and open to ideas. Of course, anyone could be open to an idea when they had no clue what it was about. She could have signed him up for Mexican mud wrestling for all he knew.

The morning passed by in a blur, and before she knew it, she was walking to Honeysuckle Street with Xander, both of them dressed up and feeling excited. For different reasons, of course.

They chatted all the way up, about school, and home. Xander wasn't keen on either, and she couldn't say that she was looking forward to facing them either. Even her job at the deli, which she did like, seemed like it belonged to another person; another version of Lucy when she was still in her little London cocoon. Now, they were here, and butterflies were everywhere. Did they really want to go backwards? She'd made an appointment at the law practice in Harrogate, but had made it for the last week of summer. She didn't want to think about it till then. It sat in her diary like a deadline, a turning point should she need it. She needed to plan everything, and make sure she was doing the right thing. If it were just her then her path forward would be easy. But it wasn't. She at least had another fortnight of denial time, and she was going to use that to help Sam, and give Xander a great summer. Those things she could do.

They neared the fire house, and Xander gasped. 'Wow, look at the trucks!'

Both trucks, Donald and Teresa, were all gleaming and ready for action, visible through the large shutter doors of the fire house. It really did look a bit like a house, all brick walls and welcoming flowers covering the grass on the side verges, the little curtains at the upper windows, where the sleeping and living quarters were. They were almost at the main doors when Sam appeared, a fireman's helmet in his hands.

'Good morning!' He plonked the hat onto Xander's head, laughing when he tried to walk around blindly. 'Hey, mate, wait just a minute.' He pulled the visor up and Xander's grinning face beamed out at him. Alan followed Sam outside, and was soon barraged with a flood of questions from Xander. Alan ushered him inside, chatting away.

'Hi,' Sam said, holding his arms out wide. He was dressed in his uniform, looking trim, fit and rather delectable. *Where did this man come from? That, Lucy, is the million-pound question.* 'I think I'll take that hug now.'

She thought about being coy for about half a second before she half ran into his arms. He didn't even flinch as she barrelled into him, holding her tight to him, his arm muscles flexing around her body. They both sighed in relief.

'Now that was worth waiting for.' He squeezed her again, and she hugged him tighter. 'Are you both okay?'

She laid her head against his chest, not answering, listening intently to his heart beating. 'We're fine. I made an appointment with a solicitor, and I told Iain by text never to come up here again like that, and that he has to call to arrange to see Xander.'

She could feel him nod in agreement. 'You didn't tell him about the solicitor though, eh? Best not to tip him off, till you know what's what.'

She pulled away a little, to look into his eyes. 'I didn't. We don't have joint money, and the house is covered, and in joint names. He can't really make a move without me knowing about it.'

He pulled her back to him, cradling her head in his hand.

'Okay, so that's the plan?'

She giggled. 'Nope, that's a bit more complicated, believe it or not, and for you, not me.'

He groaned, a low tremor spreading from his chest, and she absorbed it into her body. She could smell his aftershave, and feel him all around her. She could have stayed there forever.

'I have a feeling that this is going to be messy.'

She took a step back, and reached for his hand. 'Sure is, Fireman Sam. Shall we go in?'

The women were buzzing when they barrelled around the corner in Taylor's car. Agatha had summoned them to the manor born for a strategy meeting, and they had a few snippets of news to share themselves. As they headed through the gates and up the long drive, before pulling up alongside the front doors, near the fountain, the noise in the car was a constant stream of chatter. Sebastian Taylor was used to them all by now, after years of ferrying Agatha about as her driver. Now, he still ran her errands and played designated driver, but he was no longer on the payroll. Now, he did it for love alone, and he enjoyed every minute. Agatha was the love of his life, and he wasn't about to complain about her free-spirited and rather bossy nature. She was as big a part of Westfield as the schoolhouse that they used to learn in as children, as important in the history of the place as the fountain on the Mayweather Estate, as the big old oak that grew in the north field. She was home, to him and many others. Including the cacophony of tweeting old birds in the back.

'Thanks, Taylor, my love.' Grace patted him on the shoulder as they all got out. She hesitated a bit, looking back at him. 'The children out, are they?'

Taylor chuckled. 'They're in the kitchen, I think, with the back doors open. You're fine to go in.'

The 'children' she was referring to were two Afghan hounds, Maisie and Buster. Great big, hairy, lolloping things they were, and Agatha adored them. With her and her husband Charlie never being blessed with children of their own, Agatha had showered her love on her village instead, and on the two dogs that shared their home. The postman was terrified of them, given that they sounded like apocalyptic hellhounds whenever he deigned to touch the door knocker, but they were just like affectionate and goofy toddlers. They were perfect vessels, happy recipients of all the love that Agatha had stored up for the children she wanted but never had.

'Good,' Grace said with a sigh of relief. She pulled a leg of lamb out of her bag, wrapped in cling film, and brandished it in front of her like a knife. 'I came prepared, just in case.' Taylor guffawed, and she shook the leg at him. 'Hey, no laughing, boyo. Those things have fleas bigger than you!'

'Fleas?' A horrified prim voice came from behind them. 'My babies don't have fleas, thank you very much. Do come in, they're having their exercise time in the gardens. They're playing with Archibald.'

Archibald was one of the gardeners on the estate, although now his family did most of the work, with him being retired. Well, he was officially retired, but it would be the end of his days before he put the trowel down and actually enjoyed any retirement activities. They all walked into the house, and Archie could be heard yelling, 'Sod off, ya great big dishcloth!' out of the windows at the back of her house. Agatha's face curled up as though someone had thrust a freshly peeled lemon into her chops, but she said nothing.

They all sat down in the large living area, and Agatha stood before them, flip chart primed and ready behind her. She pulled the top off one of her coloured markers theatrically and wrote Sam in the middle of the paper, circling it with a blue wavy line, in an oval shape.

'Right,' she boomed, her eyes flashing with mischief and possibly the effects of the smelly marker pen. 'What do we know?'

'Nehhhhh–nawwww! Nehhhhhh-nawwww!' The siren blared out, deafening in the small space, but it was no match for Xander. He made siren noises right along with it, perfectly in tune, at the top of highly excited lungs. Sam was laughing his head off, and Lucy felt the pain of something deep down in the pit of her stomach. Sam pressed a button, and the fire house went quiet.

'That was awesome! Mum, can we get a siren?'

Lucy looked at Sam like any parent does when a relative buys their kid a drum kit, or teaches them to cuss in Mandarin. (Marlene did this last year over Skype, after having Mandarin classes at the community centre.) 'Thanks,' she mouthed at him, and he rolled his eyes back at her.

'Nope, houses don't have sirens, remember? They don't need them, because they don't move.'

Xander thought for a moment. 'If we lived on a houseboat, could we then? They move!'

Lucy pressed her palm to her forehead in a pretend slapping motion. 'Of course, why didn't I think of that! We have a house though, honey.'

Xander's face darkened then, and Lucy wanted to cut her own tongue out. 'The cottage?' she tried, and he relaxed.

'I like the cottage,' he agreed, the cloud of anxiety leaving his features. 'Do you like your cottage, Sam? I know you're a bit too big for a small house, but it's nice, isn't it?'

Normally, people conversing with Xander in public brought her out in a cold sweat. Xander was whip-smart and didn't miss a trick, but he also had no tact or filter either. He wore his heart on his sleeve, and said what he thought. Not everyone liked it, and often she felt like a translator, facilitating talk between the person and Xander. Trying to explain to Xander the different sayings and in-jokes he didn't understand. The day he had put his head and hands to the car window, looking for the raining cats and dogs came into her head. She cried all night that night, once he was asleep and tucked up in bed. With Sam though, she didn't have to worry.

'It is nice, and I think I'll probably look for a bigger house at some point.' He bent in close, beckoning with his finger for Xander to lean in. Once he did, Sam whispered to him. Lucy didn't catch it, and when she asked, they both tapped the side of their nose at the same time. He'd picked up his ways already. The action was so natural, so in sync that the air changed in the cab of the truck. Looking at Sam, she saw a shocked expression that matched how she felt. This was getting complicated. Xander was getting attached here. *Just Xander, Lucy? Are you sure?*

Gary came into view of the window, smiling at them all. His hair, a gelled quiff, looked a little floppy, and there were white and red stains on his apron.

'I heard we have a lasagne-loving little boy here today, so I made one from scratch. You coming?'

Xander pulled a face, pushing his back into Lucy to get closer to Sam.

'What's scratch?' he whispered. 'It sounds gross.'

Gary erupted into laughter and headed back to the kitchen.

'It's just a saying, Xand, it means that he made it all fresh, from the start of a recipe. Proper tomatoes, everything.'

Xander looked confused. 'I thought lasagne sauce came from a jar. Mum?'

Sam didn't say anything, half getting out and reaching back in to help Xander down. He ran off, heading towards the admittedly heavenly smell. He held out his hand, his eyes studying the seat upholstery intently.

'Go on then, laugh,' she said with a pout. 'I know you want to.'

He held his hand out closer, looking further down. 'I don't, honest. Let's go eat.' His hand dangled between them and he waggled his fingers.

'Look me in the face and tell me you're not laughing,' she dared. He looked into her eyes and burst out laughing. She slapped him on the arm and pushed his hand away, a full-on mini strop.

'I knew it! I can get out myself.' He stepped back a little, and she scrambled to get out, trying to maintain her modesty under the layers of cotton and tulle of the sunflower dress. He leaned forward and, grabbing her right arm with his left hand and folding her over his shoulder, he lifted her out on his shoulders.

'Ahhh!' She laughed, trying to be cross, cover up her lady garden area and slap him all at the same time. He did a little whirl, and she screeched and grabbed him tight.

164

'Sam, don't drop me!' she squealed as he danced around the bays with her.

'Drop you,' he scoffed, tickling her on one of her sides, just because he could. 'You're a tiny little woman, I've carried far bigger than you!'

Between fits of laughter, she sang out, 'Of course you have! You're like Big Foot!'

He stopped suddenly, making her body whirl into a position where she was wrapped around his waist. 'Whatever, Thumbelina.'

He lifted her then, effortlessly, so she was high above his head, his hands around her waist, holding her steady. 'Finished stropping about the sauce?' He stuck his tongue out at her and she growled, seething. He lowered her slowly, till she was level with his face. She wrapped her arms around his neck, still laughing.

'You look beautiful by the way.' He looked from her face to her neckline, and lower. 'You took my breath away when I saw you both walking up. I'm so glad you came to see me.'

She smiled at him, running a finger down his cheek slowly, not knowing why, just wanting to answer her impulse. 'I'm glad to be here too.'

He looked at her lips, and she steeled herself. *If he kisses me now, I'll let him. I want him to …*

He looked away, and lowered her down to the floor.

'Xander will be wondering where we are,' he said, his voice sounding distant, thicker somehow. She followed him, pushing down the wave of shame and rejection as best she could. She was just conjuring up a wild excuse in her head for them to leave, when he stopped at the door and looked back at her.

'I feel this.' He turned his back to the door, standing mere inches from her. The bays were empty, quiet and she could hear her own breaths coming out hard and shallow. He placed one of his hands over his chest, locking eyes with her. 'I feel what I think you feel too, but—'

She put her hand over his. 'It's okay, just listen. The girls are

165

trying to set us up, they're trying to throw us together, I think. The dress, today, their idea. The smoke alarm? When I went to sleep the night before, the smoke alarm was fine and working. I think—'

'Marlene broke it,' he replied, catching up. 'So this, all this, was them?' He looked upset, but she had to do this.

'Not the kiss, no, that was me. But they are manipulating us, putting us together.'

'So, it's not real?' It was meant as a question, but it came from him like a deflated statement, a realisation. 'My feelings can't be swayed by a bunch of women, Lucy.' He covered her hand with his other, pinning her fingers between his as he cradled it to his chest. 'I know it's wrong, but—'

'I know.' She stopped him. 'I know, Sam.' She wanted to hear him say more, say anything about how he felt about her. She was all too aware of how she felt, her whole body had an electric current racing through it, and she wanted nothing more than to jump in his arms. 'I feel it too, but it's not that simple.'

Iain and home popped into her head, and the electric zipping through her fizzled and sparked out. She felt like there was a weight on her chest, and she coughed and gasped to get rid of it. Sam was still holding her hand, looking down at her with eyes that told her he was desperate too, as desperate and as unhappy as she was. She laughed once, a small little humph, and lowered her forehead to lean against him. In an instant, he was there, wrapped around her body, his warm strong arms holding her tight.

'I wish I'd met you years ago.' A single tear fell down her cheek.

He kissed the top of her head. 'Not as much as I do, Lucy. When I saw you that day on the train, I don't know, I just knew it meant something.'

She knew it too. What were the odds that they had lived and worked so close to each other for so long, and on the day they both left for new lives, they met on the platform? They stood forever, clinging together. Just enjoying the moment with each other.

'So,' Sam said slowly, still holding her tight, 'what do the women hope to achieve with this then?'

Lucy laughed out loud, wiping the tears from her eyes. 'Oh Lord, they're the worst! They're trying to get us together, but maybe we can use it to our advantage. I wanted to tell you later.'

She pulled away, and he released her. 'I think we should use them to find your parents. It'll mean us being close to the Mayweather Mansion, and with the fundraiser coming up, it's perfect. I think Agatha was thinking of doing an afternoon ball; we could go and have a root around.'

Sam looked horrified. 'You mean, look around the house, or ask questions?'

Lucy shrugged. 'One of them, both of them. Whatever it takes.' She looked up at him and, after battling with her head and her heart, she stroked her palm along his cheek. 'I want you to find your parents, Sam. I want them to know you, like I do. To love you lik—'

His eyes widened, but he said nothing. She could hear him swallow hard.

'Like we all do. Are you in?'

'What about Xander, and Iain?' He looked conflicted, stricken. 'I don't want to hurt anyone, and this isn't a game, Lucy. I know I shouldn't have feelings, but I have.'

He slapped his hand against his chest. 'I can't get hurt, Lucy, I just can't. I don't do this, I never did. I stay alone, it's better that way. What if everything goes wrong?'

'It won't.' She shook her head vigorously. 'We'll be careful. We'll keep our distance, just concentrate on the plan. We can do this. You're my friend too, Sam, I don't want to lose that.'

Sam smiled, a goofy open smile that she hadn't seen often, and wanted more of. 'Friend, eh?'

She smiled back. 'Yes, Sam, I care.'

The door behind them pushed open and they sprang apart.

'Mum? Sam? Gary says lunch is getting cold.' He had a little bit of sauce on his face, and he was licking at it as he spoke. 'His lasagne is way better than yours, Mum, but Gary said to not tell you that.' His little face fell, a blob of sauce flicking off his chin onto his Minecraft t-shirt. 'Oops, I shouldn't have said that.'

Sam reached into his pocket and pulled out a handkerchief. *Dear Cupid, you make a man like this, and give him manners and morals like those.* Lucy watched as he stepped forward, knelt down and held up the hankie.

'Wipe your face, bud, I'll help if you need it. Your mum's lasagne is awesome, so don't worry. I'll eat your share next time.'

He looked up at her and winked, before turning back to Xander and helping him to clean the last blobs of sauce off his face.

'If I can fight fires and live, your mum's lasagne won't kill me off.'

Xander pulled a face. 'You hope!'

They fist-bumped, Xander giggling like a hyena as Sam took their hands and they headed to eat.

Xander had dropped off to sleep, chatting about fire trucks and protective gear all through his bath and supper, and eventually calming down and falling asleep as Lucy read to him. He was going through the history of the brick at the moment, and they had managed to loan a few relevant books from the local library service. He was fast asleep now, dreaming of construction and heroes chasing fire-breathing dragons. Best place for him, given the events of the last hour.

Iain had been on the phone, ringing right in the middle of bath time. Lucy had jumped for the phone, thinking it might be Sam, but her husband's name flashed across the screen instead. She'd kept the bathroom door open, so she could check on Xander, make sure he didn't wet the complete bathroom. He was a bit of a water baby, especially in the bath, but he wasn't exactly graceful or careful.

'Hello?' she said, steeling herself for the conversation.

'Hi,' he said tersely. She could hear some sports programme or other playing in the background. She could picture him now, just from that snippet of information. He was in the sitting room, a glass tumbler of his favourite spiced rum on the arm of the chair, phone in hand. He was probably sitting with his joggers on, his hand down his pants as he zoned out to the television. Same every Sunday, after golf. He only came home for Sunday dinner, and then that was it for the evening. TV, ball scratching and mild drinking. 'Can we talk, or will the coppers come knocking at my door?'

'Our door,' she clarified unnecessarily. 'I can't be on long, Xander's just in the bath. He's okay by the way, in case you wondered.'

He snorted. 'Whatever, Lucy, I'm not the one who ran off to the bloody North, am I? What's up, flat caps and bloody green fields getting a bit boring, are they?'

'What?' she asked, hearing the sneer in his voice.

'Well,' he retorted, and she heard the clink as he picked up the glass, the slurp of him taking a deep swig. 'I've had no mail, no knocks at the door. Which makes me think that you're going to come back, and be an adult again.' *Smug git.* 'Convenient that your little neighbour lad is a Londoner too, eh? Doesn't exactly talk like Jon Snow, does he? Travel together, did you?'

For a moment, she was a little taken aback. One, technically they did travel together. Not that she could or would tell him that. Probably not the best idea to mention that she shared a mattress space with him the other night either. Two, he was jealous? In all the years they had been together, Iain had never reacted to anything like that. Not that she was exactly putting it out there. She never had. She'd always played it safe, until now.

'I came here with Xander, Iain, and you know it. Have you got something you want to discuss, or have you just rung to

169

argue?' She looked in on Xander, and he was just getting out of the bath. 'I have to go, Xander needs me.'

He chuckled, a nasty laugh that made her feel uneasy.

'Well, go on then, Supermum. Just remember, at the end of the summer, he has school, you have a job. You need to come home and be a wife.'

The line went dead, and Xander came running past her, towel like a cape, naked bits wet through and on show. She threw her phone onto her bed and went off to wrangle him into some dry pyjamas.

Watching him in bed now, his little chest rising and failing with each precious breath, she could feel the rage rising inside her. When she had finally checked her phone, she'd seen a barrage of texts. It appeared the drunker her husband got, the more angry and less coherent he got in his text messaging. He was full on threatening her by the end – threatening to sue her for full custody, of selling the house and keeping all the money, of telling her boss at the deli she wasn't coming back. It was all about him, how HE felt, what HE was going through. It was mostly about work, and pride. She knew him well enough to know how he worked. She'd embarrassed him, and she knew that every argument they ever had in the future would all be brought back to this.

'You didn't put the bins out!'

'You left me!'

'You never help with your son, or the house!'

'You buggered off to Yorkshire!'

Deciding to leave had felt organised, and planned, but her emotions weren't. They had been all over the place, and here, now, she was just beginning to process them. Or she was, before Sam. Their lines of friendship grew blurrier and blurrier by the minute. She spent the next few hours ignoring her phone, not answering the incoherent rantings that Iain was sending through sporadically. He had gone out drinking by the sounds of his last voicemail. She could hear fruit machines, people laughing, the clink of glass on glass. She could hear him pulling on a ciggie as he mumbled on, pushing the smoke out of his lungs in between sentences like a toddler blowing out birthday candles. He sounded like a pretentious knob, which, of course, he was when drunk. He had no filter, and his full-on twattery came out.

The phone seemed to punctuate her evening. She could hear it vibrating on the sink when she was in the shower, sound turned off to avoid waking Xander up. She heard it buzz with texts when she was cleaning up, spritzing the house and sorting out the washing. Even now, when she was sat in fluffy PJs and a dressing gown with a cup of tea, the phone buzzed on. It lit up on the coffee table while she was watching some movie on the television, whiling away the hours till she could go to bed. If she went now, she'd lie there all night. Especially with this. If she turned it off, it would just annoy him more, and she didn't want him turning up here again tomorrow.

It buzzed again. The man was just drunk dialling now with his angry fingers. Throwing back the rest of her tea like she was drinking a tequila shot, she lunged forward and hit reply.

LEAVE ME ALONE.

She typed it all in caps, with a passive aggressive full stop at the end, just so he got how mad she was. Even in a drunken stupor or a stoner foggy haze, people knew that caps meant business. Desist and stop. Curl up and die. Bugger off and nay darken my door again, cretin.

It buzzed back straight away, and she was just typing 'FOR FU—' when she realised that Sam's name was at the top of the text screen. It read:

Have I done something wrong?

SHHHIIITT! She'd text Sam, instead of Iain. He'd got her vented anger instead. Scrolling back, she saw his original text read:

Just got home, hope you are both okay. Sam x

That kiss again. He was so sweet. She thought of him sat next door, thinking of her. Just as she was of him now.

She texted him back, ignoring the bleep that came through. Another hate text.

Sorry, I thought it was Iain. Am okay, Xander fast asleep x

After a second, she added: You okay? X

He texted back almost instantly. Am fine. Are you okay? Do you need me?

Well, that was the million-dollar question. Did she need him, want him, or both?

She wavered between saying 'come take me now!' in capitals and not answering at all. Instead she wrote:

Not really, but you get some sleep. Goodnight x

She closed his text window down, and opened Iain's. She typed out: LEAVE ME ALONE. ALL TEXTS HAVE BEEN SCREENSHOTTED. Hopefully that would punch through his wall of drunken arseholery and stop him from escalating any further. Either that, or he would pass out somewhere and then sleep it off. A nice Monday morning commute after a skinful the night before. He would regret his actions tomorrow, and she knew it. He must be in pain, but she couldn't bring herself to help him.

She turned the TV off, and was just heading up the stairs when she heard a faint knocking on the door. Turning back around, she listened for a moment.

'Lucy,' was all he said. A quiet, breathy word that filtered under the door, running over her and leaving her with goose bumps on her skin. She opened the door, and he was standing there. The glow from the porch light lit him up, the muscles tensed under his forearm skin, visible under his short sleeves. He looked tired, but his lips curled up into a smile as soon as he saw her. They both faced each other, saying nothing. Her phone beeped again in her hand, and she put it down on the kitchen counter.

Looking back at Sam, she took him by the hand and pulled him into the cottage. He looked surprised, but he came in readily, kicking the door closed behind him.

'Do you need anything?' she checked.

'Shower?' he asked. She nodded, leading him up the stairs, her fingers entwined in his. As they headed up, she heard him lock the door behind them.

Lucy was awoken from sleep by an alarm sounding at the other side of the bed from her. She felt movement in the bed, and glanced at the clock in a panic. A strong arm curled over her, smushing her back into the mattress.

'Sorry I woke you, I thought I'd better go before Xander woke up.' She turned in bed, making sure her fluffy PJs didn't twist up with her. Sam was still in his t-shirt, having got back into it after his shower. He was lying in her bed, just in his pants below the waist. It was very distracting.

Last night, she'd led him to the bathroom and then headed to her bedroom, getting into bed and listening to the sound of the running water and of Sam moving around. He came into the room in his t-shirt and boxer shorts, the rest of his clothes in a neat pile atop his boots. She didn't say anything to him, just lifted the covers. He laughed softly and she giggled back.

He got in and they both lay under the covers, and told each other about their day. She showed him the texts from Iain, and he scrolled through them wordlessly. She could see from his face that he was upset by them; little things that she had learned about him over the short weeks they had spent together. They didn't talk about the fact that they were now in bed together for a second time, both enjoying being with each other, feeling comforted by the presence of the other person. Maybe it was just too much to talk about, or maybe it just felt right. When something felt like this, did it even need an explanation at all?

'I'm heading to Agatha's tomorrow,' she told him excitedly. 'I offered to help with the charity fundraiser. Apparently she's decided to hold an auction.'

Sam's brows rose in faux shock-horror. 'That woman will probably get some decent bids too. I've only met her a couple of times, but she seems like a driven character.'

Lucy laughed again. 'No kidding, they're all as bad! Remember that film, where the women all gang up on Jack Nicholson?'

Sam thought for a moment. '*The Witches of Eastwick*?'

That got him a thumbs up. 'Yes! They remind me of that, always plotting, working together to make things happen.'

'Like us,' he said, looking across at her. 'Epic fail, eh?'

They'd fallen asleep facing each other, one hand touching the hand of the other person. She'd slept like a log.

'What time is it?' she asked now, sleepily.

'Just after five,' he replied, reluctantly getting out from under the covers. 'I'll lock up and post the key.' He put his clothes on and, boots in hand, he sat back down on the bed. 'It's funny, but I don't want to go.'

She moved to sit next to him, and brushed her fingers down the side of his face.

'Marlene is having Xander again tonight. Apparently she's bought a games console. She got Taylor to set it up, so now they're planning some big games night with Dot and Grace.'

'I'm on all day today, but I get off at six. Do you fancy doing something?' He picked a piece of her hair from where it nestled on her shoulder, playing with it absentmindedly. It felt like it was connected to her entire body, and she could feel the tremors of electricity flow through her again.

'Like what?'

He shrugged. 'Leave it with me, okay?'

Oooo! Something to look forward to. 'It's a date.' It popped out before she could filter her thoughts, but he didn't look unhappy

174

about it.

'It's a date,' he said, a soppy grin on his face. 'I'll be thinking about it all day.'

She leaned forward, and touched her lips to his. He kissed her back, reaching across and pushing his arm underneath her thighs, lifting and turning her in one smooth movement, their lips never leaving each other. She sat in his lap for a long while, the only noise in the house the sound of them kissing and the humming of her son. Argghhhh!

The two jumped in surprise, Sam standing with her in his arms, moving left, and then right, and then left again.

'Muuuumm …' Xander opened the door, and saw his mother standing in her PJs. He grinned at her. 'Morning! Can we have pancakes?' She wanted to laugh hysterically. Happily married women didn't have this kind of problem, did they? Back home, she'd be dragging herself out of bed, leaving Iain snoring in bed and making pancakes with matchsticks holding her eyes open.

'It's a bit early, sweetie. Put your slippers on, and go put the telly on. I'll be down in a second.'

He muttered something about blueberries, but did what he was asked for once.

She closed the door, and Sam came out from behind it, a sigh of relief pushing out from his broad chest.

'Close one, sorry.' He winced. 'Window?'

She looked at the window and even considered it for half a second.

'No need, I'll make sure the coast is clear, you can nip out the front door.'

He bent his head, dropping five, six tender kisses on her lips. 'See you tonight? If you need to turn your phone off, don't worry. I'll knock when I get back.'

She nodded, and headed downstairs to distract Xander with his favourite breakfast. She was just mixing the batter when she heard her front door key hit the mat.

175

'So,' Agatha said, setting down a huge tea tray in front of them on the large coffee table. The other women were all chatting away, but a hush fell on them when Agatha took the stage. 'I had rather a cheeky idea for a charity auction, and I wondered whether or not you ladies were up for the challenge.' She waved her hands around the house, as if illustrating her point. 'I did want to host an afternoon tea in the garden type event, but we wanted to make it a little different than normal, so we're holding an auction called Hot Helpers.'

'Hot Helpers?' Lucy echoed. 'What's that about?'

Agatha smiled at her. Lucy thought it was supposed to be a sincere, warm smile, but it gave her the creeps a little. Like they all knew something she didn't. Which they did, but not about the romance plans they had concocted. She was totally onto them about that. Little did they know, Sam had slept in her bed last night.

'Well, I thought that we would hold an auction, and have some of the local fireman and other residents offer up their services for say half a day, just for fun and to raise money for the community centre and the fire house. I have spoken to Chief Briggs and he has agreed to relieve the duties for some of his staff so that they can take part.'

The ladies all murmured excitedly, and Lucy nodded along.

'Great idea, do you have anyone in mind?'

Agatha's smile twitched, just for a second, but then she was back in control. 'Well, Chief Briggs will be letting them know today, and I do hope we can rely on you coming to pitch in on the day. We need some waitresses, just to serve drinks. Xander is welcome too, of course – Amanda and Lily from the village are going to run a bit of a daycare centre, movies and things, in the community centre. Do you think he'll go there?'

Xander had always loved younger children, much more than he did his peers. He tended to struggle with them, not finding friendships easy, or keeping them once he had them. Lucy knew

176

Amanda had a little one, so with that and a bit of Lego, he'd be fine.

'Yes, I think he would. It's not far either, so if there was a problem—'

'Of course,' Marlene cut in. 'You would be able to dash straight off to him, love. We don't want him upset over this. We love him to bits.'

The ladies' warm grins told her everything she needed to know. They did love him, and he loved them. He'd be fine, they'd all make sure of it.

'And when will this be happening?'

'Next weekend,' Agatha replied, looking a little panicked. 'A little close I know, but we are eager to get things moving.'

I bet you are, Lucy thought to herself. She only had two weeks left here, till her train ticket return date came around. She'd bought a return, but the closer it came to going back, the more dread settled on her. With school and work, she wouldn't be able to come back in a hurry. The cottage wasn't cheap, and between that, the money she needed to buy food etc. and the disastrous holiday she'd paid for, her savings were looking in a sorry state. Iain was changing too, getting nastier and more threatening, and if he decided to follow through with his threats, she might lose Xander altogether. That wasn't an option.

'Okay, sounds good to me! Count me in,' she said with far more cheer and optimism than she felt. She thought of Sam, and their plans, and it gave her the resolve she needed.

'So, Agatha, can I just add, about the history of the house?' The ladies were all chatting away now, Grace talking about knitting little thongs for the lads at the fire house to wear, and Marlene and Dot discussing chafing and fluff build-up. 'I'm a fan of historical buildings, always have been really. I nearly became a history teacher before I decided to study primary level.'

Agatha lit up. 'Ah well, the Mayweather Estate is steeped in history. Things have had to adapt, over the years, but I do try to keep it as traditional as possible, in keeping with the Mayweather name. It sadly died with my husband.' A bleak look crossed her features, and Lucy wanted to bite her tongue off. *Keep going, do it for Sam. Change the subject a bit.*

'So, did they keep a bigger staff here then?' She pretended to look around her, interested in the decor, the old paintings of long-dead Mayweathers. None of them bore any resemblance to Sam, so no dumb luck there.

'Yes,' Agatha sat forward, warming to one of her favourite conversations, her family home. 'We had a maid, a butler, and of course we still have Archie, the gardener. Will, his nephew, he does a lot of the work now but Archie is still the boss.'

'A maid and butler? What happened to them?' If she could speak to them, they might know what went on.

'Ah, well the butler was my Taylor's father, and Taylor, he took over. The maid, well she didn't last very long apparently. She left, and moved away.'

Damn. She needed to speak to Archie, and Taylor.

'Any idea where she moved to?'

Agatha looked sad for a moment. 'Yes, I do, although it'll not do much good now. My Charlie, bless his heart, he was ever so upset when she left. So fond of her, he was. Mary Ann Miller, she was called. Lovely girl, she didn't grow up around here. She came for work. Moved back to London, in the end.'

London. Right where Sam was found.

'Do you have an address?' she pressed. It was worth a shot. How many women had access to the house, to the food boxes and the personalised stationery? A maid would have access to all of those things. The other women were all still chatting away, Xander colouring in the corner, headphones on, happily humming away to himself. Sounded like ELO, so his musical education was still being nurtured.

'Yes, dear.' She stood and poured another cup of tea into her china cup, her hands shaking a little. 'She's in Islington Cemetery.

She was in a car accident, many years ago now. Her and her new husband. Only married a short time, they were. They're buried there together.'

Sometime and a LOT of tea later, Lucy headed back to the cottage on her own. Xander had jumped in the car with the ladies, excited and happy. He barely even waved to her as they drove off. She felt a bit sorry for the ladies, but they had brought it on themselves. All afternoon, they'd fed him milk and cookies, sandwiches and cake, all washed down with sugary tea. Xander loved to drink tea. He kept asking to try coffee, but Lucy wasn't prepared for that caffeine fest just yet. They'd offered her a lift, but there wasn't any room really, and she fancied the walk. She needed to clear her head. There hadn't been a massive amount of women at the Mayweather Mansion, and this Mary character sounded like she could be Sam's mother. Moving to London, leaving abruptly? Was that it? Was his mother so easy to find after one conversation? A big part of her wished that she had never asked. Now what was she left with? It was all going bad, and she didn't know what to do for the best. She was almost at the cottage now, but she couldn't bring herself to go in just yet. So she kept walking. The community centre had computers that she could use, and she wanted to look for some more evidence.

Sam was aghast. Even the chief looked a little blindsided, but he smoothed his moustache and carried on. Gary was cooking again, and the noise from the pots and pans had grown significantly since the start of his announcement.

'So,' the Chief said, a little louder now, trying to make himself be heard around the dining table where they were all assembled. 'It's next Saturday. All those on the list—' he brandished a suspiciously familiar piece of paper in his aloft hand '—will attend, and get time off in lieu later on. I have drafted in cover from nearby stations, so our service levels won't be affected. There is a costume too apparently, so New Lease of Life, on Baker Street, they have those and are expecting you all in at some point this week.'

The lads all looked at each other, nonplussed. Sam was the first to break the silence. 'And the funds are split between us here and the community centre, right?' Alan agreed readily, looking at the lads for a reaction. They all looked to Sam. 'Well, I think we can trim a few hedges, run a hoover round, eh, lads? That's all it will be. A bit embarrassing sure, but we've all seen worse.'

A murmur of grudging assent rumbled through the table, and Alan mouthed 'thank you' at him. He nodded once respectfully. He would have done it anyway, but he felt like he had to lead the charge, really. He really needed this event, to get closer. He knew that Lucy would be involved too, thanks to the ladies. Seeing her every minute he could this summer was becoming his favourite thing. The summer was over in two weeks, and school would be starting. Things were so up in the air, they needed as much time as possible. While they could.

Gary, still slaving away in the kitchen, wasn't impressed. 'Why am I not on the ruddy list? What about me?' He lifted up his t-shirt to show off a rather impressive set of abs on his skinny frame. 'Two per cent fat, mate, that's me. Women love it! Sod 'em, I tell ya. Sod 'em!'

He went back to serving, every portion of chicken stew being sloshed into bowls, dumplings plonked on top as he chuntered on to himself. Sam went over and picked up a tray full of steaming hot bowls.

'Looks lush. Gary, listen. I bet we could auction you off, like a Naked Chef type thing?'

Gary's face lit up, his mouth opening in a wide gasp.

'YES! I'd bloody rock that! Do you know him, like? Would he mind?'

Sam was confused. 'Know who?'

'Jamie Oliver!' He slapped Sam on the arm. 'He comes from your neck of the woods, doesn't he?'

Sam laughed. 'Er, no I don't know every cockney, besides he's an Essex boy. Do you know every famous Yorkshire person?'

Gary thought seriously for a moment. 'Well, I did meet a few of the Dingles once, at a farming show.'

Sam's raised brow was enough to silence him on the point. 'Am sure we can sort something out, I'll speak to the chief.'

'Well, good luck with that. I have a feeling that he's the monkey, not the organ grinder.'

Sam chuckled, patting Gary on the back. Gary, with his 2 per cent fat and tin ribs, flew into the wall and face-planted into the plaster.

Sam was due to come round in ten minutes, and she was still staring into her bedroom mirror, trying to work out what shade of lipstick to put on. She'd packed light when leaving London, and her little make-up kit was sparse. Had she known she would be going on a date with a fireman, then she would have perhaps been better prepared. She was wearing her best dark blue denim jeans, a cream blouse that flowed and hung off her body in all the right places, and her little dusky pink jacket. She'd topped it off with a pair of cream kitten heels, and curled her hair so it hung in loose, beachy waves. She was all ready, except for her naked lips. She'd lined up the two options, and was looking from one to the other, back to her reflection in the mirror. She felt sick with indecision. Nothing had felt right since she'd spoken to Agatha. Nothing could ever feel right again. She looked again at the sticks of pretty lip gloss, and grabbed the deeper shade, slicked it on over her lips and tucked it into her handbag. She checked her phone, but thankfully it was still quiet. After her last text to Iain, she hadn't replied to him at all, and eventually he had stopped. This morning, around the time Iain would be sitting down at his work desk, she got a text.

'Sorry' was all it read. She didn't reply. He should be sorry, but she knew it was more than drunken ramblings. He was upset, and she needed to sort things out. Less than two weeks now and she would be due home. Whatever happened, she would be tied to Iain for life, through their son. She had to decide what she was doing, and stick to it. Rip off the plaster, wait for the stinging of the skin, the feel of the fine hairs being pulled from their roots. She checked her reflection in the mirror, and was satisfied that she looked good. Showtime.

She was barely downstairs when she heard the knock at the door. She went over and opened it, finding her legs shaky as she walked.

'Hi.'

Sam was standing there in grey slacks, a white patterned shirt and grey tie covering his torso, a bunch of flowers in his hands, and a bar of chocolate.

'For Xander,' he explained, passing it over with the flowers. 'The flowers are for you.' She took both with thanks, murmured 'come in' and headed to the kitchen. He followed her in, dipping his head as he walked through the door.

She busied herself by arranging the flowers in a vase she found under the sink, putting the chocolate out of reach for Xander to have later. She could feel him watching her, but she couldn't bring herself to look at him again. When she'd set eyes on him at the front door, he'd taken her breath away. He looked so attractive, so cute, she couldn't bear it. He had a happy expression on his face, one that she had come to enjoy and even try to coax out of him in their time together. She didn't want to be the one to break that mood. She'd rather die than cause him pain. She took her time, slicing the bottoms of the stems, arranging them neatly in the glass vase.

'Everything okay?' he asked softly. She could tell by his voice that he was close by, close enough to touch. She sighed and turned around. He was standing behind her, a concerned look on his face. 'Do you not want to go out? If you've changed you mind, I get it … with Iain and everything, I nearly cancelled myself. I'm not this guy, I'm—'

'I found your mother,' she blurted, stepping half a step closer and placing both hands on his chest. 'I think I have anyway, but …'

She'sdeadshe'sdeadshe'sdead rang in her head over and over on a loop. How could she say the words? And what if she was wrong?

He reached up with his hands, covering one of hers with one and cupping her face with the other.

'It's okay,' he urged, a sad little smile on his features. 'I'm okay. Just tell me.'

The kitchen table was full of printouts of old newspaper articles. Sam was poring over them, reading each line.

'Mary worked at Mayweather Mansion as a maid, but she left abruptly one day, no one knew why. I found an advert in the local paper for a new maid, only six months before you were born. Her old job, and she left in the summer, so it tallies. You were left in the fire station six months later, so I think she got pregnant and left, moving to London. She must have taken the box and the stationery, so maybe she wanted you to find home.'

Sam was reading each piece, till he came to a headline a little different, with a photo.

'I look like her.' He was looking at a photo of a husband and wife on their wedding day, smiling and happily posing for the camera. It told their story, of the fact that they had met in London, mere miles from the fire station where Sam was left, fell in love, and married within a year. They'd been travelling to see his family when the accident had happened. Black ice on a dimly lit road late at night. They'd both died instantly. Two years after Sam was born.

'I think that she came to London, had you and then tried to move on. She stayed close, right till she met her husband, then they moved to Islington, to his house. They're in Islington Cemetery together.'

183

Sam nodded numbly, his eyes not leaving the photo. She knew how he felt, she'd cried when she'd seen it herself. Looking at her, all she could see was Sam. His eyes, the way his nose curved, the smile, open, happy. It was like looking at a ghost.

'You see it right? That I look like her?' He sounded so panicked, she couldn't bear it. She held his hand on the table.

'Yes, Sam, I see it. You look just like her, it's so obvious.'

He smiled then, running his fingers along the page.

'She's beautiful. She looks really happy with him.' She'd married a man called Thomas Jenkins, becoming Mrs Mary Jenkins. He was laughing in the photo, his face turned towards his bride with a look of devotion etched on his features, clear as day. They looked the very image of youthful love.

'I wonder if he knew?' she wondered aloud.

Sam shook his head.

'Even in those days, it would have been awful for her. I was all over the news, and living close by, she must have known how and where I was. She was on her own, no money, no house. I get it.' He swallowed, his jaw flexing. 'I don't like it, but I get it.'

Lucy couldn't believe he was taking it so well. Shock perhaps. He started to fold up the papers, tucking them back into the Manila folder she had put them in to transport home. 'Can I keep these?'

'Of course, they're yours. Can I get you anything?'

He looked at her then, a look of gratitude on his features.

'No, you have done enough. Thank you so much, Lucy, you don't know what this means to me.'

She felt her eyes water, the familiar burning sensation of unshed tears. 'I'm really sorry, I feel like I upset you.'

He squeezed her hand tight. 'No, you could never upset me. You found my mother, I'm grateful. Are you ready?'

'Ready?' she echoed. 'Oh, I thought that you wouldn't want to go now.'

He frowned. 'Not go on a date with the sexy neighbour who

found my family? Are you mad?' He stood up, taking her by the hand, and led her to the door. 'Come, my lady, your carriage awaits.'

He led her outside the door, giving her just enough time to grab her bag and lock up. There was no waiting taxi, no car parked up.

'How are we getting there?' she asked, fearful for her kitten-heeled feet. He was striding down the path, and then she saw it propped up against the fence. 'A tandem? You have got to be kidding me!' He laughed, passing her one of the two bike helmets that leant against the seats.

'Chicken are we? Norman lent me it. He and his wife love it. I thought we could use it, just this once.'

Lucy was about to have a girly strop when she thought about it again. They had no car, and this date was something she was looking forward to. She never took chances till recently, why stop now? She put the helmet on, silently praying it wouldn't kill her hairdo, and grinned at him.

'Right, let's go!'

After a shaky start, where they both misheard what the other said and ended up stuck in a bush, they were off. It was hard at first, and Lucy's legs started to burn, but Sam soon found his groove and then it felt like her feet were being spun by the pedals, not the other way around. He was on the back, and she silently thanked her wardrobe choices. Having her bum crack pop out at him wouldn't exactly be sexy, but the blouse was tucked in, and she felt comfortable enough to concentrate on steering. Sam guided her through the village, passing the cottages and houses, the vet's surgery, the rows of little shops. They were heading further away from the pub, not closer, and her interest peaked.

'Where are we going?'

'Snapdragon Street, just a bit further.' Lucy, still at least pretending to pedal, thought of what she remembered being up there.

'Snapdragon Street? There's not much there, you know.'

'Oh, I know.' He kept going, and she led the way. Snapdragon Street was a long windy one, playing fields carved out of the hills on one side, with football and rugby pitches further still. The only other thing there was the school …

They neared the school gates, and she saw a man in the doorway. He was dressed in casual clothes, a bottle green parka over jeans and a jumper, and he was waving them through the school gates.

'That's Lionel, he caretakes here. Lives in the cottage across with his wife. I came to do some safety checks here the other day, and we got to chatting. His wife, it turns out, is a big fan of role play. I gave him one of our old fire house jackets, one that was never used, and he let me have the school for the night.'

Lionel gave them a little wave, closing the gate behind them as they rode through.

'We have it till ten,' he said, helping her off the gate and waving back at Lionel. 'My lady?' he said, offering his arm. She laughed and put her arm through his.

'Lead the way, kind gentleman.' They headed through the main doors, and the smell lit up Lucy's grey matter. The smell of the school equipment, the little seats everywhere, the displays on the walls. She was hit by a wave of nostalgia, and she breathed in every little detail.

'Nice, isn't it?' he said, still leading her through the school. The lights were on in the main corridors, and when they got to the gym doors he stopped. 'They're looking for a teacher you know. One of the teaching staff is leaving next year, retirement. I saw the ad in the local paper, but Lionel says the head's not keen on the applicants so far.'

She looked around her. A job, her dream job, in the place she had run to?

'How many pupils?' she asked.

'Currently, eighty-seven,' Sam answered without hesitation. 'They are an inclusive school too, so Xander would fit right in.'

So, he had a reason for all this. 'You asked about all that, for us? Xander and me, I mean.'

'I asked for all of us,' he breathed, moving closer. 'I wanted you to have options. I thought that you were finding out the answers to my life, I wanted to do the same. I know the deli job is not what you dream about, Lucy. You're a mother first, of course, but why can't you be happy too? It's a small school. You could travel here every day, and be together. You know Xander inside out, you can help them to help him.'

In his current school, there were six times that many students, and the numbers only rose when high school came around. He hated school, but loved the lessons. Maybe this would be the answer. Was it really that easy though? She'd still be homeless, after all.

'I'll let you think about it,' he said, sensing her inner monologue was not ready to be shared. He opened the hall doors, and there, in the middle, was a table, set with a white linen tablecloth, flowers, silver cutlery and candles. The whole hall was dimly lit, and music was being piped in, a low murmur of romantic ballads. The smell of heavenly food wafted in, and she felt and heard her stomach growl.

'The lads helped a bit earlier, and Gary's in the kitchen. I got him into the auction, so he offered to cook, get a bit of practice in.'

It looked beautiful, and she was so moved by the effort he had made. That afternoon, finding out what she did, giving it to him, she never expected this to happen. Let alone being led to a table by a handsome man, someone who was trying to help her live the life she wanted.

Back home, when she'd offered to give up her teaching job, to look after Xander and be around more, Iain had never once tried

187

to help. He'd agreed readily, seeing her sacrifice as better for him. Someone to be home cooking his tea, running his errands, dealing with the brunt of parenting, leaving him more time to work and play. He'd honestly never even asked her if she minded, or if she was upset to leave the job she had studied and worked at for years to get.

They'd had a lovely dinner, the starters and mains simple, elegant and tasty. No jars of sauce to be found in this food, and Lucy and Sam devoured every morsel readily, their talk small and of no consequence. They didn't mention the real world at all, instead talking about their childhoods, their likes, dislikes. Favourite movies, aspirations for the future. Sam wanted to be fire chief one day, and head up his own team and fire house. He was happy where he was, but worried about being far from his mother Sondra. He was looking for a house to buy, which surprised Lucy, but she said nothing.

'What about your father?' she ventured when the conversation had dropped to a lull. 'Will you keep looking to find him? Agatha said that Mr Mayweather was devastated when Mary left.' She was careful not to say 'mother'. 'He looked for her, too. I even found an advert he put in the papers locally, looking for her. He was really cross when he found out she was looking to hire a new maid.'

Sam looked down at his empty plate, pushing together his cutlery and reaching for his glass of wine. Between them, they'd run through nearly two bottles of white, topped up by Gary, who kept running in and out with various delectable bits to eat. The bike ride home would be fun.

'Mr Mayweather did that, for a maid?'

Lucy nodded, taking another sip of the cool white wine.

'Yes, so someone might know something. I can ask my aun—'

'That's not necessary,' he said, cutting her off abruptly. His face was closed off, cold even. 'I think we should head home, it's getting late and Lionel will want to close up. Gary's on clean up.'

With that, he stood and started to walk towards the kitchen. She was left alone, wondering what the hell had made him so mad. After waving goodbye to Gary and Lionel, the bike ride home should have been fun. They were both a bit tipsy by now, and when the fresh air hit Lucy, she felt a bit pissed. Riding through the village by tandem bike should have been a laugh. Instead, Sam never spoke, and he pedalled like a maniac, leaving her pushed along and very confused. They got to the cottages, and he helped her off the bike. She turned to him, passing him her helmet and leaning into him a little. He smiled, but it didn't reach his eyes. He bent his head, and kissed her on the cheek.

'Goodnight, Lucy.' He pushed the bike into his own garden and closed the gate, leaving her standing outside hers. He disappeared around the back with it, and she was left alone for the second time that night, wondering how the evening had changed so abruptly.

CHAPTER 13

The next few days passed by in a blur. The head teacher of the local school had called her, having been given her number by Sam, and they had met for coffee in the local café. Mrs Holliday was a lovely, happy woman. She turned up dressed as the Queen of Hearts, putting down her sceptre and handbag and apologising for her attire. Her lips were painted to look like a heart, and her eye make-up was bright green and shimmery.

'I've been at the community centre, we hosted an *Alice in Wonderland* tea party for the children. Some of the teachers came as the characters. They didn't moan, but, to be fair, if they had, it would have been off with their heads!' She made a regal movement with her hand, bowing before them. Xander, looking very taken aback, burst out laughing.

'Off with their heads, Mum! Like the real Queen of Hearts!' He laughed again, Mrs Holliday joining in.

'That's right, Xander, have you read the book?'

Xander beamed. 'Yep, Mum read it to me. It's good, but I like *Harry Potter* better.'

Mrs Holliday grinned at him. 'Me too, honey, truth be told. Have you read this one?' She pulled out a book from her handbag. '*Gulliver's Travels*.'

Xander's eyes widened. 'No, but I've heard of it.'

She passed it over the table to him. 'Well, you tell me what you think, okay? And if you want any more, I have plenty you can borrow.'

She winked at Lucy, asked her if she'd ordered, which she had, and headed off to the counter to place her own.

By the end of their lunch, Lucy and Xander left happy, full of cheese toasties and tea, a job offer and a school place all sorted out. There would be a lot of paperwork of course, but Mrs Holliday didn't see a problem.

'We have the place, and our provision will suit Xander perfectly,' she'd said, after listening to everything that was in place now, and wasn't working. 'Our class sizes would be perfect for him, and our staff are amazing.' She looked pointedly at her, and Lucy blushed. 'You say the word, I'll make it happen.'

She could have kissed her there and then, but she held off. After all, she still had no money, nowhere to live, and the cottage had bookings through till October. Then there was the little fact that she had an angry husband back down south who was fully expecting them to return.

She hadn't heard from Sam all week. She'd put the Manila folder about his mother through his letterbox, but heard nothing. She'd texted him a couple of times, just simple things like 'good morning' and 'how are you?' All breezy, gentle texts that opened up communication. Except they hadn't, because he'd kept his ruddy distance. When they got back, his lights were never on, and she didn't hear a peep from next door. He was ghosting her, and she felt his apparition around her at every moment. She'd kept herself busy, chatting with the ladies, joining in with their crafting sessions, helping to set up Mayweather Mansion for the big day. She had six days left till her train tickets became due, and she needed to make a final decision. It was as though the two men in her life had changed overnight. Sam was ignoring her, and when she had taken Xander to the fire station so that he could give them some cookies they'd baked together, Sam had spent time with Xander. Showing him the trucks and the gear, making a fuss of his cookies, declaring them to be the best things ever, both of them giving Gary one and letting him be judge (he loved them, of course). He'd said hello, but in a formal way, using her married name. Mrs Walsh. Who even was that any more? She'd never been Mrs Walsh to him. It hit her like a bullet, leaving her standing there, bleeding profusely and looking for the sniper. It was harsh, and deliberate, and she hated him for doing it. He'd made her feel cheap, and that was awful.

Iain, on the other hand, was kindness personified. He'd offered to send her some money, which she'd declined. He'd asked about Xander, about how he was feeling and coping on holiday. He'd apologised for his drunken rants and explained how he'd felt powerless, and abandoned. Him him him still, but he was trying. He'd even offered to hire a cleaner and have one weekend a month at home, so that they could spend time as a family. Baby steps, and probably bullshit, but he was trying. Trying to make it harder for her to pull the plug. She'd cancelled her legal advice appointment, and spent her nights lying awake, wondering how she would feel if she returned home. Would she BE returning home, or leaving it?

The day of the charity auction was no different. After a pitiful night's sleep, Xander had executed his dawn raid, and was halfway down the stairs screaming 'Pancakes, pancakes!' when there was a knock at the door. She heard Xander shout up the stairs, 'I'll get it!' and jumped out of bed.

'No, Xander, wait for me!' She threw her dressing gown on, running down the stairs.

'Dad!!' Xander shouted, jumping into a very shocked Iain's arms. Iain reached for him, saying 'Hi, buddy,' but instead of pulling him closer, he set him back down on the ground. 'I came to talk to your mother, can you go watch TV?'

'But … but … it's pancake time,' he said, pointing towards the kitchen. 'We always have pancakes when I get up.'

'Well not today, okay?' He took him by the shoulders, and gently pushed him in the direction of the living room, where the couch could be seen through the open door.

'It's okay, Xander. Go sit at the kitchen table, I'll make them.' Xander slid past his father, looking a little fearful, and slipped into the kitchen.

'What are you doing here?' she hissed at him, angry at his treatment of his son. 'You know he has a routine, and you could have at least hugged him. He's missed you, you know.'

Iain sneered. 'One late breakfast won't bloody kill him, and whose fault is it that he misses me, eh? It's your bloody fault we're here.' She ignored him, heading to the kitchen. In the corner of her eye, she could see Sam heading down the path to his gate, a suit bag hung off one of his shoulders. Iain's car was parked right outside the cottages. She cringed, but Sam looked at it once, and kept walking. Not even a backward glance. He pulled his phone out of his pocket, and she felt jealous. She knew he wouldn't be contacting her. Her phone was on charge upstairs. Could she resist? She started to make the pancakes, and ignored Iain who was standing in the kitchen doorway, arms folded, watching her. A second later, her phone trilled and she had to fight the deep primal urge she had not to drop-kick him out of the way and race up the stairs.

Iain looked towards the staircase. 'I'll get it.' He was off and up the stairs before she could stop him, and she didn't want to make a scene, so she just stood there, making breakfast. Waiting for the men to decide her fate. OfIain. That's what they'd call her if she went back. Look at him now, only two minutes he'd been here, and she already wanted to scratch his eyes out, scream at him to leave them alone. She looked at Xander, and he was reading the book Mrs Holliday had given him. He looked subdued, hunched over. She hated Iain again.

She could hear the phone still ringing, and then Iain's voice saying hello. SHHHHHIIIITT! Her heart was pounding hard, flopping and flinging itself against her ribcage like a wild bird trying to escape her cage. She wanted it to be Sam on the phone just as she prayed it wasn't him. Iain walked into the room and passed it to her, a smug little grin on his face.

'Your auntie,' he stated, before going over to sit at the table with Xander. She whisked the batter, her phone in the crook of her arm.

'Hello? Marlene?'

'I was told he was there, but I didn't believe it till I heard his voice. Why is he answering your phone?'

'I'm making breakfast, yeah,' she said as nonchalantly as possible. 'Pancakes. Everything okay?'

'No it bloody well isn't okay, my girl. Why is he there?'

'Hmm-hmm,' was all that Lucy could say. Big and little ears were listening.

'You can't talk can you! Oh, the gall of that man. Listen, leave breakfast, Grace is on her way for you and Xander now. She's bringing you both here, I'll make pancakes. Bring your stuff for today, and don't tell him what you are doing, we don't want him there.'

She was just saying okay to Marlene, grateful that an escape plan was mapped out for her, when she heard Xander telling Iain about the auction.

'It's so cool, you bid money and then people clean your house for you! My friends are all in it. Gary's going to cook, and I think Sam might cut down trees with his bare hands.' He leaned forward, right into Iain's face. 'He's so strong, and muscly! He's like an actual giant. I'm going to play though, Mummy says she's helping out there, and it might get a bit rude, so I'm going to be somewhere else.'

From the mouths of autistic babes. They tell it like it is, and he had sold her right out. She couldn't be mad though, and watching Iain's face drop at the mention of Sam's physique was priceless to her.

'Er,' she said into the phone. 'We'll be ready but the cat is out of the bag.'

She heard Marlene swear under her breath, and steeled herself for the day.

'Welcome, dear residents of Westfield, and to all our dear visitors. Thank you so much for coming out today to help our very worthy causes!'

Mayweather House was transformed, and the great hall was packed. A runway was centre stage with seating to both edges, all placed around circular tables. Waiters were milling around with drinks and fruity jugs of juice, Pimm's and champagne. Canapés were being walked around by waitresses.

'Also, a very big thank you to our volunteers!'

'Tributes, more like,' Grace quipped. The ladies were all sitting around one of the centre tables. Dot, Grace, Marlene and Lucy, all sat around with a few of the other craft and chatters from the village. Agatha had gotten them a pretty good table too. Lucy had started handing some things out, canapés etc., but Agatha had ushered her to a seat on the table.

'You rest, dear, I don't want you to miss the auction!'

They were all listening to the speech with interest.

'Ha! May the odds ever be in your favour,' Dot guffawed, earning a high-five from Grace. Agatha, ever the pro, looked across and gave her an evil look so hidden, so well-timed that no one else would have even seen it, before turning back to the audience. Dot shrank down in her seat, taking another glug of her champagne. 'Oops. I'll get it in the neck for that later.'

Lucy laughed. She had been on edge since Grace had turned up, but she was starting to relax a little now. She'd ushered Iain out of the cottage, locking up behind her, and Xander was settled at the community centre. Mrs Holliday was there, and she knew

195

not to hand him over to anyone but her or Marlene. Iain had roared off in his car, none too happy. She had been on edge when they'd first arrived, but his car wasn't there when they arrived at Agatha's.

Agatha went on to talk about the community centre, the swimming pool, and the plans for community services in the area.

'Now, we move on to the fun part of the event, the auction! As part of their efforts to raise money for the Westfield Fire House, our lovely firefighters are here to cater to your every whim!'

She raised her hand, and the music started. It was then that they noticed a DJ booth in the corner, her husband Taylor standing next to the DJ. Probably planted there by Agatha to make sure the poor bloke hit all the cues he was supposed to.

'First of all, we have the wonderful Norman! Norman likes long walks in the village, cask ales and sparkling conversation! What will you bid for an afternoon with Naughty Norman?'

The guests, mainly women, with a few bored-looking men, all whooped and cheered. Norman's wife stood up with a handful of cash, screaming, 'A hundred pounds for cleaning the gutters round ours!' Norman groaned. 'Woman, shut up! Get back home!' He pointed to the woman next to her, who was laughing hysterically. 'Hilda, I told you, she's not to have the Prosecco!'

Agatha pursed her lips and ploughed on. The whole thing was hilarious, and when Norman's wife was the victor, she came and carried him off the stage, yelling, 'I told ya I'd get my odd jobs done, now home! Hilda, grab that bottle!' The three of them headed out to loud applause and approval, and that set the tone for the rest of the event. Lucy was on her second glass of Prosecco, savouring the taste and the feeling of being relaxed and in adult company, when she noticed Iain standing at the back, looking intently at the stage. He'd been there a while by the looks of it, a side table nearby holding a few empty glasses. It was orange juice though, she noticed with relief. A waitress offered him a glass from her tray of Prosecco flutes, but he waved her away.

'Iain's here,' she said to Marlene, and she looked around her.

'Where?' Her auntie was scanning the crowd. 'Shall I get security? Taylor will make him leave.'

'Make who leave?' Iain said jovially, having come over unseen. 'Lucy, can we talk for a minute?'

Marlene and the other women all shook their heads at her, but she didn't want to make a scene, and Agatha was moving on to the next poor auction victim.

'Just a minute, outside the hall,' she stated. She stood up, pushing her chair back as quietly as possible, and navigated the exit. Just outside the doors, she moved to one side and he followed her.

'What is it, Iain? I'm a bit occupied at the moment.'

'Yeah, watching men get sold like pieces of meat, while your son is carted off God kno—'

She held up a hand. 'You don't talk to me about parenting. Ever. What do you want?'

He sighed. 'I'm sorry, I know you look after our son, that was a cheap shot. I want you to come home. I have the car, we can travel together.'

She was already shaking her head, an involuntary movement that her body put into action before she could even process what was said.

'Our train leaves in six days, and you know that Xander hates travelling long distances in the car.'

She didn't tell him that she hadn't made her mind up yet whether they would be on the train when it left. She hadn't banked on him being here today, to have to answer this question.

'So, change the tickets. I'll bring your stuff home, and meet you there.'

'It's not that easy, Iain, I don't know—'

'It is that easy! You have a job, and a home, and a husband.

You can't just gallivant off up the country when you feel like it. What is it, a midlife crisis or something?'

'No, Iain, people tend to do shit things like play golf, and get their teeth capped in midlife.'

A deliberate dig at him, and he narrowed his eyes. 'Change the tickets, buy new tickets. I don't really care, Lucy, you need to come home, both of you do. How can you manage on your own?'

The fact that she wasn't sure herself wasn't lost on her, but she would die before she told him that.

She heard a cheer come from the crowd, and she pushed past him. 'I have to get back, please just go home!'

She opened the doors just as the next act was coming down the runway. Iain bolted after her, shouting, 'I want you both back, Lucy, I still love you!' Just as there was a lull in the music. All eyes fell on them, and she headed straight for her chair. The man on stage was looking at her, and she turned around, her breath catching in her throat.

Sam was stood still on the runway, wearing his firefighter standard-issue trousers, and a pair of black boots. That wasn't what she noticed first though. Or the fact that he was bare-chested, his trousers held up by a pair of red braces. What she noticed was him looking at her, an expression on his face she'd never seen before. Not like this. Pain. Pain, pure and simple. Iain reached for her arm behind her, and she shrugged him off. She saw Sam's eyes narrow, his gait change, his chest pectorals tense, along with his fists. Agatha was spluttering into the microphone.

'Sorry about that, technical hitch!' She cleared her throat, looking at the ladies and nodding her head towards Lucy. Was she kicking her out? 'Take a seat, Lucy dear,' she said kindly. No, she wasn't trying to get rid of her. She wanted to support her, show her she wasn't alone. She turned back to the rest of the crowd, turning up her kilowatt smile.

'So, our next offering is single and ready-to-mingle Sam Harper! London born and bred, he is our newest fire officer and he's certainly fitted in around Westfield already! At over six feet tall, our gentle giant is quite the Adonis, I'm sure you'll agree. We have a bid already, from table ten, of £150!' Lucy closed her eyes, cringing inwardly. Their table was number ten, and it looked like the ladies were not done meddling. The crowd was loud again, shouting out comments at Sam, and offering wads of cash.

'Now he doesn't need a ladder for those gutters!'

'He's a big un, isn't he? Do you think he's in proportion?'

Grace stood up, and shouted, 'Two hundred pounds and all the jumpers you could ever need!' She raised her Prosecco glass aloft, stabbing it in the air and sloshing half the table in the process. She took a swig and moaned. 'Awww, running low again. Waiter!'

Iain grabbed Lucy again, and she yanked her arm back. She could see Sam jump off the stage, and in a second he was over to them. The crowd went wild, and it slowed his progress, having to pick his way through a sea of quite tipsy and rather excited women to get to them. Iain saw him growling at them and pulled her through the doors, Marlene shouting and swatting at him with her handbag as they went past. They burst through the doors, and the pair stood looking at each other.

'It's him isn't it,' Iain said, his face a mix of frustration and rage. 'All this bad Iain this, bad Iain that. Truth is, you've bloody cheated on me with someone else. You're nothing but a slut!'

Mid rant, the doors had been flung outwards, Sam charging through. He looked so sexy and menacing, Lucy didn't know where to put herself. He had a novelty blow-up axe in his hand, which made him look all the more the part.

'Don't you dare call her that! She's done nothing wrong.'

Iain laughed, but he took a couple of steps back, pushing Lucy between them.

'Whatever, Magic Mike! Why don't you piss off and go find a woman of your own, there's plenty in there that'd climb your greasy pole!'

'Shurrup,' Sam spat, his teeth clenched tight. His eyes were black, shark-like and the look he gave Iain was one of great warning. 'Leave, now!'

The doors flung open again, and Agatha, Taylor and the ladies all came piling through.

'I'll second that,' Taylor said, standing next to Sam. 'Leave the establishment. We don't need people pulling people about here. You're not welcome, this is a private event. Invitation only.'

Iain looked around him, Lucy taking the opportunity to step away from him. Marlene, Dot and a wobbly Grace all picked over her like monkeys looking for fleas.

'Are you hurt, love?'

'I'm fine,' she soothed them, and saw Sam out of the corner of her eye. He was still standing like he was ready to throw a punch at any moment, but she saw the flicker of relief in his face at her words. 'You need to go, Iain. It always ends like this with you, doesn't it? Just go.'

He looked like he was going to fight his corner, just for a second, but then he relented. Looking at the faces behind her, she knew that he must realise that he was beaten.

'I'll see you both in six days,' he said airily. 'I'll pick you up from the station.'

Taylor stepped forward, pointing to the exit and Iain allowed himself to be seen off the property. The ladies all encircled her, hugging her, kissing her, saying nice things and generally making a fuss. Agatha stepped forward and parted them like the Red Sea.

'You'll be fine, my dear, you're made of good stock. We'll look after you. You are a Westfieldian, after all.' She dropped a kiss on her cheek before enveloping her in a sweet fragranced hug. 'Come along, ladies, we have men left to auction. The women all headed back in, Dot murmuring something about being an oiler backstage, and then Sam and her were left alone again. He was standing there, rubber axe still in hand, facing the door that Taylor and Iain had just exited.

'I'm so sorry, Sam,' she started, 'I ruined the auction.'

He turned around and she was in his arms. He hugged her so tight, and she could feel and hear his heart hammering all around her.

'You've nothing to be sorry for. That guy is a dick. I wanted to kill him, Lucy.'

'I'm not defending him, but he's just out of his depth. He was from the minute Xander was born, really. I wanted kids and I thought he did too, but when the baby came, it was different.' She thought of all the nights that Xander had been up screaming, refusing to eat properly, or sleep. Something was wrong, and they knew it.

'I retreated into research and work, to look after Xander. In the end I just stopped including him, because he didn't want to hear it.' He'd worked later and later, and then he was working and out seven days a week, leaving Lucy alone with the appointments, and the therapy, and trying to raise their child. 'He doesn't get it, Xander is not the son he had imagined. He doesn't like sports much, and he argues every little point. He's not go with the flow, and Iain never got that.'

Sam shook his head. 'No excuse, and I hate him putting his hands on you like that.'

'He's never hit me, and he'll never do that again. It's over.' As soon as the words left her mouth, she felt the weight lift off. It was over. There was no coming back from this. They were different people. The puzzle of their family didn't fit together any more, and she couldn't shave off any more parts of herself to make it work. Seeing the change in Xander, she knew it would work out.

'Xander needs a father though. You'll let him try, won't you?'

Lucy shrugged. 'If he wants to see Xander, we can make a plan, a legal plan, get things in place.'

Sam looked placated, but still troubled. 'Good, he deserves the chance to have a father at least. I wish I'd had that chance. Still, I inherited some things from him.'

Lucy looked at him in shock. *Did he suspect what she did?*

'What do you mean?' she asked tentatively.

'I think you know what I mean, Lucy, you're just too nice to say it.' He tucked the axe into the waistband of his trousers, running both his hands up over his face and head, sliding them down the sides of his broad neck. 'My father, Mr Mayweather. It makes sense, he was here, he knew my mother. There was no one else it could have been. Mary is my mother no matter which way you look at it, and Agatha said he was upset when she left. Tried to look for her even. It fits. He cheated on his wife, got poor old Mary Miller pregnant, she couldn't cope with the shame, so she left. Whether he wanted to find her to silence her, pay her off, or if he really loved her, I'll never know. Either way, I'm not taking a family and ripping them apart for my own needs and wants. I just won't.'

Everything clicked into place, and she wanted to scream.

'That's why you changed, on the date, isn't it? You think you're like him?'

He looked at her, and smiled sadly. She felt like her heart was breaking, she could almost hear the tinkle of the shards splintering off as he spoke.

'I don't know, Lucy, but I have my answers, and I just want to move on now. You should too.'

He came close to her, and dipping his head, he kissed her fervently. Passionately. Like it was the last kiss. She felt a splash on her face, and when he pulled back, a tear track shone down the side of his nose. 'Take care of yourself and Xander, Lucy, and, for what it's worth, thank you.'

He left straight through the doors to the hall, and a cheer sounded his arrival. She started to cry, really sob, and saw something in the corner of her eye. Taylor was standing there, looking guilty. *How much had he heard? Oh God.* He walked over to her, pulling a set of keys from his pocket.

'Come on, love, I'll take you home. We'll pick the lad up on the way.'

CHAPTER 14

Two days had passed since the charity auction, and Lucy woke up with the heaviest sense of dread she'd had since arriving. Today was the day she went home.

She'd holed herself up since Taylor had dropped them both off that night, trying to make sense of what had happened, what it meant. She felt like she'd ruined everything, and brought Sam along for the ride and hurt him too. Now he didn't want her at all, and he had no family left to find. It was all a huge mess.

She'd rung Iain the day after, and had it out with him. They'd talked on the phone for hours, hashing it all out, but, ultimately, they knew it was over. She'd known before she left, she just needed to work it out in her head. He'd agreed to move out into one of the company apartments in central London, to not disrupt Xander any more than he needed to be. He was already going back to a school he hated, and now his parents were splitting up. They'd put the house up for sale, and go their separate ways. She needed to go home, to sort everything out, and escape Sam. She just couldn't live in a village where he was every day and cope. She had to sell up and move on. The deli owners had been lovely, and she had a job as long as she wanted. It wasn't teaching, but it would do for now. Once they were settled in a new house elsewhere then maybe she could find something better for Xander

AND her. Marlene had tried to talk her out of it, but Lucy couldn't be swayed, so that was it. She'd even refused their lift offer to the station. She'd get a cab, and get out of Westfield as fast as she could, new train tickets in hand. She looked out of the window for a long time, at the views beyond her window, taking them in and sealing them in her memory vault. This was her last day in Westfield, and she would miss it dearly.

'What's wrong, Agatha? You look like you've seen a ghost!'

Amanda ran to doorway of New Lease of Life and ushered Agatha into a nearby comfy chair. The four ladies all looked at her. She was dressed in canary yellow today, looking rather like the Queen, and the colour palette was currently doing nothing for her complexion.

'Ahh, nothing really. A bit of a late night with Taylor, that's all.'

Grace tittered. 'I bet you did, you filthy woman! Use some of the props from the auction, did ya?'

Agatha didn't raise a smile, just sagged into her chair.

'Lucy's leaving today, with Xander,' Marlene said sadly. 'I offered to drive them to the station, but she wouldn't hear of it. I'm going to miss them so much. They'll be gone in an hour.' She sniffed, and Dot passed her a silky hankie. 'I've tried Sam, but his phone's just going to voicemail. I had such high hopes for them too.'

Agatha sat forward. 'Lucy's leaving today?' She rose to her feet, her colour returning a little. 'She can't go! Sam ... er ... er ...'

'What?' Grace said. 'What?'

Agatha stuttered again, her head bobbing as she tried to form the words.

'What is it?' Grace pressed. 'Timmy stuck down the well? Spit it out, woman!'

She took a deep breath, and hung her leather handbag, also yellow, over the crook of her arm.

'To the car, ladies, now!'

They got in the car, Grace throwing a stack of knitting pattern books into the footwell. 'Sorry, had a bit of a charity shop binge.'

Agatha practically shoehorned the women into the back seat, slamming the door on them, and grabbed her mobile from her bag. It rang twice before someone answered.

'Taylor darling,' she said, her telephone voice coming into force despite her heightened state. 'Come to the fire house now, my darling, Lucy's leaving. It's time.'

She didn't wait for a response, shoved the phone back into her handbag and jabbed Grace none too gently with her elbow, making the car swerve. 'You heard me, the fire house! Quick! Try bloody sixth gear!'

'I don't think it has a bloody sixth gear!' Grace bellowed. 'And watch my tit next time! You've got elbows like Gollum!'

They careened up to the fire house, straight in front of one of the fire engines. Chief Briggs came running out, waving his arms.

'Move your car, you're blocking the engines.'

Grace ignored him, pointing to indoors. 'Sam here? We need him.'

'He's just getting ready to go out. He and Norman are taking part in a fun day in Leeds, showing the kids in the local area our Bessie and teaching them about fire safety.' He looked proud. 'Our Bessie will turn some heads I can tell you! Now move please, unless you have a fire emergency or a crowning baby!'

'I shall crown you, Alan Briggs, if you carry on,' Agatha cut in, getting out of the car and heading into the fire station. 'Grace, park in the car park, but don't you let Sam leave without me seeing him.'

'Aye aye, captain,' she said, saluting her out of the window and sticking her tongue out at Alan. 'Have that Briggsy!'

Sam was just heading out of the door to the engine bays when Agatha came around the corner, smiling warmly at him.

'I never saw it before now, Samuel, but I see it now. You have his eyes.'

Sam stopped, swallowing hard. 'Do I?'

She came closer, and held out a hand tentatively. 'May I?'

He gave her a sign of assent, and she reached up, touching his cheek. 'Ah yes, you are more like him than you know. He's a good man, you know.'

Taylor walked in behind her, looking as though he'd run a marathon. Agatha waved him over.

'This is my husband Taylor, you've met, of course. My second husband that is. He worked at the estate with myself and Charlie, my first husband, God rest his soul.'

She reached for Taylor's hand and Sam's and put them together, wrapped in hers.

'He worked with your mother, Mary too,' she added gently. 'He really liked her, actually. Charlie's not your father, sweetheart. Taylor is.'

'What?' Sam was standing on the corridor at work, being presented with a father, something that he thought he had lost forever. 'How do you know?'

'I heard what you said to Lucy, at the auction. I was seeing your mother, but our families were never keen really. My dad was all about the work and the traditions. Me courting the maid wasn't acceptable to him, and I was destined to take over when he retired. She just upped and left one day, I swear I never knew.'

'Charlie and I both looked for her,' Agatha said sadly. 'She was a big part of the house, but she just didn't want to be found. That night, I looked through all the newspapers, the stuff my father kept, and I found this.'

He held out the same newspaper clipping that Sam had seen many times before, the story of his being found. 'I think my father suspected, or she told him. I think he paid her off, and she took the money and went to London. Last time we heard news, it was of her death.'

Sam leaned against the wall, bending over and resting his hands on his knees. He couldn't believe it.

'I didn't know, Sam. If I'd known, there would be no way I wouldn't have raised you.'

'We,' Agatha added. 'We would have had you in a heartbeat.' She looked at the tiny ornate gold watch on her wrist, and tutted. 'We don't have time for this now, Sam dear. Lucy and little Alexander are heading to Leeds Station as we speak, in a taxi. They're going back home.'

'What?' Sam yelled. 'She's not supposed to leave yet!'

Taylor took his keys out of his pocket. 'I'll drive you there, if you let me. It's none of my business, but you can't let her go, son.'

He winced at his use of the word 'son'. 'Sorry, didn't mean to.' Sam reached forward and pulled him into a hug. 'It's okay. I guess we have a lot to talk about.'

'Later,' Agatha said, chivvying them both along towards the door. 'Come on, we need to go!'

'I have a better idea,' Chief Briggs said when they told him. 'The event doesn't start till two. Leeds traffic at this time? We'll give you a lift. Gary can fill in for you. He's been somewhat of a celebrity since his nude baking thing. He'll be a big hit with the mums!'

Bessie flew through the traffic, sirens blaring. The cars and trucks on the road parted for them, making their journey fast and exciting. Behind them, staying close and keeping pace were Dot, Marlene and Grace. Grace had asked for a stick-on siren for hers but Chief Briggs had politely declined her request. Agatha and Taylor were in the fire truck, sat in the back with Sam, Gary and Norman up front.

'Woo!' Taylor said, looking out of the window at the traffic scattering. 'This is some adrenaline rush!'

Sam laughed as he whooped and cheered, Agatha clinging

to him, whimpering slightly. Taylor grabbed her tight, comforting her, and Sam's heart shifted, as though something had clicked into place. He was a good man, Agatha was right. He found himself looking forward to getting to know him, to hearing about his mother when she was young and in love. They pulled round to the side of the train station. Sam jumped out and helped Agatha get down with her canary yellow class intact.

'Good luck, Sam, bring her home, eh!' Gary shouted out of the cab as Norman pulled off. 'The chief's going to send you a ride, so keep your phone on, eh?'

They tooted on the horn, and drove away. Sam looked at the pair stood next to him.

'Go Sam! Run!' Agatha screamed at him.

'We're right behind you,' Taylor added, their eyes locking. Sam nodded once and was gone, racing to the train platforms.

Lucy settled Xander onto the train, making him comfy and giving him his iPad, snacks and Hedwig. He hadn't said much all morning, and even his pancakes had been left untouched. She knew that he was thinking of the bustle of home, the school he hated, his dad. They had called a truce for now, deciding that legal help was needed to sort everything out, but it was still going to be hard on him, to move house again. He'd lit up in Westfield, and she couldn't help adding his mood to the list of things that she had destroyed this summer.

'It'll be fine, honey. We'll look for a new school. You won't be there forever, and we can decorate your new bedroom how you want it.'

'I want Great Auntie Marlene back,' he said honestly, his open innocent eyes boring into her with their disdain. 'I liked it there, and Mrs Holliday said—'

'I know what Mrs Holliday said, but we can visit, for Christmas maybe?'

She hated lying to him, and promising a child, especially a child like Xander, anything and not following through was terrible. He would remember. Maybe that's why she said it. *Truth be told, Xander, I don't want to leave either.*

'Sam!' A shadow fell over them both, and Xander hurled himself out of his seat, headphones flying everywhere, and barrelled straight into him. Sam picked him up easily, tucking him into his side.

'Hey, buddy! Where do you and your mummy think you're going?'

'Home,' he said glumly. 'I don't wanna go though, and Mum cried all night.'

Sam's eyes fell to her. 'Is that right?'

'Might be,' she said cautiously. 'Why are you here?'

Sam put Xander down and squeezed himself in the vacant seat next to her.

'Sebastian Taylor is my father, not Mr Mayweather. He didn't know about me. He heard us, the day of the auction.' He pointed out of the train window, where a bright dollop of sunshine stood with Taylor, platform tickets in their hands. They waved wildly, hugging each other tight. 'They brought me here to get you.'

'Get us?' Xander checked. 'To go to Great Auntie Marlene? Cool!'

Xander grabbed his bags and off he ran to the doors, fluffy owl in hand. Sam looked at the pair on the platform but they were already running to meet him. Watching them walking him over to a doughnut stall, his bags tucked under his father's arms, he relaxed and focused on what else he came here for.

'I was a dick,' he stated, for lack of anything else to say. 'But I love you, Lucy. I love you and your son, and I don't want you to leave.'

'You were a dick,' she confirmed, before a small smile played on her lips. 'But I love you too. I'm so sorry.'

'Will you stay, with me? I know it's hard but—'

'Yes,' she said, crying now. 'I'll stay. I never wanted to leave in the first place.'

He kissed her, and the train carriage broke into applause as he picked her up, bags and all, and carried her off the train.

ACKNOWLEDGEMENTS

This is the eighth book I have completed now, and I still pinch myself that I get to write the books I loved as a child, and adore as a woman. My first thank you goes to my readers, who have loved this series and kept me writing more. I love you all, and you are welcome for a cuppa in Westfield whenever you like. Xander might even let you have a piece of cake. Watch this space, more books are coming!

A huge thanks to the wonderful, energetic team at HQ Digital, who worked on this book with me and made it what it is. Gratitude to Nia Beynon, Manpreet Grewal, Cara Chimirri, Helen Williams and Dushi Horti at HQ for dealing with my rambling emails and occasional brain fart and also to the design team who create the wonderful eye-catching covers I adore. Big thanks to you all, and keep doing what you are doing.

A huge shout out to my author buddies in crime and the RNA, my Yorkshire writers, and my school mum friends Gina, Nicola, Rita, Sara, Tracy, and Waseela. Thanks for being there.

A big hello to my agent Lina Langlee from the Kate Nash Literary Agency, who is currently banging her head against a wall somewhere because I sent her another rambling email, or wacky book idea. Thanks for taking me on! #sorrynotsorry

Autism is something that is present in my life every day, as a mother and a teacher, and I wanted to tell Xander's story. Every autistic child is unique, so I modelled Xander on my own two boys, and their uniqueness. The hardest thing is the judgement of others, and hopefully this book will go some way to combat that, and help a parent struggling realise that they are not alone. Hit me up on Twitter if you need a friendly face, or a rude joke. You got this. They haven't walked in your shoes, so you don't deserve their judgement. Keep fighting, let them hear you roar.

Also thanks to WHSmith for hosting my book signings, to Rickaro Book Shop in Horbury, Wakefield for being my local champion, and to Stanley Library, who are utterly amazing, and make us feel right at home whenever we step through the doors shouting 'sanctuary, sanctuary!' Wakefield Library Service rock in general, and I am honoured to have my books on your shelves.

Finally, as ever, the biggest thank you to my family, who put up with me and cheer me on. I love you all very much, even the ever elusive resident Phantom Pooper.

Dear Reader,

Thank you for taking the time to read my book. I hope you enjoyed it as much as I enjoyed writing it and, like me, fell in love just a little bit. I love to engage with readers, so feel free to contact me on Twitter and Facebook and let me know what you think, and to find out what else I might have written that tickles your fancy. I am already hard at work on the next book, so watch this space!

If you do get a moment, popping a review onto Amazon/iBooks/Kobo would be much appreciated. It not only brightens my day, but also helps other readers who might enjoy my stories to find me and take a chance on my books, and that's just brilliant all round!

🐦: @writerdove
f: https://www.facebook.com/RachelDoveauthor/

Thank you for reading!

Thank you so much for taking the time to read this book – we hope you enjoyed it! If you did, we'd be so appreciative if you left a review.

Here at HQ Digital we are dedicated to publishing fiction that will keep you turning the pages into the early hours. We publish a variety of genres, from heartwarming romance, to thrilling crime and sweeping historical fiction.

To find out more about our books, enter competitions and discover exclusive content, please join our community of readers by following us at:

🐦 @HQDigitalUK

fi *facebook.com/HQDigitalUK*

Are you a budding writer? We're also looking for authors to join the HQ Digital family! Please submit your manuscript to:

HQDigital@harpercollins.co.uk.

Hope to hear from you soon!

Turn the page for an exclusive extract of
The Wedding Shop on Wexley Street ...

Turn the page for an exclusive extract of
The Wedding Shop on Wexby Street ...

CHAPTER 1

August

The heat from the summer sun kissed the tanned and freckled skin of the wedding guests as they walked up the long path to the beautiful Grade II-listed church, the best Harrogate had to offer in terms of the ultimate IT wedding venue. One where God had a front-row seat anyway. Behind an oddly discreet line of police tape, a scoop of journalists jostled against each other, all dressed in their best uncrumpled clothes. All eager to snap the incoming guests, the first glimpse of the happy couple.

Quite the guestlist was walking up this pebbled drive too. The hottest reality TV stars, fresh from the villas and beaches, the latest hot things to rock football shorts on the field, today all suited and booted with the local glitterati, were all here to see the modern love story. Meghan and Harry had nothing on Harrogate's very own playboy and tea baron, Darcy Burgess, who was today set to marry the girl of his dreams or, as the press had come to know her, the elusive girl next door. Uncharacteristically, Darcy had kept his lady out of the spotlight, so today, in the sumptuously beautiful and historic surroundings of St Wilfred's, all eyes would definitely be on the bride.

Past the line of paps, inside the church, the pews were festooned with flowers, laced into intricate ribbons and designs at the end of the aisles. A large, imposing centrepiece full of calla lilies, white roses and the best that taste and money could buy stood on a pedestal near the altar, and the whole church was fragrant with the scent of expensive perfumes and the ambience of flowers. Everything shone and gleamed, from the brass lectern to the cheeky sparkle in the excited guests' eyes.

Today would be talked about for months, a real gem on the Northern social calendar. Taken up by the South, the Burgess wedding was certainly a networking event like no other. No one could wait to finally see the girl who had tamed the great player, Darcy. The girl next door. The young lass from the little village shop. A day of new beginnings, in more unexpected ways than one.

New beginnings came in all shapes and sizes. The day Maria Mallory was due to be married would be the first day of her new life too, but for reasons very different to those the average bride would ever think of. In fact, had she known what was coming, she might have stayed in bed that day, quivering under the duvet and throwing holy water on her wedding gown to expel the demons.

Ask any beaming child in the playground what they wanted to be when they grew up and you would get an enthusiastic answer. Thomas wanted to be an army man, Benjamin a vet just like his dad. Cassie wanted to be a ballet dancer, Alex to help sick people.

Kids wanted to be everything, from astronauts to bakers. But Maria had always been different. She didn't dream of a job. She dreamt of a status, a milestone. Maria Mallory had always wanted to one day be a bride. She'd spent hours at home poring over her parents' wedding albums, legs dangling off the couch as she studied the happy, radiant faces of her mother and late father on their special day. While other kids played video games and rode bikes, Maria made scrapbooks filled with magazine cutouts, scraps of fabric from her mother's workbox, recipe ideas for the wedding breakfast. Elizabeth Mallory worked from home as a seamstress, and her daughter would check her diary fastidiously, looking for bridal appointments. Women would come to their house all the time, requesting custom gowns, having their dresses altered, looking through her mum's designs for the perfect bridesmaid dress to match their perfect white gown. Maria loved every minute, and couldn't wait to get married. When she hit her teens, her determination to be a bride hadn't changed. She helped her mother after school, and eventually took over when her mother got sick, running the business and helping at home while doing her own business degree. Even with the bumps in the road, Maria had never once lost sight of her goal: to get married. To have the life her mother and father once had. In sickness and health, true love, till death do us part. To have the wedding of her dreams.

And what a wedding it was shaping up to be! Every man, woman and dog had been chatting about the nuptials for months, and the moony-eyed public were all rooting for the unlucky lovers to finally say I do, and prove that love really did conquer all. What girl wouldn't want that? Even the tomboys among the fairer sex still had an odd glistening tear at the thought.

But today, as she stood waiting in the wings of the church, missing her parents, sheltered from the view of the baying press outside, with Cassie moaning about her pale peach silk dress beside her, she was … well … disappointed. It seemed everything in her life had been leading to this point, so why didn't it feel that way? Why did it feel like an anticlimax? She told herself it was just down to wishing her parents were there with her. More so than anxiety. She was still having flashbacks to the dream she had had the night before, when she was wheeled out into the church, dressed like a whipped-cream meringue, with make-up Gene Simmons would deem 'trowelled on'. She had woken in a deep panic, covered in sweat and in the tight grip of fear. She needn't have worried, though. With her designer gown, make-up artist and professional hairdresser to the stars, all hired by the Burgess family, she looked more than catwalk-ready.

Maria felt like she had reached into the pretty chocolate box and pulled out a disgusting orange cream. She tried to shake off the feeling she was having. It was just nerves, that was all. She had been waiting for this day for ever, since she was old enough to wrap a sheet around her head and marry her teddy bears. Today was the day, and nothing was going to spoil it, least of all her own silly niggles. She felt a prod and looked around, annoyed.

'What?'

Cassie was staring at her, fixing her with a look she had never seen on her best friend's face before, and Maria felt the emotions of foreboding all over again, in stereo.

'Cassie? What ... what is it?'

Cassie swallowed hard and, looking around, Maria noticed they were alone. The other bridesmaids, on the side of the groom, were suddenly noticeably absent, and the vicar was standing there, looking very uncomfortable indeed. Maria's heart dropped from her chest, nestling in her sparkly ivory court shoes.

'Cass, what!' She gripped her bouquet tighter in her hand, causing a calla lily to break from its stem. It fell to the floor between them, and Maria's eyes narrowed as she focused on the lone bloom.

'He's not coming, Mar, I'm so sorry.' Cassie's voice was uncharacteristically soft, at odds with her usual ball-busting, divorce-solicitor persona. Maria nodded, and her head kept nodding away.

'Mar, can you hear me?' Cassie stepped forward, taking the bouquet from her and dropping it onto a table nearby. Maria kept nodding, sinking into the chair that appeared like magic from behind her. Turning around, she saw the vicar, his hand on her shoulder, a kindly expression on his face. She could hear the murmurs of the congregation outside, no doubt sensing this wedding wasn't going off without a hitch. In fact, there would

222

be no getting hitched today. Maria's cheeks flamed and tears started to run down her face. She jumped when Cassie slammed her fist down hard on the table, making her bouquet flip on the wooden surface.

'That utter bastard! I swear, I am going to staple his nards to the wall!'

Maria wiped at her tears, frowning when her make-up left a smudge on the pristine, white, long-sleeved glove she was wearing.

'Stay here, okay. I'll see what I can find out.' Cass manhandled the vicar out of the door, muttering things about God and angels and pitchforks to him under her breath. 'Stay put, okay? Don't come out till I know what's what.'

Maria nodded to the already-closed door, feeling like her head was separate from her body. It felt like it was floating somewhere, free, above her head like a balloon. Shock. It must be. Either that or she was about to pass out. A beep shook her from her thoughts. Cass's purse was on the table. *Her mobile phone!* Maria leaned forward and snatched it up, fumbling through the contents to grab the phone and bring up the call display. Before she could talk herself out of it, she dialled Darcy's number and held her breath. *It must be a mistake, Chinese whispers. He was probably stuck in traffic. Last-minute nagging from his mother, perhaps.*

He picked it up on the third ring.

'Hello?' he asked lazily. He sounded a little drunk even. 'Hello, who is this? Hello?'

'Darcy?' It came out as a cracked whisper. 'Where are you? Are you okay?'

A tear ran down her cheek and she went to dab at it, trying not to ruin her expensive face paint.

'Maria.' It came out of his mouth, just like that. Flat, monotone. No excitement, no rushed explanations, no desperate plea for her to wait for him. He said it like he was disappointed it was her, regretted taking the call from a number he didn't recognise. Cass and he had never been that close. 'It's you.'

223

'Of course it's me! I'm at the church. Are you here yet? The vicar said you're not coming? What's wrong?'

At first, she didn't hear anything, and she thought the call had dropped till she heard the ching of the glass. A sound she recognised. The glass coffee table in their apartment made that noise when she filled his favourite whisky tumbler and set it down next to her glass of wine as they settled down for the evening.

'I'm not coming, Maria. I'm sorry.'

At first Maria couldn't decide whether to cry, wail or laugh. The words sounded so absurd, so silly. She half-expected him to start laughing, that laugh she loved to hear. The one that came from his belly as he celebrated another successful prank.

'Don't be daft, of course you're coming. We're getting married!'

The glass clinked again, hard.

'I can't do it, Maria. I'm sorry. I … Mother … we …'

Maria felt her heart break. 'Darcy, I …'

'I'm sorry. I have to go.'

The line clicked, and he was gone. She went to press the button, to call him back, to shout, to cry, to ask him why he'd said those things. Why her Darcy, the man who should be nervously passing wind at the altar, chewing the fat with his best man to stay calm, was at home, drinking instead. Leaving the woman he loved sat in a dress, in an imposing church setting. Trapped. Stranded in her very own fairy tale. Maria pushed the phone back into Cass's purse, throwing it onto the table as she heard her friend's loud voice coming closer outside.

'Mate, that best man is a total jackass, I tell you. I almost decked the arrogant swine!'

'Cass,' she whispered.

'He won't tell me where Darcy is, or give me his number, and apparently his family didn't even show!'

'Cass,' she tried. Harder this time. Fighting to push the words out of her mouth, amidst the mess of her scrambled thoughts.

Her friend turned and knelt before her again. Maria looked

into her eyes and swallowed hard, trying to dislodge the huge lump in her throat. The more she swallowed, the thicker it felt.

'Cass,' she tried again, her voice betraying her. 'Get me out of here, okay?'

Cass nodded. Marching over to the window, she wrenched it open, looking outside. Seemingly satisfied that they had an escape route, she beckoned for her friend.

'I scoped this out too, just in case. Come on, my car's outside.' Maria nodded and five minutes later she was in the passenger seat of her friend's Mercedes, hunched low, being whisked away from her own wedding. For the first time in her life, she was glad her parents weren't there to see how her life was going. Cassie placed a warm hand over hers.

'Stay with me, okay? I'll arrange for your stuff to be collected from Arsy's.'

Maria nodded, too numb to even complain about her friend's nickname for her would-be groom. Darcy Burgess of the Burgess Tea empire, a well-respected Harrogate institution. Currently about to corner the Yorkshire market in herbal teas, they sold everything from ginger snaps to ornamental teapots to go with their amazing tea blends. Beatrice Burgess, the head of the family, was an all-encompassing woman, driven and one hundred per cent committed to making sure her children, Laura and Darcy, didn't do anything to embarrass her beloved empire. She made the Godfather look like small potatoes, and her wrath wasn't something to seek out.

Darcy, who had just jilted her at the altar, in front of their friends. Darcy, who, up until yesterday, she had lived with in his plush apartment in Harrogate. She started to sob quietly. Cassie swore under her breath and turned on the radio, jabbing at the buttons as though they were part of Darcy himself.

'Poncey git. Who wants to marry a Darcy anyway?'

Maria looked across at her in exasperation. 'Millions of women,

Cass. Millions. Mr Darcy, Mark Darcy? Come on, I know you have that poster of Colin Firth on your fridge.'

Cass's lips pursed, and she grinned at her mate. 'Okay, okay – but seriously, Mar, you'll be okay. Everything will work out.'

'I called him.'

Cass looked at her, but said nothing, flicking her attention back to zooming through the streets.

'And?'

'He said sorry.'

Cass's lips clamped together, as though trying to ward off something unpleasant from being rammed between them, or trying to escape.

'Oh, he'll be sorry all right.'

Maria nodded, looking down at the engagement ring on her finger. She didn't think for one minute he would be, but what else could she say?

'I'm hungry,' was all she could think of. 'I didn't eat a thing this morning, I didn't want a podge in my dress.'

Her friend smiled. 'I know just the thing to cheer you up.'

Ten minutes later, a very startled food server was taking an order from a weepy bride and a very angry woman in a flouncy peach dress. They took a booth in the back, ignoring the stares of the lunchtime crew and the mothers feeding their children a junk-food treat. Cassie put the tray down in front of them, and Maria sank her teeth into a cheeseburger, a napkin shoved into the front bodice of her couture gown, one Darcy's mother had insisted she wear, rather than one of her own designs. A glob of ketchup dripped from the side of the napkin onto the ivory material, and Maria wiped at it half-heartedly, leaving a small red dot on the fabric. *Oh well*, she thought to herself. *Not like I'll be saving it for my daughter, eh?* She swallowed the last of her burger and looked across at Cassie, who was shovelling fries into her mouth while barking orders into her phone. She reached for hers out of habit, before realising that her bag, containing her keys and phone, was still in the hotel. *In the space of a morning, I have lost my fiancé, my home and my sanity,* she thought to herself glumly. The reality of her situation dawned again, and she felt the threat of her cheeseburger coming back up. Cassie barked out a final command and stashed the phone back inside her tiny peach purse. Her face paled as she looked at the current state of her childhood bestie.

'Maria, you doing okay?'

Maria looked across at her. 'Cass, what the hell am I going to do?'

Cass gripped her hand in both of hers, squeezing it tight. 'Mar, you are going to pick yourself up, get a new place, go back to work, and never speak to Arsy again.'

Maria smiled weakly at her, looking away quickly from the builder who was looking her up and down while devouring a family-sized box of chicken nuggets.

'That easy, eh? Just like that?'

'Yep.' Cass's eyes flashed with determination. 'You can do it. And tonight,' she continued, smiling devilishly, 'we are going to get you very, very drunk.'

Maria rolled her eyes. 'I can't go out tonight. I don't even have anything to wear.' She looked down at her wedding dress, to point out the elephant in the room. Cassie smiled weakly.

'No night out. PJs, boxset, and copious amounts of Chinese food and alcohol.'

Maria nodded. Not quite the night she had planned, but it sounded good right about now.

'Deal,' she said, slurping her vanilla shake. 'But no Colin Firth.'

CHAPTER 2

One Week Later

'What the hell! You have got to be kidding me!' Maria slammed the local newspaper, the *Westfield Times*, onto her desk and stomped over to the kettle. She stabbed at the button, throwing ingredients into a mug. She reached into the biscuit barrel, shovelling a triple chocolate cookie into her mouth, mumbling as she chewed, before turning to the wall.

'I mean, I am the ONLY wedding planner in Westfield! The only one! How could Agatha Mayweather go elsewhere, when all she does is prattle on about community, and giving back, and fighting big corporations!' She thrust her arms out wildly as she spun around, cookie crumbs flying from her mouth. 'I mean, seriously! I am going to ring that woman up and give her a piece of my mind!'

'Who are you talking to, dear?' a voice at the door asked. Maria whirled around, seeing her part-time assistant, Lynn, standing there, a large flask in hand. Maria flushed and pointed to the wall, where a picture of her mother was framed and hung up.

'Sorry, Lynn, I was talking to Mum. The Baxters got married again, did you know that? From Love Blooms, the florist? They

228

had a big event on Agatha's estate, and I wasn't even approached to help!'

Lynn smiled kindly, closing the door against the slight breeze of the weather. It was quite autumnal already. She put the flask down on her desk and strode over to the wooden coat rack, taking off her cream faux fur coat.

'I know, dear, they seem so happy now, and about time too. I did worry about them, when they passed the shop to Lily. Idle thumbs and all that.' She waggled her own very busy thumbs in the air.

Maria glared at her. 'And!?'

Lynn sat at her desk, pouring a slurp of tea from the flask into one of the many bone china mugs she kept at work. She sighed and looked at Maria as she stirred, trying to find the words.

'Darling, Agatha didn't want to bother you about planning a wedding when your ... er ... when you were supposed to be on honeymoon. Your diary was full, so she didn't ask.'

Maria's shoulders slumped as realisation set in. 'She didn't want a wedding planner who got jilted at the altar, did she?' It came out as more of a defeated statement than a question, and Lynn's heart went out to her. She had watched Maria grow from a tiny baby to the beautiful woman standing before her, and whenever she thought of that wretched Darcy fellow, she found herself planning grisly things against his man parts with a crochet needle.

She waved her hand, cutting off Maria's rant. 'No love, not at all. No one thinks that.'

'Oh no?' Maria shouted, dashing over to the appointments diary. 'So how come I have no bookings then, for the rest of the month? Eh?'

Lynn sighed slowly. 'Maria, I know you're upset, but think about it. The diary is empty because you were supposed to be on holiday, that's all.' She took a sip of tea and eyed her furtively, obviously expecting horns to sprout from her head at any moment. Maria sagged over the diary, deflated. 'Oh,' she said softly. 'Of course, yes … sorry, Lynn.'

Lynn raised her hand to wave off her employer's apology. 'Don't give it a thought. Why don't you take the time off anyway – go away somewhere or something? Nice change of scene, eh?'

Maria shook her head. 'I should be in St Lucia now. Somehow a week in some caravan in Skegness on my tod just doesn't sound appealing.' Lynn opened her mouth to speak again, but the phone on her desk started to ring. She smiled kindly at Maria and dealt with the customer. Maria went to the just-boiled kettle, pouring herself a huge mug of steaming hot coffee. As she added more sugar, she had to admit, if only in her own head, that she shouldn't be at work. She felt like the angry wedding performer in that Adam Sandler movie. A movie she loved, and now couldn't watch for fear of murdering someone, or herself, with a noose made from the finest lace she possessed. She should be glad she didn't own a hardware store, the way she was feeling, but Lynn was right: work *was* going to be tricky, to say the least.

She listened to Lynn discussing venues and prices with the person on the phone as she took her coffee into the back, to her office. Once there, she closed the door and sagged to the floor behind it, the steaming beverage clutched in her fingers. She took a gulp and, setting it on the coffee table, crawled across the floor and curled up on the couch in the corner. She covered herself over with a blanket, and promptly fell asleep.

Lynn came in an hour later, tucked her in, and pulled the phone socket from the wall so she wouldn't be disturbed. Maria looked exhausted, even in sleep, and Lynn frowned as she looked down at her. *The poor girl*, she thought as she brushed a strand of blonde hair away from her face. Closing the office door behind her, she went to the diary and looked over the next three months. Christmas was coming, and with it the party season, bringing a very welcome set of clients that had nothing to do with weddings. Lynn would book the diary up with these, and try to avoid doing any events. The business was doing well – if a little stalled since the wedding as regards the bigger, more lucrative jobs – so a couple of months off the wedding circuit wouldn't do them any harm, and Lynn was determined to protect her employer as much as possible. She bit her lip as she fired up the computer, checking for any incoming enquiry emails that might derail her plan, but it appeared to be blissfully quiet on the nuptials front so far. It was a stroke of luck that Maria had put her own wedding at the end of the main season. Had this happened in spring, it would have been even worse. She just hoped Maria would be feeling better by the time the season was in full swing again. Being a jilted bride, wedding planner and owner of wedding boutique Happy Ever After wouldn't bring Miss Mallory peace any time soon. *Men*, she thought to herself, seething at her feeling of helplessness. *They really did have a lot to answer for sometimes.*

**If you enjoyed *The Fire House on Honeysuckle Street*,
then why not try another delightfully uplifting romance
from HQ Digital?**

9 780008 330910